W9-AWG-102

STACKS
MAR 15 1999

Circles of Confusion

Circles of Confusion

April Henry

HarperCollins*Publishers*

HarperCollins books may be purchased for educational, business, or sales promotional use. For information please write: Special Markets Department, HarperCollins Publishers, Inc., 10 East 53rd Street, New York, NY 10022.

FIRST EDITION

Designed by Kyoko Watanabe

Library of Congress Cataloging-in-Publication Data

Henry, April.
Circles of confusion / April Henry.
p. cm.
ISBN 0-06-019204-6
I. Title.
PS3558.E4969C57 1999
813' .54—dc21 98-21820

---

99 00 01 02 03 ❖/RRD 10 9 8 7 6 5 4 3 2 1

Acknowledgments

Special thanks go to three women in my life: Nora Merle Meeker Henry, for always believing in me; Wendy Schmalz, for sticking with me; and Cathy Humble, for serving as midwife.

For research help, I'd like to thank Laurie Dodge, Prudence Roberts, Sonja Sopher, Matthew Weigman and the folks at the Multnomah County Library. At HarperCollins, Carolyn Marino provided invaluable editorial assistance, while Robin Stamm kept everything organized.

My appreciation also goes to the many people who have been loyal readers throughout the years, including Carole Archer, Pat Bell, Jan Bellis-Squires, Fran Gokey, Robert Goldberg, Jan Hallbacka, Hank Henry, Nancy Husbands, Lauren Shapton, Sonja Steves, Melody Swift and Aileen Willis.

Thanks to Kaiser Permanente for a flexible work schedule, and to the folks at Rocking Horse Day School and West Hills Child Care for letting me take full advantage of that schedule. And thanks to Randy and Sadie, who could always be counted on to team up to give Mom some free time at the "puter."

Acknowledgments

PUZZLD?

At the end of each chapter, you will find a vanity license plate puzzler. See if you can decode these hidden messages. Look for the glossary key at the end of the book to check your detective work.

Circles of confusion:

The luminous spots caused by imperfections in a camera lens. In painting, refers to the effects of the camera obscura, a pinhole device that projects an image upside down and backward, a forerunner to the camera. Vermeer was perhaps the best-known painter to use the camera obscura. Many of his paintings are marked by circles of confusion.

New York City, New York, October 3, 1997

Dante Bonner grinned a little in satisfaction as he contemplated the portrait on the easel in front of him. Golden light, curly beard, the left side of the face in shadow. He set down his delicate paintbrush, stood back and looked at the painting critically, one eye half-closed. No one could ever doubt that Rembrandt's hand had painted those lines, that the great master himself had laid those bold brushstrokes. He snapped off the magnifying light and went to lunch.

Buenos Aires, Argentina, October 3, 1997

Rudy Miller found the one-inch article buried on the last page of local news, just before the want ads began.

Local Woman Found Dead

September 30 (White City)—Cady Montrose, 80, was found dead in her home in the Tarrymore Trailer Park on Tuesday.

> Neighbors said they had not seen the woman for several weeks. Ms. Montrose, who never married, retired from the head teller position at Jackson County Federal Bank in the early 1980s. During World War II, she served as a clerk in the Women's Army Corps, and was stationed in Germany after the war in Europe ended. No funeral is planned.

Rudy closed the paper with a satisfied snap. It hadn't been cheap, having the *Medford Mail Tribune* mailed to Argentina. But as usual, his forethought had been rewarded. If his grandfather and namesake had only put as much care into what he had done, Rudy would never have been forced to go to these ridiculous lengths. He pulled a cellular phone from his breast pocket, unfolded it and tapped out a number.

"Tell Karl I have a job for him."

NEW YORK CITY, NEW YORK, OCTOBER 3, 1997

Troy Nowell placed the picture, encircled by a golden frame, on a velvet-covered easel. Fifi regarded the painting with the perpetually surprised look of a too-taut facelift. Her real name was Margaret Montgomery, but Troy privately thought of all well-dressed Park Avenue women as Fifis.

"It's beautiful," he said. "And very rare. No other Pieruccini angel displays such joy at seeing the Christ child." And until recently, neither had this particular angel, who actually had begun existence as a dour-looking saint. It had been John who had suggested that the addition of a joyful expression and some gold-leaf wings would make this painting fly right out the door.

"That hair. It's the exact same color as my Toby's."

"Toby?" Troy inquired politely.

"My apricot AKC-registered teacup poodle. He is everything to me. Everything."

Troy nodded his appreciation of this completely unforeseen selling point. Then, with a few carefully chosen words of praise, he began to reel her in. If he applied just the right amount of pressure, Fifi would prod her husband, a man who had made millions selling low-flow toilets, into buying this painting of a rather insipid-looking angel, his hair not blond exactly, but instead a pale shade of red.

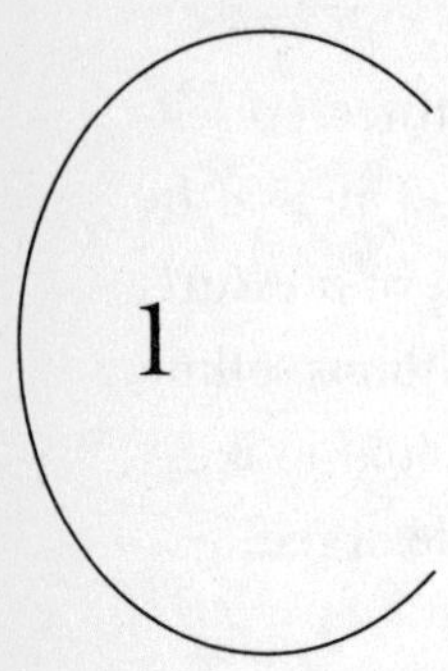

1

Portland, Oregon, October 3, 1997

". . . And as a lot of our listeners out there remember, next weekend will be the anniversary of Oregon's Columbus Day storm . . ."

Claire Montrose quickly snapped off the radio (brought from home, tolerated if played at a low level) that sat on top of her state-issued gray metal desk. Great. It was that time of year again. She was tired of hearing about the Columbus Day storm that had ravaged the West Coast nearly thirty-five years before, the day before she was born. Each year, Claire's mother could be counted on to remind her about how she'd suffered to bring Claire into the world, trapped at home with all roads blocked and no telephone, no lights, no heat and no assistance except for an elderly neighbor.

The great windstorm of 1962 had left dozens dead and hundreds more stranded for days on end. Huge fallen trees had blocked Portland streets, crushed cars and homes, and turned power lines into spitting snakes. The wind had peeled back roofs, pushed trucks off highways, and snatched up small animals and patio furniture. Of course, Claire didn't have any of her own memories of this, but she felt as though she did. Every October, the TV stations could be counted on to trot out the grainy file footage to pad a slow news day.

It served only to remind her that she was getting older, rusting into place, with most of her waking hours spent in a cubicle that resembled a cross between a cattle pen and a prison cell. Sometimes Claire thought her dramatic entrance into the world had been the last exciting event of her life.

The phone on her desk shrilled into life. Claire used a neon-orange Chee•to to mark her place in the department's Spanish-English dictionary.

"Oregon Motor Vehicles Division, Custom Plate Department. How may I help you?"

Claire had been looking up "AMORT"—the request of an accountant—to see if it meant anything in translation that couldn't be put on a license plate. "Amort" hadn't been in the Spanish dictionary, but "Amor"—love—had. Claire had become sidetracked considering how limited both Spanish and English were when it came to words for love. There were dozens of kinds of love—platonic love, love from afar, love for one's family, love for a pet, love for food or other inanimate objects, hopeless love, passionate love, unrequited love. Why wasn't there a separate word for each, the way the Eskimos were supposed to have seventeen different words for snow?

"Hi, Claire. It's me."

"Mom!" Claire pressed the phone closer to her face. There should definitely be a word for the mingled love and annoyance she felt for her mother. "I told you not to call me at work unless it was an emergency." She hoped Frank wasn't listening on the other side of their shared cubicle wall. Each time she received a personal call, she half suspected him of making a hatch mark on a clandestine list of her failings.

"But this *is* an emergency."

"What did you buy?" Please, not another thousand-dollar Kirby vacuum cleaner. Even though Oregon law allowed a three-day cooling-off period for major purchases, the last time it had been nearly impossible to extract her mother from the clutches of the contract's fine print.

"I didn't buy anything," her mother said, stung. "I'm calling about your great-aunt. I just got a call from her lawyer. Poor thing died last week."

"Great-aunt? What great-aunt?"

"Don't you remember Aunt Cady? My father's sister who lives in White City? I guess you probably haven't seen her since your grandmother's last group birthday party for you kids."

Claire was beginning to picture her now, a thin woman standing on the sidelines of family gatherings, her graying hair pulled back in a bun. "Wasn't Aunt Cady the one who was in the WAVEs or the WACs or something?"

"WACs, I think. She ended up in Germany after the war."

"How old was she? What did she die of?"

"About eighty. The lawyer guy said they think it was a heart attack. She lived alone, you know. Nobody's too certain exactly *when* she died." Claire suppressed a shiver. "Anyway, she's left everything to you."

"Me? Why me? I can barely remember her."

"Evidently she liked you the best of all us relatives. I don't think she was really close to anybody. The lawyer guy said that she'd been living like a hermit for years. Anyway, he wants you to go down there and go through her trailer. Sort it out. He says the park manager is anxious to rent out the space, so I promised him you'd come down this weekend."

"This weekend? You mean tomorrow?" Claire echoed incredulously, forgetting to keep her voice down.

Her mother's voice took on the wheedling tone that Claire knew all too well. "You know what they say about old people who live alone. Maybe she's held on to a fortune in pesos from the war."

"Marks, Mom." Claire effortlessly collected scraps of facts, and she pulled one out now. "I think the Germans use marks. But that's not the point—the point is, I'm sure Evan won't want me to go on such short notice. You know how he likes to plan things in advance."

"Oh, Claire, it's not like you're married to him or anything."

∾

Claire waited until twelve, and the beginning of her lunch hour, to call Evan from the pay phone in the break room. No sense giving Frank any ammunition by making a personal phone call on company time. She sketched out the problem for Evan, fully expecting him to be annoyed by this change in plans.

"My mom tried to tell me it would be like a treasure hunt. I guess the lawyer says the place is piled high with all kinds of stuff." Claire turned to pace, but was brought up short by the absurdly short metal phone cord. She suddenly felt trapped, tied by a rigid umbilical cord to the hospital-green wall. "What's that squeaking noise?"

"I'm Lysoling the phone. Someone asked to borrow it after a meeting. There's a courtesy phone in the lobby, but no, he had to ask to use this one, right at the beginning of cold and flu season." The squeaking stopped, and then Evan began to outline a plan. In her mind's eye, Claire saw his long pale fingers methodically ticking off the steps. "If we leave Portland at six tomorrow morning and drive straight through, we should be there by eleven. We'll spend the day cleaning things out, make a trip or two to Goodwill, pack up anything of value, and drive back to Portland with it tomorrow night. We can rent a U-Haul trailer if we need to."

She was surprised by his impulsiveness. "You want to go with me?"

"I'm not letting you drive that car of yours on a five-hundred-mile round trip. And who knows, it might even be worthwhile. If your aunt was anything like your mom, she'll have ephemera from the forties and fifties tucked away, still in its original boxes. Stuff like that could fetch a fortune now."

"Since she's related to my mother, it's more likely that we'll find some Jack LaLanne fitness plan still in its original 1957 packaging."

"That's exactly what I mean. Have you checked out those stores in Multnomah lately? They don't just sell Navaho rugs and Depression glass. People will buy anything if it reminds them of their own past—Howdy Doody mugs, old *Life* magazines, NIXON NOW! buttons, handmade quilts, cast-iron frying pans. There are times when it pays to be related to someone who holds on to everything, and this may be one of them."

Claire sometimes thought in the shorthand of license plates, and she summed up Evan's hopes now: BG BKS.

~

After lunch, Claire tried to concentrate on work. A flock of birds flying by the floor-to-ceiling window caught her eye. They beat their wings so powerfully that she could see the muscles in their shoulders moving. Flying didn't look effortless, but it did look worthwhile. After the last bird disappeared, she watched the clouds sliding by. She could see herself reflected faintly, a ghostly figure with red-gold hair and appropriately pale skin. Around her, a beehive of identical cubicles hummed with the sound of ringing phones and the *click-clack* of computer keys.

She pulled a new application from her in-basket. The owner of a gold-colored Mercedes was requesting WHYWALK for her license plates. Claire ran down the checklist automatically: not an obscenity, not sex- or excretory-related, not slang for an intimate body part, didn't promote religion or drugs, didn't mean anything dirty in another language. She even halfheartedly took it into the bathroom to check out the words in a mirror, but the letters said nothing when reversed. Clearly, the owner was simply expressing an opinion, the opinion of a forty-three-year-old matron who lived in Portland's West Hills and thought her car was everything. And since the computer showed that no one else had the plate, Claire stamped the application APPROVED and put it in her out-box.

As she picked up another application, Claire remembered the last time she had seen Aunt Cady, at one of her grandmother's infamous birthday parties. Claire had been fifteen. It was the year before her grandmother died, and the last year she held one of her parties. Grandma Montrose—known as that even after her last name became Clabberwhite and then Woods and then Eastwood and then Reese—had been unwilling or unable to remember the exact dates of her twelve grandchildren's birthdays. She had solved the problem by hosting one giant birthday party for all of them every Fourth of July. Presents were always wildly inappropriate, reflecting whatever bargain Grandma Montrose had stumbled across in the weeks prior to the big event. One year it had been queen-sized pantyhose for the seven girl cousins when none of them was obese—or over the age of nine. Another year they were handed grab bags of items from the dollar store. Claire had gotten a canister of garlic powder, a flea collar and a pocket mirror.

That particular July 4th, her mother had driven Claire and her sister, Susie, south from Portland to Medford, where Grandma had moved after her latest divorce. The freeway was an endless straight line to nowhere, and five minutes into the drive Claire opened the copy of *Gone With the Wind* she'd checked out from the library the night before. She ate mechanically from a box of Pizza Spins, transported to another world, a world of eighteen-inch waists, hoop skirts and green-eyed jealousy. Even when they stopped for lunch at a McDonald's outside of Eugene, Claire walked into the restaurant blindly, her eyes on the book she held open before her. After lunch, she clambered back into the front seat of their beat-up Pinto. Susie's response was immediate.

"That's not fair! Who said you could ride shotgun all the way to Medford? Mom! It's not fair! Make Claire give me that seat!" Susie's voice held a whine that only a twelve-year-old was capable of. Her hair, carefully hot-rollered that morning in frank imitation of Farrah Fawcett, was already beginning to lose some of its bounce.

"Your sister's right, Claire. You should trade seats with her. Besides, you haven't even looked out the window once. I'd be surprised if you even knew where we were."

Claire didn't bother replying. Rhett had just asked Scarlett to dance, scandalizing the entire populace because Scarlett was a widow in mourning. Still reading, she picked up the book and got into the back seat. Susie used her new proximity to the radio to begin to hunt for a station that played rock and roll, and soon the interminable strains of "Stairway to Heaven" filled the car.

By the time they took the exit for Medford, the stunning heat of southern Oregon had sucked the energy from their bones. Portland and Medford lay at opposite ends of the state, and they had exchanged their lush, green and frequently wet city for a town cradled by tawny hills and capped by a hard, hot blue sky. As they drove down Jackson Street, the electronic temperature sign on the Far West Bank sign read 106 degrees. Once in Hawthorn Park, Claire kissed her grandmother's wrinkled cheek, trying not to inhale the scent of Virginia Slims. She nodded hello at the uncles, aunts and cousins clustered around Grandma's camper, with its not so secretly stashed keg. As soon as she could, Claire took shelter under an oak tree several hundred yards away. All around her, knots of people were barbecuing or playing Frisbee, but Claire was once again in the world of Rhett and Scarlett.

"Claire, dear, is that you?"

Reluctantly, Claire tore her gaze from the page. Her mom's Aunt Cady stood over her, a tentative smile on her face. Despite the heat, there was a faded cardigan over her bony shoulders. Her straight back and the prominent wings of her collarbone gave the impression that Aunt Cady had left the coat hanger in the sweater.

"Hi, Aunt Cady." All Claire knew about her was that she had been dead Grandpa Montrose's sister, that she had never married, and that she had had something to do with World War II, a million years ago.

"What are you reading?"

Claire turned the cover of the library book toward her.

"*Gone With the Wind.* I loved that book." She smoothed the back of her dress—the dress another thing that set her apart from the rest of Claire's relatives—and then settled down beside Claire. "I read it when it first came out. I was just about your age, and I had to hide it from my mother."

This was a brush with ancient history. When it first came out? Claire had looked at the copyright date, which was 1935. "Why did you have to hide it from your mom?"

"It might seem quaint to you, but even though I was nineteen she didn't think it was appropriate for an unmarried girl to be reading about a woman who is involved with man after man. She hadn't read it herself, of course."

"I love to read. I wish I could read all the time."

A garbled shout made them both look up. Cousin Bucky, clearly having paid a few too many visits to Grandma's hidden keg, had just fallen down in the parking lot. Uncle John, who insisted on cutting his son's hair so short that sleepy-eyed Bucky resembled a confused but amiable badger, looked on indulgently as Bucky attempted to stand. Boys would be boys.

Claire exchanged a glance with the older woman. Her great-aunt's eyes were a washed blue, deep-set in a pale, narrow face. Aunt Cady reached out to tap Claire's book. "Reading is wonderful. But you have to be careful it doesn't become a substitute for real life." Her voice dropped to a near-whisper, as if she were speaking more to herself. "I wish I had learned that lesson when I was your age."

People were always telling Claire that she read too much, but it seemed better than the alternative. Did her great-aunt mean that instead of reading a book about made-up people living a long time ago, Claire should be with people her own age? She looked again at her relatives in the parking lot. Her cousins were willing to hang out with the adults as long as the beer held out. Claire felt alien around other teenagers, with their conversations about smoking pot, drinking and streaking. Susie was more than happy to try to fit in. Claire saw that Bucky now had his arm looped around her shoulders. It looked as if he needed her for balance, but Susie's face had lit up as she experienced her first brush with romance.

"But if reading makes you forget your real life, isn't that good? Especially if you don't like it?" The people gathered around the camper seemed only technically her family. Grandma Montrose, who had spent the years before the war traveling around the country as a "Hormel Girl," now seemed to be demonstrating one of her old routines. In the middle of the parking lot, she gyrated her narrow butt and gestured broadly, singing about the wonders of Spam in a cigarette-roughened voice. Claire's mother was laughing so hard that she had crushed her paper cup, spilling beer down her T-shirt.

Aunt Cady had taken a while before she answered. "Maybe. But it's better to find a way to live in the world you want."

Now Claire supposed the reason she remembered the conversation so well was that it had been one of the first times an adult had spoken to her as an equal. But had she heeded Aunt Cady's warning? Did she still live only through books? Her life was boring, even to her. Two weeks before, she had been grocery shopping when she had suddenly been seized by the desire to live dangerously. Freeing a nested shopping cart, Claire saw that someone had left behind their grocery list. With a surge of exhilaration, she had exchanged it for her own. She bought some other person's Lite beer and Velveeta, spent the week trying to make meals out of lemon yogurt, Tater Tots, hot dogs and cream of mushroom soup, while her roommate Charlie watched bemused. By the end of the week, Claire had been forced to admit that it was easier to be herself.

Claire picked up another application—ANGLBB—and tried not to feel depressed. She had worked for the State of Oregon for over ten years, yet she still held basically the same job. When she had first taken the position as a verifier, she had thought it suited her. She had understood and appreciated the little jokes hidden in people's vanity plate requests. Now Claire was bored by the whole thing, bored by her life, with its treadmill of work, exercise, and a standing Saturday date with Evan. Every ten minutes it seemed as if her car was thumping over the same pothole on the Marquam Bridge as she drove to work.

ZTHSIT?

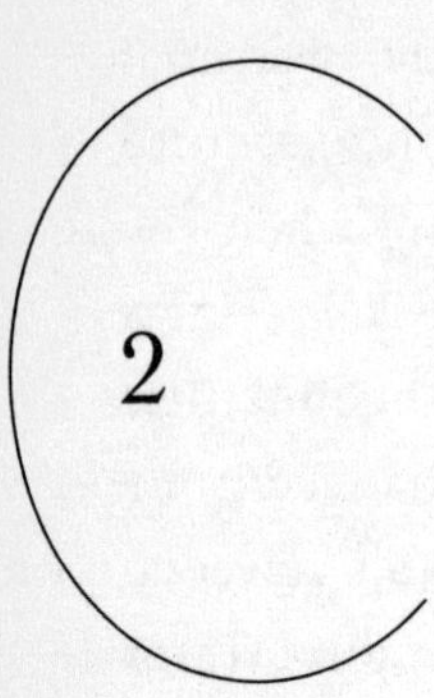

2

"We're starting a new insurance line," Evan said. He kept his gaze steady on the road, his hands in the ten o'clock and two o'clock position on the Volvo's steering wheel. "Executive coverage."

"Executive coverage? What's that?" Claire asked. Evan must be happy with the time they were making, because he seldom allowed himself to be distracted by conversation while he drove.

"A lot of companies are really predicated on a single man. What would happen to the Turner empire if Ted were killed in a car accident, or to Microsoft if Bill Gates became an alcoholic? Companies are finally starting to realize they need to take steps to insure against such a huge loss." Evan shook his head. "Accurate rating is going to be a nightmare, though. It's going to have to be completely individualized." Claire could see he was secretly looking forward to being alone with his risk tables and expensive multifunction calculator.

"It seems like a lot of those maverick CEO types like dangerous sports. Racing. Helicopter skiing. Hang gliding." Claire tried to picture the nebbishy king of Microsoft behind the wheel of a rocket-like car. "Well, maybe not Bill Gates."

"He's the smart one. If those other guys really looked at the statistics they'd know they should stick to something safer, like golf." As an afterthought he added, "Just as long as they stay off the course when it's raining."

Evan had probably been a worrier even as a child, but his job as an insurance adjuster had only heightened his continual calculations of risk. He refused to go canoeing because statistics showed that spending six minutes in a canoe cut fifteen minutes off one's expected life span. Smoking just two cigarettes cut nine minutes, as Evan had pointed out to a complete stranger who lit up behind them at a sidewalk café. But even avoiding risks brought with it its own agonizing set of risks. Take the advice for reducing the risk of catching colds: frequent handwashing. Yet handwashing itself was a risky activity, because most soaps contained potentially carcinogenic cosmetic additives.

Evan worried about everything. Earthquakes. X rays. Pesticide residues on his food. How close he lived to the now-decommissioned Trojan nuclear plant. Whether a sneeze heralded the beginning of a cold, which might turn into antibiotic-resistant double pneumonia and drag him inexorably down to death.

So many things were outside his control that Evan tended to be obsessive about those that were. He took a brightly colored handful of vitamins each morning. His diet consisted almost entirely of organically grown fruits and vegetables. He exercised six days a week. (Evan had met Claire at the health club when, after mentally estimating the strength of the three other people in the room, he had asked her to spot him on free weights.) He was the only person she knew who had electric socket covers even though he didn't have children. He didn't even have any friends who had children.

The same cautious appraisal that now sometimes drove Claire up the wall had been what had originally attracted her to him in the first place. It had been months before he even ventured to kiss her goodnight after a date. She had welcomed the contrast to other men she had known. Dates where you went out to dinner and a movie? Goodnight kisses? Up until Evan, most men she met seemed to want to skip all that and just move in with her.

To Claire, Evan represented steadiness, steadfastness. He had plans, a future all mapped out. He would never vanish the way her father had before she was even born. He would never lie to her. So what if he were honest to the point of being blunt? He would always have a job, a good job that paid well. And Evan had chosen her. Knowing how he calculated and weighed everything meant that he had also found her worthy.

She studied him as he carefully piloted the Volvo down the far right-hand lane, only reluctantly moving into the middle lane to pass the slowest of motor homes. Because it absorbed all his concentration, driving with Evan gave Claire the luxury of observing him. She liked watching his thickly lashed large hazel eyes as they flicked back and forth from his rearview mirror to the lane ahead of him and then to each sideview mirror, as regular as a metronome. His eyes redeemed Evan from the ranks of the ordinary. Everything else about him was unremarkable—he was neither fat nor thin, his hair was somewhere between brown and blond, he was tall enough that Claire could wear medium heels.

Today he wore a moss green sweater, a birthday present from Claire that brought out the gray-green cast of his eyes. It wasn't unknown for Evan, left to his own devices, to wear white socks with his dress shoes. Secretly, Claire liked this flaw in him, with its inherent proof that he wasn't perfect. At the same time, she also knew that he didn't see it as a flaw at all. Evan resented dressing up. It seemed very impractical. Why should he spend good money simply to make an impression? Couldn't people admire his mind and how well it worked?

The sign ahead read MEDFORD—20 MILES. "Get out that lawyer's fax and tell me which exit I should take," Evan said.

RUD14ME

ᘓ

The place where Aunt Cady had lived and died was tucked on the edge of a vast parking lot for a brand-new shopping mall. The trailer park was sheltered by a huge spreading oak, the turning leaves a welcome antidote of color to the black acres of macadam. Fast food places bordered the edges of the shopping mall's parking lot. Burritos Now! was the closest, standing only a half-dozen yards away. Every night, Aunt Cady must have gone to sleep listening to the sound of cars pulling away from the drive-up window of the turquoise-and-adobe-colored plastic box.

Claire had arranged to meet the lawyer in front of the trailer. A tall young man was already walking toward them, hand outstretched, as they climbed out of the Volvo. He looked more like a teenager than a lawyer, with limbs as loose and floppy as a handful of rubber bands.

"Claire Montrose? Justin Schmitz, your aunt's attorney. I appreciate your coming down on such short notice." He shook both their hands as they introduced themselves. The cuffs of his too-short navy blue suit exposed the scuffed heels of his black shoes.

Evan went straight to the point. "My understanding is that Claire inherits her aunt's entire estate. Is there anything in addition to this trailer home and its contents?"

"That's about it, I'm afraid. What little money she had in her accounts went for her cremation." He turned to Claire. "The terms of her will stipulate that I am to pay all her bills, close her checking and savings accounts, sell this trailer and then transfer the net proceeds to you. But I'm afraid the total won't amount to more than a few hundred dollars. Two thousand at the outside."

She found herself apologizing. "That's okay. Really, I hardly knew her. I'm surprised she left me anything."

Evan looked at his watch. "Well, we might as well get started." He held out his hand for the key.

"Wait a minute." Claire turned to Justin. "Tell me something about my great-aunt. What was she like?"

"I'm afraid I only met her once. Last year she fell and broke her hip. When she was discharged from the hospital, she came to see me."

"Why did she choose you?"

Although she hadn't meant to sound critical, the base of Justin Schmitz's throat flushed. "I run a little ad in the Yellow Pages. I charge a flat fee for the basics—wills, prenups, divorces, that sort of thing. Your great-aunt was very definite. She said she wanted a will and a neutral executor so that no one in your family would end up having to decide what to do with her possessions."

Claire didn't tell him that her relatives were legendary for dying intestate, leaving the survivors to assuage their grief by tussling over the dear departed's earthly belongings. The morning of Grandma Montrose's funeral, for example, Claire had stood on Grandma's lawn and watched as relatives scuttled out of the house with their arms full of afghans and antimacassars, TV trays and old 78 records. Uncle John hit Uncle Chester in the jaw as they fought over possession of a color TV set. Cousin Bucky scurried past, clutching a battered plastic AM radio. Claire's mother had not been immune to the fever of acquisition, managing to lay claim to a huge old KitchenAid mixer and a little doll designed to sit on the back of a toilet. The doll's red skirt, crocheted by Grandma, hid an extra roll of toilet paper. Claire didn't remember seeing Aunt Cady there, but perhaps she had sat in her car, watching her relations scurry over her sister-in-law's property like bugs over roadkill, and vowed it would never happen to her.

Evan waited until the lawyer had gotten into his rusting Chrysler K car before he put the key in the trailer door. The key turned, but the door refused to yield until he pushed on it with his shoulder. With a lurch and a squeal, they were in.

"Oh, my God."

Evan's normally matter-of-fact voice was filled with something like awe. A tiny path wound from the door back into the recesses of the trailer. On either side of this narrow opening were piled magazines, books, newspapers and odds and ends, in some places as high as their waists. The air was thick with dust and the smells of ancient cooking. One swift glance was enough to tell Claire that while Aunt Cady had saved everything, she had kept nothing of value.

Claire looked at Evan's face for his reaction. He was allergic to dust and hated disorder. But she had to give him credit. He didn't say a word, just went to the trunk of his car, where he retrieved a small suitcase and a stack of flattened boxes. As always, Evan had come prepared. Before they even got started, he stood just inside the closed trailer door and changed into his oldest, grubbiest clothes (which, being Evan's, weren't old or grubby at all). He settled a dust mask over his nose, offered her a second one, and then they went to work.

Claire followed Evan's lead, working methodically and in near silence. She was amazed at the sheer variety of what they unearthed and then quickly discarded. The living-dining room area alone yielded dozens of snow globes, a tiny vase in the shape of a lady's boot, sheet music from the forties and a two-inch-long plastic vial of gray ash labeled "Mt. St. Helens, May 18, 1980." Everything wore a thick fur of dust, and even beneath his mask, Evan was soon snuffling.

While a few things—like the snow globe collection—were set aside for Goodwill, nearly everything went into the brown Dumpsters that sat in the middle of the trailer park. When the Dumpsters filled up, Evan neatly stacked boxes beside them.

Next to the worn armchair was a clock radio. Impulsively, Claire pressed the ON button. Classical music filled the trailer, and they worked to the sprightly sounds of a harpsichord until Evan unplugged the radio, wrapped the cord around it, and put it in the Goodwill box. Then they both carried the armchair to the Dumpster.

It was clear that Aunt Cady had continued in the love of reading she had talked to Claire about nearly twenty years before. In addition to the towers of magazines and yellowing newspapers, there were stacks of hardbound and paperback books, some dating back fifty years. A few were hard-boiled private eye novels of the type that Claire had seen for sale behind glass in Multnomah. She found one of these books—*The Corpse Wore Black*—under a pile of *National Geographics*. On the cover a red-haired beauty, very much alive, stared out at the reader through kohl-rimmed eyes. She wore an artist's salacious interpretation of widow's weeds, cut low and tight to show off breasts shaped like artillery shells. Claire placed it in the box of things she planned to take home, along with *A Mind for Murder, Death in a Dark Place,* and *A Debt to the Dead.* Maybe she could sell them to one of the antique stores in her neighborhood.

In the early afternoon, Claire took a break to use the tiny bathroom. While she washed her hands, she studied the snapshots tucked in the frame of the mirror. With a small shock, she recognized one as her own senior high school photo. It was traditional for seniors to go to a studio to pose for portraits, but there hadn't been any extra money from the welfare check for that. Claire's earnings from her nearly full-time job at Pietro's Pizza were being carefully portioned out to keep the electric and gas companies at bay. So instead of posing under an artificial tree or against the backdrop of a muraled sunset, Claire offered a tentative smile against the blank wall of every school picture.

She compared the photo with her reflected face. It was depressing that she hadn't changed much. More than fifteen years later, and she still had the same flyaway curls, the same pale skin—only now a few laugh lines framed her mouth. A part of her had always hoped that someday she would figure out how to make herself look glamorous, how to tame back her hair into a sleek chignon (a word she had read but had no idea how to pronounce). But she had only gotten older with nothing to show for it. With a little shock, she realized that if she pulled her hair back tight and lost twenty pounds, she might look something like Aunt Cady.

Claire took down her own photo and then began to pull the other photos from around the mirror's frame. Here was another school portrait, this one of Suzy at sixteen, the last year she went to school, taken just before she moved out of the house and in with her motorcycle-riding boyfriend. Underneath a wing of hair made brassy by an overlong application of Sun-In, her gaze was wary, sidelong. Next in the circle of photos was a picture of a slim young woman with her head thrown back, caught in mid-laugh. She wore a Jackie Kennedy-ish outfit, complete with a pink pillbox hat. Claire looked closer. It was her mother, back in an age before teenagers tried so hard to set themselves apart from adults. Mom had given birth to Claire when she was just sixteen, seduced and abandoned by a man she had met in line at the movies who had dropped her two weeks later. Claire had always pictured some lecher sweet-talking a blank-faced child, but in this yellowing photo, her mom looked more adult and sure of herself than Claire did now.

The last two photos in the mirror frame were cracked black-and-whites of a man with movie-handsome good looks, his blond hair cut short as fur. In one formal photo he posed in a military uniform, chest out, teeth gleaming, cap set at just the perfect angle. Next to that photo a snapshot showed the same man standing hipshot, his arm draped casually around a young Aunt Cady's shoulder. Her face was lit by a smile that completely transformed it, turning her sharp-edged features into beauty. In neither photo did the man smile. Instead he lifted his chin like a challenge. His eyes must have been pale blue, but in the old black-and-white photos they glowed like quicksilver.

Claire slipped the photos into her pocket, but the other things in the bathroom—a hairbrush, sample bottles of moisturizer, a cardboard-colored cardigan sweater nearly worn through at the elbows—she gathered up to carry to the trash.

"Is anyone at home?"

A barrel-chested man in a too-tight jacket was just stepping through the open trailer door. "I'm Karl Zehner." He spoke in a precise, fussy voice that was at odds with his size. "And you must be dear Cady's son." He offered his hand to Evan, who had methodically been stacking newspapers in a box.

Evan slipped off his dust mask. "I'm afraid you're mistaken. She didn't have any children." He nodded at Claire. "This is Claire Montrose, her great-niece."

Claire thought she saw the man's expression tighten, but when he pivoted to her, his face was again smoothly jovial. "I occasionally took your great-aunt to church."

Church? Claire was a little surprised. They had sorted through hundreds of books, but she didn't remember seeing a single Bible.

Karl Zehner clasped his large-knuckled hands piously in front of his chest, while his eyes roamed about the trailer. "I was so sorry to hear about dear Cady's untimely demise."

"Maybe you could tell me something more about her. I haven't talked to her in nearly twenty years. What was she like?"

He blinked rapidly. "A sweet, God-fearing lady. Of course, now I can see why she never invited me in. She must have liked to hold on to things, and it got a little away from her." His eyes found the two boxes that held the few items they had deemed worth keeping. "She used to talk about some art she owned." His voice was muffled as he leaned over to finger a yellow Bakelite bracelet carved with leaves.

"Art!" Evan snorted. "Maybe she was referring to her collection of frogs. She had frogs made out of stuff I didn't even know you could make frogs out of." They had found frogs carved out of soap, macraméd out of twine, even a frog made of little pieces of macaroni fitted together and spray-painted gold. Evan picked up a stack of boxes. "Those frogs were about as close to art as she got. Now, if you two will excuse me, I'm going to take these out to the Dumpster."

"What kind of art?" Claire asked the other man.

He shrugged. "Oh, she never really said. Perhaps it could have been . . . a painting?"

His speculation was interrupted by the sound of raised voices from outside. Evan stormed in, the screen door slamming behind him.

"The manager says we're going to have to take all those boxes to the dump. He refuses to have this be, and I quote, 'on his ticket.'" He pulled his keys from his pocket and turned to Karl Zehner. "So where is the dump, anyway?"

He stepped back. "The dump? I'm afraid I've never been there."

"Well, surely you know where it is?"

The man's huge feet, like pontoons covered in oxblood leather, jigged nervously. "No, sorry, I have no idea." He made a show of looking at his wrist, already walking out the door. "Look at the time! I'm afraid I must be going." He called back over his shoulder, "So sorry for your loss!"

"What a strange man!" Claire said after he left. "He reminded me of my relatives when somebody died—like he was looking for whatever he could carry off."

"Well, I wish he'd have gotten here before us. Anything he took would have saved us the trouble of throwing it away." Evan sighed.

"I guess I'll go see if I can find a neighbor who knows where the dump is."

Standing in front of the kitchen faucet waiting for the water to run cold, Claire looked out the window just as a long dark car pulled out from the parking lot behind Burritos Now! Even in a Cadillac, Karl's huge bulk looked crammed behind the wheel. The car had a vanity plate, A-1 35. Claire remembered at the beginning of the year she had approved a series of plates that went from A-1 1 to A-1 78, with a few gaps here and there where other people had already claimed the plate for reasons of their own. The series had begun with A-1 because the cars had all belonged to a Portland company that specialized in luxury cars: A-1 Rent-A-Car.

H2OUUP2

∾

The trailer was nearly empty and Evan was on his third trip to the dump when Claire found the battered tan suitcase pushed far underneath Aunt Cady's narrow bed. Brushing away a half-inch of dust exposed cracked leather covered with decals from distant, long-vanished destinations.

Claire opened it, expecting another of Aunt Cady's collections, perhaps matchbooks or music boxes. Instead it held a jumble of odds and ends, making it resemble a small-scale reflection of the trailer's interior. On top lay an upholstered pink satin book, about the size of a paperback, bound with a band of brass. It was like the diary Claire had gotten for Christmas when she was twelve, the one she had filled with nothing more exciting than the fact she had made Appian Way pizza for dinner again because her mother was on another strange diet and refusing to cook.

She picked up the diary, eyeing the moldering brass mouth where a key would go. Already knowing the key was surely lost, she riffled the sheaf of yellowing papers that had been underneath it. They seemed to be pamphlets written in German, the old-fashioned impenetrable lettering looking appropriate for a King James Bible. Her breath caught. The cover of one leaflet bore the broken cross of a swastika. Claire thought of the delicate tracery of numbers on her roommate Charlie's wrist and shuddered.

A bracelet set with dark blue stones caught her eye. The metal must be silver, but it was tarnished so badly that it was almost black. A small black jewelry box was tucked in the corner of the suitcase. Claire opened it, thinking she might find an engagement ring from a long-ago liaison. Inside, a silver ring gleamed against a black velvet lining, but instead of a diamond it bore a square death's head. Claire snapped the box closed and tossed it back into the suitcase.

The whole thing, Claire decided, would go straight to the dump on Evan's next trip. She no longer cared what her great-aunt had written in the diary, or that the suitcase—with its decals of hotels and even countries that no longer existed—would be snapped up by any antique dealer in Multnomah.

A flash of yellow at the bottom of the suitcase caught her eye. Claire pushed aside a sheaf of crumbling papers and there it was, a small, nearly square painting in a red and gold wooden frame. Her breath caught.

In the painting, a young woman stood in front of an open window that washed the scene with tones of pale light. She was half-turned toward the viewer, her lips slightly parted, her eyes wide and luminous. The expression on her face was enigmatic, although Claire thought her lips were beginning to smile. Light shimmered off her blond hair, which was caught up in a smooth bun wrapped with strands of her own hair. Side curls fell over her ears and dangled to the hollow of her white throat. She wore a lemon-yellow satin jacket that fastened at the throat and then fell away from her body. Its wide sleeves were trimmed with black-spotted white fur that she had pushed back above her elbows. In her hands she held a letter.

There were some other elements to the painting—a brass-studded chair in the corner of the room, an oriental carpet that lay bunched in folds on a table between the woman and the viewer—but it was the woman's enigmatic expression and the way the pale light poured into the room that mesmerized Claire.

The woman was clearly from another age, but the scene looked so fresh, so real. Claire ran her fingers across the hard swirls of paint, her heart skidding.

She sat back on her heels and lifted the painting to her lap. Only a little more than a foot tall, it was surprisingly heavy, the thick and bulky frame a contrast to the still, small beauty it held. Claire had seen real paintings before, on school field trips to the Portland Art Museum, but there she had certainly never been allowed to touch one. Again she ran her fingers across the ridges of paint that still showed the brush marks of the artist, whoever he or she had been. She knew suddenly that it was a man, a man painting a woman he loved. It was in the light that shone on the woman's luminous face, and in the sheen of the pearl eardrop she wore.

She stopped cleaning and simply waited for Evan to return to the dump. As soon as she heard the screen door squeal, she ran to him. "Look at this!" Claire's hands jittered as she held the little painting toward him.

"Where did you find this?" He took it from her, angled it to the light.

"Underneath the bed in a suitcase."

Incredibly, he shrugged and handed it back to her. He indicated the three boxes behind them. "It's your call. Keep, Goodwill or trash."

"Trash?" Claire echoed, unbelieving. "It's beautiful." She looked down at the painting again, at the woman's face and the molten light.

"Some little paint-by-number job? It's a miracle that your great-aunt managed to get all the right colors on top of the right numbers. Look at that frame! It looks like a wood shop extra credit project painted by someone with an overactive craft gene."

Claire had to admit that the garish frame did not match the trapped beauty it held. The thick, rough-hewn frame was painted a chipped red, with gold wooden stars stuck every few inches around it.

"Maybe this is the painting that man was asking about. Do you think it could be real?"

"Real in what sense? That you are holding it in your hands? Then yes. In the sense that it is a valuable painting? The chances of that are near zero."

"The frame may be ugly, but I think the painting is beautiful. I don't care who painted it, even if it was Great-Aunt Cady from a kit. I want to keep it."

Evan turned away, although Claire could tell from the way he held his shoulders that he thought she was being foolish. "I already said, it's your call."

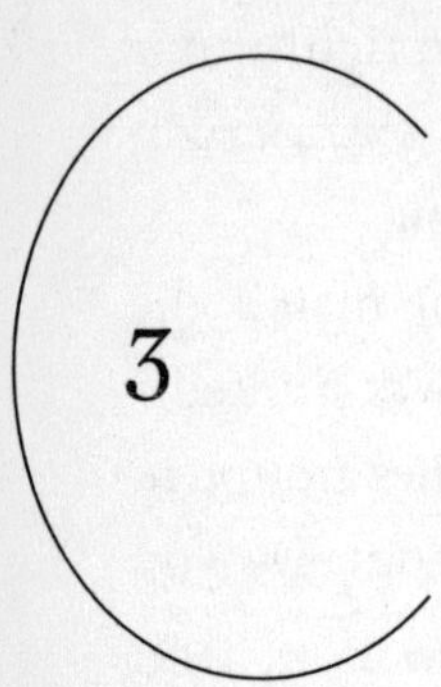

3

It was nearly nine in the evening when Claire stepped over the huge ceramic dog dish that lay on the front porch of her house. The dish was nearly a foot wide, and along its edge it bore the legend DUKE in gold script. Charlie had bought the bowl at Saturday Market and paid the dollar extra to have it personalized. She said it was a lot cheaper than a burglar alarm—or a real dog.

With the box of items rescued from Aunt Cady's trailer—including the old suitcase—braced on her knee, Claire turned the knob of the front door. She pushed it open with her hip, and set the box on the white oak floor. Behind her, Evan's tires crunched on the gravel as he backed out of the driveway. The strings of Claire's body loosened. She rolled her shoulders and stretched her arms overhead, relaxing the kinks of a five-hour, nearly silent drive.

Charlotte Heidenbruch—Charlie to her friends—came bustling out of the kitchen, wiping her hands on her apron. The enticing smell of baking bread wafted after her. She was seventy-eight and just four-foot-eleven, but she managed a quick waddling stride. Charlie was the star of her Self-Defense for Seniors class.

"How was your trip, Clairele?" she asked, giving Claire's name the affectionate "le" ending that was one of the few things she had kept fifty years after leaving her hometown of Vähingen. Her English, although nearly flawless, was still flavored by the cadences of southwestern Germany. But no matter how persistent any questioner might be about what she was, Charlie always insisted that she was, of course, an American.

Claire bent down to be enfolded in a quick, fragile hug. Next to Charlie she felt huge and ungainly, galumphing around in her size ten shoes. To top it off, her stomach let out a growl loud enough that even Charlie could hear. Evan's lunch of five-spice tofu, whole wheat pita bread and knobby organically grown carrots had left her starving. In the midafternoon, Claire had discovered an unopened bag of Doritos in a kitchen cupboard, and she'd crammed handfuls into her mouth each time Evan took a trip to the dump.

"Could I tell you about it after I eat something?"

Charlie made a little scooting motion. "Take a shower, and by the time you are done, I'll have something heated up for you."

Claire did as she was told, feeling the peacefulness of the house enfold her. Built in 1919, it had the kind of craftsmanship that was unheard of now—gumwood and mahogany trim, all corners perfectly mitered, and built-in everything. Built-in bookcases flanked the living room fireplace, there was leaded glass in the dining room's built-in china cupboard, and the master bedroom even boasted a built-in vanity. Like everything else in life, the house's greatest attraction—its age and style—was also its largest drawback. The old pipes were always developing mysterious leaks. The five-foot-wide front door had gradually shifted on its hinges so that all winter long a cool breeze skidded around their ankles. On weekends, Claire haunted the aisles of nearly identical warehouses, each as big as an airplane hangar, that housed Home Depot, Home Quarters or Home Base. Each store carried thousands of items, but never exactly what she needed, some part hand-lathed seventy years before.

Claire had moved in with Charlie shortly after turning thirty. She had met the older woman by literally running into her. Claire had been hurrying downstairs to the weight room at the Mittleman Jewish Community Center. MJCC attracted a lot of non-Jews from the surrounding neighborhood, like Claire, because of its convenient location and reasonable rates. A flyer on the bulletin board at the turn of the stairs caught Claire's attention. The next thing she knew, she had crashed into a tiny old woman in pink tennis shoes. Even sprawled on her back with her head resting against a concrete wall, Charlie had insisted that she was fine, fine, and that there was no need to help her up. A remorseful Claire had insisted on buying her a cup of coffee (while surreptitiously monitoring the older woman for any sign of injury, shock and/or heart attack), and what had begun as an accident had eventually led to a friendship.

When Charlie had invited her to share the house in Multnomah Village, Claire had said yes without even having to think about it. They made a good team. Charlie gained a renter who paid enough to cover the property taxes and who also kept the old house from falling apart. For Claire, the benefits had been even greater. She was thirty years old. Before she moved in with Charlie, she had feared that she was already in others' eyes, if not quite yet in her own, the kind of woman who lived alone with her mother. Now, while she stood in the white claw-footed tub under the showerhead she had installed herself, Claire remembered how her mother had panicked when she told her she was moving two miles away. "But what will I do without you?"

ULIV 1S

∞

"Heating something up" turned out to be a savory stew redolent of herbs from Charlie's window box, accompanied by freshly baked bread. Charlie had taught Claire to bake the European way, not hurrying the dough, but allowing it to rise overnight in the refrigerator, where it tripled in bulk. The result was like nutty brown velvet. After one bite of Charlie's bread, Claire had forever abandoned the store-bought white loaves she had grown up eating, the kind where a single slice could be rolled into a tiny grayish pill.

Charlie poured them both another glass of red wine. "So, what was it like, cleaning out your great-aunt's trailer home?"

"Incredible. There was junk everyplace. I thought my mom was a pack rat, but this was worse. Aunt Cady must have saved everything she ever owned, and it was all covered in dust. You can guess what that did to Evan's allergies."

Charlie made a muffled snort, but Claire heard it, as she was meant to. It was no secret that Charlie thought she could do better than Evan, with his thin mouth and calculated approach to life.

"Evan was a saint, Charlie. He just kept shoveling through all this, this—*crap* she had saved, just methodically clearing one space and then moving on to the next."

Charlie sat back in her chair. She was so small that her shoes dangled two inches above the floor. She looked like an aging little girl playing dress-up. "And your aunt, she had no friends, no family of her own? She had lived like a hermit?"

"Well, she never married."

"No lovers?" Charlie arched an eyebrow. Even at seventy-eight, she could still draw men to her.

"Before this trip, I would have said no." Claire got up from the table. "I found something that I want your opinion on. Evan didn't think it could be real, not if Aunt Cady owned it."

Kneeling on the floor, she unfastened the suitcase, which she had carried on her lap all the way back to Portland. She lifted the lid and began to set aside the papers that cushioned the painting. A low moan interrupted her.

"*Nein.*" Charlie's face had gone pale above the edge of her rose-colored sweater. Her eyes were fastened on one of the pamphlets. It showed a half-dozen men in close-cut, neatly pressed uniforms, their backs to a bonfire spitting flames into the darkness that surrounded them. Behind them, another soldier was tossing a stack of books into the flames.

Charlie's mouth fumbled. She raised her hand to cover it, the hand that still bore an obscene embroidery of green numbers along her wrist, ending in the web between her thumb and forefinger. One human being had done that to another, the better to keep track of inventory.

Claire was conscious as never before that the older woman had walked through another world that to her was only a brittle pamphlet, a yellowing photo, a documentary. Charlie had labored in Dachau, that much Claire knew.

"Why do you have these?"

"The papers were in the suitcase, but I don't know why she had them. Maybe she didn't even remember they were there. All this had been untouched for years. Maybe even since the war. Aunt Cady was over there, in Germany. But that's not really what I wanted to ask you about." Claire lifted the last of the papers that cushioned the painting. Its beauty struck her with fresh force, and she heard Charlie gasp.

Across time, the woman's liquid gaze met theirs. She seemed as real as the two women regarding her. Together, Claire and Charlie bent over the painting. For the first time, Claire began to look closely at the things that lay around the woman. The chair, topped by lions' heads, had a row of brass studs across the top, and a pattern of gold diamonds painted on its back. At the edge of the picture, a fringed oriental carpet, patterned in red and blue and cream, lay bunched in folds on the table beside the woman. Claire ran her fingertips across it, almost surprised to feel tiny brushstrokes instead of thick tufts of wool. On top of the carpet a white jug with a curving handle and brass lid rested in a shallow brass basin. The basin held an exquisite mosaic of reflections from the room, tiny chips of paint in all colors.

The dominant colors of the painting were shades of blue and yellow. What could be seen of the woman's dress under the yellow jacket was a deep ultramarine blue. There were echoes of color in the blue tracery of the carpet's flank and in the shadow of the open window's frame. The room was not merely revealed by light, but constructed by it. Even the shadows of the table and the chair shone.

"Look," Charlie said, her finger tracing the wall behind the woman's back. "Do you see what is missing?"

Claire narrowed her eyes. The chair and the table, the pitcher set on the carpeted table—all cast shadows in shades of blue and gray, but the woman herself, the woman who stared back at them with half-parted lips, she cast no shadow at all. This should have made her look one-dimensional, a flat figure painted on top of a real background, but instead it gave her a greater reality. It was as if the woman existed someplace halfway between the painting and the room where the two women returned her gaze.

"She is beautiful," Charlie said. Claire heard the tiny click of her manicured nail as it tapped the dried paint. "And, I would say, genuine. Of course, you would need more confirmation than an old woman's memories." Charlie sat back in her chair, closed her eyes. Her skin was so translucent that Claire could see the delicate blue threads of veins in her eyelids. "We were, you know, a bourgeois family. Before." Claire didn't have to ask before what. "I grew up surrounded by old manuscripts, medals, golden fans, Louis the Fourteenth furniture, vermeil flatware with precious stones on the handles. And paintings. Paintings that had been with the family for generations. All gone now. When I married, I had as part of my dowry a Rembrandt. Or at least a painting from his school. A little painting of a woman sewing. Four hundred years old, and it was as if she were there in the room with you. Like this woman." Charlie opened her eyes, but they remained unfocused, cloudy. "Of course, what do I know, just an old woman with memories."

"What happened to the painting?" Claire knew enough of the answer not to ask what had happened to the family.

Charlie's mouth tightened against the answer. "Göring collected art. Sometimes, it was said, he was willing to trade rather than to simply take. My husband traded the Rembrandt to someone who worked for him, traded it for safe passage to Switzerland. But the official said it was only worth papers for two, not three. When he came back, Richard said I must go, take our son." She pronounced her dead husband's name the German way, with the "i" a guttural long *e*, followed by a hard *k* sound and the second *r* rolled in the throat. Ree-kard. "I argued. I said I would not go without him. Our son, he was just four. Finally I took our son and went away, as we knew I must. But at the border we were turned back, told our papers were no good. And when we returned home, Richard was gone."

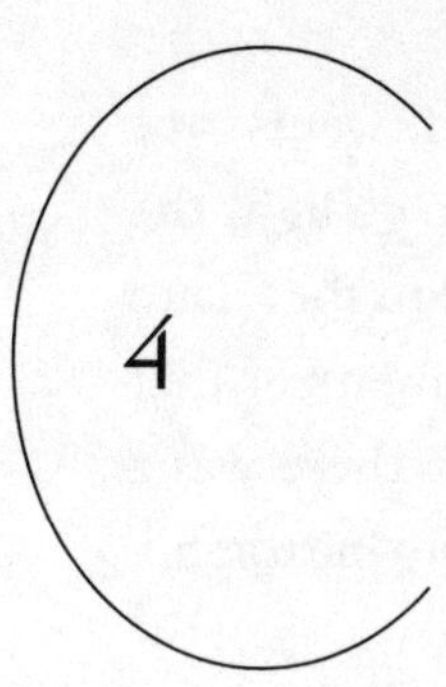

4

That night Claire took a nail file to the mouth of Aunt Cady's diary, prepared to force it open, but the brass band sprang apart as soon as the point slipped inside. She flipped through the pages, reading entries at random. The diary started in 1943, when her great-aunt had joined the Women's Army Corps. Claire counted backward in her head. Aunt Cady had been 26, but in the first few dozen entries she sounded more like a high school girl, listing everything in breathless detail, from the items that made up her clothing ration (*"rayon khaki underwear pants—ick!!"*) to complaints about GI soap (*"horrible brown stuff that is mainly fat and lye"*). As Claire read further, she began to recognize the story beneath the surface, the story of a woman considered an old maid destined to take care of her aging parents, who had grabbed her one chance to get out in the world.

Claire skimmed the first third of the diary, which covered basic training and a few months of clerical work at Fort Des Moines, Iowa, as well as Aunt Cady's reassignment to Fort Oglethorpe, Georgia. Gradually, Cady began to sound older, seasoned, not such a giddy girl. Diary entries grew further apart in time, appearing only when something had deeply disturbed her. She was sent to England as a typist, survived the buzz bombs.

As the end of the war in Europe drew near, she and twenty-one other WACs had been sent to Munich to free up men to go fight the Japanese—or as Aunt Cady put it, "the Japs." It was hard for Claire not to color each entry with her own knowledge, to remember that when Aunt Cady wrote in her diary she did not know there was a fixed date for the end of the war that events were moving inexorably toward, that even winning itself had been no sure thing.

Claire began to read more carefully. She was certain that the secret to the painting's past lay in Germany and what had happened to her aunt there. Aunt Cady had evidently worked as a secretary to one of the men overseeing the newly conquered enemy. "I keep track of things, from Harold's meetings to his parties. It's like being his wife with none of the perks. He is short with me unless he wants something, and then he is sweet."

May 10, 1945

They have billeted us in someone's old home. The rain comes in where the tiles are partially smashed or blown away, and the wind whistles through the dormer windows. My blanket has a peculiar smell. When I go into the courtyard, glass splinters grate under my feet. Our quarters are surrounded by barbed wire, and if we leave the area, we're supposed to be accompanied by an armed escort. But I'm so tired of never being alone.

The barbed wire can't keep out the smell of lilacs that still grow in the fire-blackened ruins. This last winter, when there was nothing to eat at all, they say children were dying with bloated bellies. People dug for roots in the woods. Old people ate grass, like animals. There is still a great hunger, pent up after years of want. We're not supposed to fraternize with the enemy, but we do a bit. Ordinary people—never were they Nazis, never!—are our servants and our translators, our cooks and our washing women. And they all hint around or come right out and ask for chocolate, milk powder, cigarettes. Things go missing, laundry soap, cheese, even flour. People—our side and theirs—search through empty apartments, looking for something useful. Nowadays it seems like everything belongs to everybody. You see something you need, you take it. I don't complain. And people's lives were hard, you can see it in their eyes, dark and hollow. Our cook has a little girl, about four, and presumably no husband, since one is never mentioned. The two of them are pale and blonde and so thin their knees and elbows show like knots in a string. When I have something sweet, I often find myself giving it to the child. She can make a single chocolate bar last for hours, nibbling on it like a faded little mouse.

Sometimes I feel so lonely here. The other girls go about in great gaggles, inseparable. They are overjoyed at the idea of going home. They borrow lipstick from each other and fix each other's hair and those who aren't married are plotting to be.

The only person I really know here is someone from home, Al Patten. It's funny that I should say "know," because I didn't, not really. He moved in a different crowd, one of the boys who was destined to drop out and go to work in the mill, pulling green chain and making lots of money as long as he was strong. I used to see him standing on the street corner before class, smoking a cigarette, his face already needing another shave. He scared me a little. But war changes things. When he learned we were both stationed here, it was like we were old friends.

May 11, 1945

Went for a walk today, just down the block to what used to be a park, but still, strictly forbidden. The streets were empty and silent. Houses have been replaced by ruins, charred shells, masses of rubble and sometimes even mass graves. Everywhere remnants of the war, disemboweled cars, burned-out tanks, twisted gun carriages. Very few people. Once in a while a miserable figure staggered past me, a man in shirtsleeves, a ragged woman in bare feet. An old man rattling along on the metal rims of a tireless bicycle. They look at my uniform and they look away.

The park has been transformed into a desert. The trees have become stumps, lost to the need for firewood. You have to watch your step because of the trenches that are now filled with rags, cans, bottles, coils of wire, spent shells. It was a terrible place, but it was still good to be alone.

While I was in the park, I saw a group of POWs in the distance, trudging silently, dragging their feet. Some of them limping. Stubble-faced, sunken-eyed, out of step. They didn't look anything like the Germans in the posters at home, who were square-jawed and square-shouldered, with gleaming red eyes. These men were either very young or very old, *Volkssturm* men in patched uniforms sent out to guard the barricades, the last terrible harvest the German officials made from the male populace. Filthy, gray-bearded faces, or boys who had no need of a razor. I heard two of them talking to each other in high voices. Thin in their far-too-loose uniforms, they couldn't have been more than fifteen.

On my way home, I passed a hill of broken brick and stone, and two shaky old women trying to remove some of the rubble with dustpans into a little wagon. At that rate it will take them weeks to dispose of that mountain.

An elderly civilian was digging up corpses from a makeshift plot in front of what had once been a cinema. I guess he planned to rebury them properly in a cemetery. One corpse already lay on the rubble—a long, clay-covered bundle wrapped in canvas. I was aware for the first time what a dead body smells like. A smell too thick to be inhaled.

The digger wiped the sweat from his brow with his shirt sleeve while he stood half-supported by his shovel. When he looked up, he saw me, and my presence enraged him. Maybe it was our bombers who had killed whoever lay at his feet, maybe he was angry to see an enemy looking so well fed, but whatever it was, he started yelling at me. *"How op!"* it sounded like. *"How op!"*

Then he began to rush at me, waving his shovel over his head. My feet were nailed to the ground, but then a man I hadn't even noticed was nearby, an American GI, rushed in and put himself between me and the man. He rattled off a string of German, his hand on his holster, and finally the man dropped his shovel and began to back away.

My savior began to scold me. "You girls are not allowed out of the barracks, and certainly not on your own," he told me. "You could have been killed!"

"All I did was go for a damn walk!" I yelled back at him, and then surprised myself by bursting into tears. And was surprised even more when he took me into his arms and patted me on the back. Strong arms, a rough cheek against my own, the smell of cologne. I stepped back as soon as I could, feeling more than a little off-balance. I'm not like the other girls. I didn't join up thinking it would be a great way to meet men. I'd finally gotten free from my parents—and I didn't feel like cooking or cleaning again for anyone but myself. But still, this man intrigues me. Rudy. Rudy Miller. He has eyes like silver. And he asked if he could see me later.

The next few entries were again like a schoolgirl's as Aunt Cady began to spend time with Rudy—the man, Claire guessed, from the photos. *Rudy said this, Rudy said that, I think Rudy likes me, Rudy kissed me,* then more circumspectly, *Rudy took me to a room.*

June 5, 1945

Our cook, Frau Lehman, invited us—me and Rudy, who she slyly referred to as my "beau"—to a little party tonight. They held it in what remained of their house—the cellar. After walking through a wasteland of rocky rubble, the moonscape that was once their neighborhood, I began to appreciate what a miracle it was that even their cellar had survived. We brought wine with us, and crackers, and some American cheddar, which they thought was funny because they've never seen cheese dyed orange. Our contributions turned out to be all the food there was, which may be the reason they invited us. There was plenty of black market booze, though, something that seared the back of your throat. I didn't drink more than a sip, but Rudy had a fresh glass in his hand every time I looked.

Frau Lehman and her friends were quick to reassure us that they had never supported Hitler, and that they had suffered for their beliefs. I have yet to meet anyone in Germany who admits to having been a member of the Nazi Party. They will look you straight in the eye and say that they never joined, when you know they must have. That they hid their Jewish neighbors in their cellars when the truth more likely is that they looked the other way when someone came for them.

But now everyone is in the same boat, desperate, lying and scheming to find work, to find food. The whole economy here is run on cigarettes. For a few Camels, you can buy anything from a cabbage to a painting. It all depends on how hard up the seller is. Rudy doesn't smoke. At first I thought it was because he considered it a vice, since he so clearly looks down on people who do smoke. Then he told me it's as foolish as a man rolling tobacco in a ten-dollar bill.

On our way home from the party, we passed a group of men—liberated forced laborers and displaced persons—with faces like animals, the skin stretched over the bones, their eyes shifty. They smelled like animals, too. On seeing us, they conferred in a babble of languages—Polish, I think, and French, in addition to German—and then approached us. Rudy pulled his service revolver and they decided to go looking for someone else. One of the men stopped and stretched out his hand to me in a hopeless kind of way. The night was so silent you could hear the sound of the hammer of Rudy's gun being pulled back. They turned and left. I was shaking, but Rudy wasn't frightened at all. I've never seen him scared.

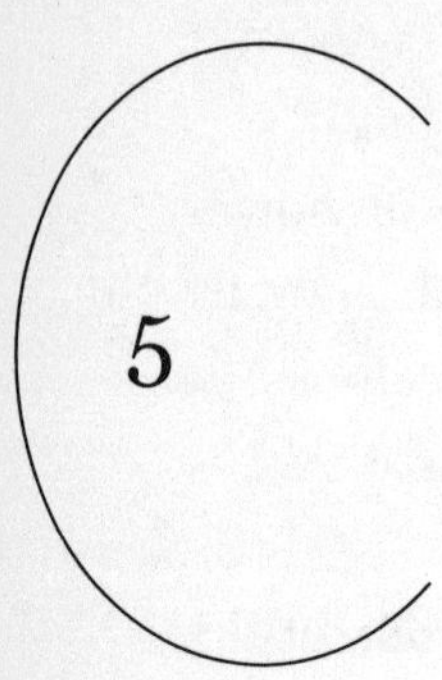

5

In Claire's dream, Evan had just completed building a new bed for her. In real life, tools were foreign to him. His long-fingered pale hands were meant to be tapping the buttons of a calculator, not being turned to bloody pulp under the missed stroke of a hammer. But in her dream, Evan had become an accomplished carpenter. The finished bed was newly painted a red as bright as blood, the glossy color of Chinese lacquer. Evan encouraged Claire to lie down and try it out. Obediently, she climbed in. But in her dream, the bed seemed to shrink, so what had once been a roomy double now seemed barely wide enough to contain her.

Still dreaming, she rose up on her elbows. The bed had shaped itself around her, angling sharply from her shoulders down to her feet. As Evan approached her, smiling a dead smile, she saw that he carried the missing piece—the lid to the new "bed" he had built her. And now Claire recognized the familiar shape that surrounded her. Evan had built her a coffin.

Waking tangled in ropes of sheet, Claire was relieved to find herself in a real bed. Then she looked at the clock and groaned. It was six-thirty on a Monday morning, time to get up and gird her loins for another week at the Custom Plate Department.

TI—3VOM

~

Claire tried to distract herself from the fact that her week was beginning all over again. As soon as she got into the car, she inserted a Spanish language tape into the cassette player on the passenger seat and began to dutifully echo the instructor. The words rolled off her tongue without engaging her brain. Her thoughts were still taken up with the painting and Charlie's reaction to it. Talking about her past had left Charlie looking drained, reminding Claire of how old her friend really was.

As she drove past the neighbor who lived two blocks away, Claire exchanged waves. The other woman was just getting into her car, a Mazda the exact same model and color as Claire's. They shared this ritual greeting every weekday, although they had never spoken. The woman looked a little like Claire, only Hispanic, with high cheekbones and a halo of wiry long dark curls. Claire imagined that she came from someplace exotic like Costa Rica, perhaps spoke with the same lilt and rolling *R*'s as the instructor on the cassette tape.

At the stoplight, Claire pushed back her cuticles with the corner of the Chevron card she kept in the car's otherwise empty ashtray. It was another part of her current self-improvement campaign. She was going to learn conversational Spanish, get her nails manicured and swear off junk food for good.

Nothing ever quite worked out, though, the way Claire had originally envisioned it. For instance, the Spanish tape seemed to have been designed for some nightmare vacation. So far, she had learned to say in Spanish, "My suitcase is lost," "I have been assaulted," "Why do you wish to search the car?" and "My wallet has been stolen."

The line of cars waiting for the ramp signal to the freeway had already backed up onto Multnomah. Claire inched past the mini-mart, which had a new red banner stretched over the entrance. FROM DONUTS TO DIET COKE, START YOUR DAY WITH 7-ELEVEN. Claire felt a little sick as she tried to imagine what that would be like. In front of her was a black pickup truck jacked up on huge tires taller than the Mazda's roof. At the wheel sat a tiny blond with a bad perm. On the back of the truck was a bumper sticker saying, ENJOY LIFE! THIS ISN'T A DRESS REHEARSAL!

Even on the freeway, traffic was still crawling. It thinned only as she pulled out of the Terwilliger curves. With a cough and a jerk, the Mazda finally found fourth gear. "Bump-bump," Claire muttered along with the car as the tires thumped over the same pothole on the Marquam Bridge that she crossed every weekday morning.

Claire's ten-year-old Mazda 323 drove Evan crazy. She had bought it used shortly before she met him, another step on her road to independence, even if she was doomed to always be years behind anyone else her own age. To her, the car's interior, which smelled like the previous owner's Shi Tzu, held the invigorating scent of freedom.

Even when it had been new, the car had been cheap, occupying the lowest rung of Mazda's offerings. It lacked a passenger sideview mirror, and the wipers didn't have an intermittent setting. In the summer, Claire had to peel her thighs from the vinyl bucket seat. The "sound system" consisted of a radio that squawked and squealed when turned up above a murmur. The dash was pock-marked with holes where gauges on the more expensive option package would have gone. There was even a rectangular recess in the center of the dash (helpfully labeled QUARTZ) meant for a clock—if the original owner had ponied up for much more than four tires and an engine.

But the Mazda did get thirty miles a gallon. And even more important, it was paid for. Claire had spent enough years with her mother to know that debt was a trap. So no matter how much Evan badgered her, she refused to get another car.

To compensate, he seized any opportunity to cushion Claire against the random blows of fate. The car's trunk was filled with his gifts. The first Valentine's Day after they met, he had given her a neon yellow banner that read CALL POLICE in three-foot-tall black letters. Last Christmas, Evan, who knew less than nothing about tools, had taken the advice of a Sears salesman (who must have met his sales goals for the month in a single hour) and bought her a red metal tool chest full of Craftsman tools. She guessed Evan had been seduced by the foldout drawers, by the way the tools marched in silver order from smallest to biggest. Claire, who was just beginning to understand how Charlie's old house worked, had little idea of what to do with these mysterious wrenches and widgets. If she ever did break down by the side of the road and offered her toolbox to the first stranger who stopped to help her, he would probably turn out to be a psychopathic sex killer who would turn her own tools on her in unspeakable ways.

Evan (who had his own set of the U.S. Army Corps of Engineers maps of the fault lines that ran under Portland) had even supplied Claire with a backpack filled with emergency earthquake rations. In the event of an earthquake, Claire was to find her way to her trunk, shrug on the backpack and stagger to clear ground. The backpack's offerings included plastic pouches of water, a space blanket and a first aid kit with a sticker trumpeting that it contained 137 items. Closer inspection had revealed that 120 of those items were miniature Band-Aids. For nourishment, there was an intriguingly heavy foil-wrapped rectangular package about the size of a deck of cards. According to the label, it contained enough dehydrated food to feed five people for three days. The fine print cautioned that the contents were to be consumed with plenty of water.

Claire pulled into the parking lot and then glanced at her watch.

Two minutes to make it into the building before Roland and/or Frank would note her as tardy. With a sigh, she shouldered her tan leather backpack, left over from years of riding the bus. Then she had been forced to lug around a whole day's worth of needs, instead of using her car as a closet on wheels. The backpack still held every necessity: Band-Aids, Advil, a flashlight, snacks, a toothbrush, foil-wrapped towelettes, a sewing kit, matches. Her co-workers joked that she probably had a hand grenade in there someplace, too, but whenever anyone needed something, they came to her.

Every now and then, Claire tried to imagine herself as the kind of woman who could pare down her needs into a few things that would fit into a tiny sleek evening bag. A lipstick and a gold card, perhaps. But the backpack held more and kept her hands free.

Outside the building's doors a clump of smokers huddled in solidarity. More and more, it seemed to be only the secretaries, security guards and housekeepers who smoked—no suits among them. One plump older woman in a red polyester miniskirt was taking alternate sucks from a cigarette and a purple lollipop. Next to her stood one of the building's security guards, broad, squat and neckless, a blond crewcut young man who obviously lifted weights in his spare time. He looked at Claire with a half-smile, and she started to return it until she realized he was only admiring his reflection in the windowed corner of the building.

In the elevator, Claire pulled out her card key. She hated the picture of herself on it, which more closely resembled a Catholic high school girl gone bad, a schoolgirl's face with one eye half-closed in what appeared to be a slutty wink. She flashed it over the sensor and then pressed the button for the thirteenth floor. When she had first come to work for the state, she had found it disconcerting that the state rented space in a building with a thirteenth floor and that she had to work on it. Now she no longer thought about it.

The doors opened and she stepped out onto the flat orange carpeting that covered the floors of the Portland outpost of the License Plate Division of Oregon's Motor Vehicles Division. While others in the department dealt with the minutiae of ordinary license plates (new, lost, stolen, missing, damaged), Claire, Frank and Lori, and their supervisor, Roland, made up the section that specialized in vanity plates.

On the way to her desk, Claire passed a homemade sign on purple posterboard that was taped to the wall. In wobbly lines of gold sparkles it spelled out YOU DID IT!!! The triple exclamation points particularly grated on Claire. She could imagine Roland, the tip of his tongue protruding between his crowded teeth, as he struggled to keep the three lines of Elmer's glue parallel to each other. The poster celebrated the month of September, when they had managed to meet their "quality target" for issuing vanity license plates within a certain number of days after the application was filed. Roland and Ed, who was the manager for the entire division, never did any of the actual work involved in issuing license plates themselves. Instead Ed went to a number of "meetings" (most of which the office had long ago discerned took place in his parked car, where his only company was a paper-bagged bottle from his glove compartment). And Roland spent his hours devising a series of "motivational tools" for his staff of three. Hence the poster.

Despite management inefficiency, their little section was a lucrative one. For a fee, Oregon motorists could order license plates containing their chosen word or phrase, up to seven digits. People were vain, but that vanity brought in a lot of money for the state. There were 78,988 vanity plates on Oregon vehicles, each of which had cost $45 initially and then $30 a year to keep.

Most requests for personalized plates were for a person's hobby, occupation or first name. Others were more creative. That was where the problems began. People were always trying to slip something past you.

It was Claire and her co-workers' job to approve or deny the applications, deciding if words were obscene or otherwise objectionable. Their tools were a set of dictionaries (including specialized ones for slang and obscenities), the bathroom mirror, a good eye for vulgar and otherwise offensive words, and a Rolodex. The Rolodex held the numbers of various people who knew specialized slang, like the doctor who could advise them if a proposal was an obscure word for a certain body part.

Doing this job required a dirty mind and a big vocabulary. In ten years, Claire had learned how to say "fuck" in thirty-eight different languages. When she first started, the process had seemed interesting. Claire knew a little bit about everything, which meant she caught on to the hidden reasons behind plate requests faster than anyone else. Unfortunately, most people weren't very clever. Take the request that was waiting on top of her in-basket: COWPOO. The applicant had tried to justify this witticism by claiming he was a cowboy.

First stop for any new application was the "Vulgar List" of several hundred forbidden words, phrases or alphanumeric combinations. Each had either been rejected outright or recalled after a citizen complained to the department and a second look determined that a word or phrase was offensive.

In addition to the obvious no-no's, the Vulgar List included "ethnic" words, if they referred to a definable class of persons and ridiculed or supported superiority of that class. A few years before, it had taken Claire several hours to decide if VIKING counted as an ethnic word. She finally approved it. GOD was on the list because it had been deemed a bit sacrilegious. But there were always gray areas. The whole task of rejecting or accepting these messages involved detecting perceptual crime, a difficult area for the government to regulate. No bathroom vocabulary was allowed—but what about PP DR for a urologist? Claire had been inclined to allow it, but had been overruled by Roland.

COWPOO, however, was an easy call. Claire stamped Rejected on the form and tossed it in her out-box. The next applicant wanted BUNDY, the last name of the Northwest's notorious serial killer. Rejected. GETNAKD. Get real. What did people think the department was going to do? There were kids out there learning to read by looking at these plates, and older people who didn't have a sense of humor about some of this stuff. The next applicant wanted RESQ ME. On the optional explanation lines, the applicant had written that he was a fireman, which made the plate even more appropriate. After checking it out to make sure it didn't contain any hidden messages, Claire stamped Approved on it and tossed it in her out-basket.

The year before, a woman had appealed for the right to use a feline nickname on her set of plates. She had even sent a photograph of her car—a Mercury Lynx adorned with cat decals and with stuffed kitty toys in the back window. A nervously giggling Roland and a blasé Ed had finally approved the plate, with the result that the state of Oregon now had a PUSSY roaming the roads.

Claire spent the first part of the morning approving DEVORSD, SWMR, and IMHERE, plus applications from two people requesting their first names who were lucky enough that they weren't already taken. Then she came upon a more problematic request.

"Frank?" she called over the gray burlap cubicle wall. To stay on Frank's good side, Claire made it a point to occasionally ask for his advice. "What do you think I should do with 'Y-R-U-F-A-T?'" Too late, she realized how it might sound to him.

She heard his sigh and the squeak of a chair being pushed back, and then his slow footsteps around the corner. Finally he appeared at the entrance to her cubicle, nearly eye to eye with Claire although she was still sitting. As if to make up for his height, Frank had gradually gained weight over the years they had worked together, until now he was nearly square.

"Here's what you should do, Claire." Frank, like a used car salesman, tended to insert his listener's name frequently into any conversation. "Deny it."

Even though that was exactly what she had planned to do, Claire felt herself rebelling. "On what grounds? It's not on the Vulgar List."

Frank shrugged, considering the case already closed. "So what? Claire, if we approve it, then chances are someone will complain, it will be yanked, and in six months YRUFAT will be on the Vulgar List anyway."

"Maybe I'll talk to Roland," Claire said, not intending to do any such thing.

"Maybe there's no need to talk to Roland." Frank gave her a knowing smirk.

"Why not?"

"Maybe pretty soon there won't be any Roland to talk to."

"What do you mean? He's leaving?" Claire felt a lightening in her bones. No more arm around the shoulder in the guise of "team-building." No more clumsy comments about her hair or clothes, no more looks that lingered on her legs.

"Not exactly. I hear he's being kicked upstairs."

"Promoted? Are you serious?"

Frank nodded, his expression managing to convey both the smugness of an insider's knowledge and a patronizing amazement that Claire was out of the loop.

"Promoted to what?"

"I heard they were letting Ed retire on disability. Roland's got the experience to replace him."

"Experience? How can you say that? He's twenty-five and he's only been here two years. The only reason we *have* a Roland is that the state believes people can't make decisions on their own. What does he do all day besides stay in his office coloring and sprinkling sparkle? It's like being managed by a first grader who somehow acquired a college degree."

Frank had folded his arms during this outburst, his expression unreadable. Now he said, "I've never said this before, Claire, but I think those charts add a lot of value. It's like Roland has helped us all to know where we are going and what vehicles we need to get there."

Too late, Claire saw which way the wind was blowing. "Who do you think they'll replace Roland with?"

"You have to admit it's a fantastic opportunity for the right person."

There was no question as to who Frank saw as the right person. "If that's what you want, you should go for it." Might as well stay on the good side of the man who would probably be her new boss. Claire switched the subject to buy herself time to think. "Um, did you have a good weekend?"

"It was great. Liz and I have decided to make it permanent."

Liz was Frank's longtime girlfriend, just as short and pale as he was, although she was thin and also very quiet. Over the years, Claire had seen her at a variety of strained staff picnics and Christmas parties. Each time the woman had done nothing but mumble hello while keeping her eyes downcast.

"Congratulations! When are you two getting married?"

"Married?" Frank echoed incredulously. "We're getting tattooed. That's the only thing that's really permanent."

2RU LUV, Claire thought, making a mental note to tell Lori at break time.

The fifteen-minute midmorning coffee break was religiously observed by everyone who worked for the state. Managers stayed in their offices, while the rank and file drank stale coffee in the glow of the break room's vending machines. Today, Claire and Lori traded sections of the *Oregonian* while Frank sat at a table in the far corner of the room, reading a science fiction paperback and eating an overripe banana, the same snack he had had every day for the last ten years. Claire felt a little guilty taking a break when she planned to pad her lunch hour, but if she didn't take one everyone would notice and ask her about it.

"Hey, Lor, weren't you supposed to go to the doctor this morning to see what was wrong with your stomach? What did he say?"

"Oh, yeah, that was real useful," Lori said, resting her hand on her abdomen, which was perfectly flat even when she was sitting down. Her hair hung down in two dark wings, a contrast to last week's bleached blond Madonna look. Every so often, boom, Lori was a brunette. Or she came to work a redhead. Claire had no idea what her natural color was. Lori continued, "No wonder my stomach hurts. According to this booklet the doctor gave me, my digestive system is run by tiny cartoon elves."

"Elves?"

"And they've got it in for me. The booklet has illustrations that show how these elves can turn the wheels so everything goes faster or instead go on strike so nothing works at all. I guess mine are evil elves."

Claire had a quick image of Lori's insides populated by elves that looked like the Snap! Crackle! Pop! trio, only with their smiles replaced by sneers.

"My stomach's not doing so hot today, either. Just the thought of seeing Mr."—Claire pitched her voice soft and high—"Mr. 'Maximize the Output So We Can All Avoid Redundancy' this afternoon makes me feel queasy." She was good at mimicry, but Roland's prissy way of equally accenting every syllable made it easy. She tapped the front of the Metro section. "Do you think there's something wrong with Portland? All the local stories are about sex. Here's a guy, this social worker, who had sex with a thirteen-year-old client. His defense is that it was her idea. And this story here says the city's prostitution-free zones are just pushing it out into the suburbs. And here's a school superintendent who got fired for using school money to buy pornography."

Lori leaned over to read out loud. "Including videos entitled *The Adventures of See More, Virtual Vixens,* and *Mom, Sis and Spot.*" She grinned. "That one should be a question on *Jeopardy!* 'What X-rated video violates at least three sexual taboos in its four-word title?' 'Alex, what is *Mom, Sis and Spot*?'"

A disapproving sigh came from Frank's corner, which they both ignored.

Claire pointed to a story below the fold, next to an ad for bargain fares to New York City. "At least this one isn't about sex. ANIMAL RIGHTS ACTIVISTS DEMONSTRATE AGAINST THE WIENERMOBILE."

"The Wienermobile?"

"You know, that car that looks like a giant hot dog in a bun? They were holding auditions at the Coliseum for a new kid to sing the Oscar Meyer wiener song in the next commercial." Claire read aloud from the article. "A costumed 'pig' and a companion 'butcher' greeted the Wienermobile to protest what People for the Ethical Treatment of Animals called 'cruel intensive pig farming.' But Oscar Meyer representatives were on hand to give the youngsters a 'warm wiener welcome.'"

"'Warm wiener welcome?'" Lori raised one eyebrow. "Are you certain that story isn't about sex? When I was in college, all the guys were hoping to give you a warm wiener welcome." She turned to the comics. "Oh, I clean forgot to ask you. Did you find anything interesting in your aunt's trailer this weekend?"

"Most of it was junk. There was a little painting I liked a lot, though. And my aunt's diary of when she was in Munich after the war."

Lori perked up. "A diary? Really? That's cool."

Claire had impulsively tucked the diary in her backpack while she was getting ready for work, and she pulled it out to show Lori.

She flipped it open at random. A fusty smell rose from the pages, which were etched with a delicate filigree of blue-green mold. Claire read aloud.

> *May 27, 1945*
>
> Rudy [that was her boyfriend] gave me the most beautiful inlaid bracelet today. It's a silver cuff etched with flowers. At the center of each flower is a blue stone that he says is lapis lazuli. He traded a pair of boots with a DP for it.
>
> We got in an argument, though. I said I didn't know if it was right to take advantage of someone who had nothing.

"Do you know what a DP is? Was?"

Lori shrugged.

Claire looked over at where Frank sat, still engrossed in a battle between the mutants and the humans on the planet Zorgan. "Frank, aren't you a World War II buff?"

He spoke without looking up from his book. "Troop movements, battles. I've re-created the battle of Arnhem in my basement."

"What?" Claire was beginning to lose track of the question she wanted to ask.

"The battle of Arnhem. With toy soldiers and little silk parachutes and plasticine mountains and some miniature trees from a train set. It's all done to a one to one hundred scale. Sometimes I spend all weekend in the basement working on it."

No wonder Frank was so pale. "If someone who lived in Germany during the summer of 1945 used the term 'DP,' what would they mean?"

"A displaced person—a refugee. Europe was crawling with them after the war." Frank, never a curious sort, didn't inquire why she had asked. Instead he folded down a corner of his paperback to mark his place and stood up from the table.

Claire looked up at the wall and saw that it was already 10:15. Reading more of Aunt Cady's diary would have to wait.

∾

Claire felt sneaky, devious—and damp, since she was coatless on a rainy day. Her lunch hour was nearly half gone, and all she had done was drive to Multnomah Village and find a place to park. She was hoping that her co-workers wouldn't notice her absence. If anyone did come looking for her, the coat she had left behind should serve as a decoy. With luck, they would just think she was in the bathroom.

A bell jingled above her head when Claire pushed open the door to Eclectica. The shop lived up to its name, selling everything from novelty salt and pepper shakers to Native American rugs to Depression glass. For a time an elaborate rattan elephant saddle had filled the front window. And once or twice Claire had seen a painting for sale.

A fiftyish-looking man looked up from behind the glass counter that doubled as a display case for old jewelry. The store was otherwise empty. "May I help you?"

"I'm not sure. I recently inherited a small painting. I guess it's an oil, but I don't know much more about it than that." Her words seemed inadequate, somehow disloyal to the woman in the painting.

"I'll have a look at it if you want. If you want it appraised, I'm *not* your man, but I've been kicking around this business a long time. I might be able to tell you something."

Claire had cushioned the painting with bubble wrap. Now she freed it and laid it on the counter.

The man sucked in his breath. He slipped on a pair of half-glasses that hung from a silver chain around his neck.

"You're a *beauty*, aren't you, dear?" he murmured, addressing the woman in the painting. "But what are you? Not English, no, definitely not that. Possibly French?" He paused. "*That* doesn't seem right, either."

With his fingertips he picked up the painting and walked from behind the counter toward the window. His eyes never left the face of the young woman in the painting. Claire was struck by the contrast between the real man and the painted woman—his middle-aged body in Dockers, with a tan polo shirt pulled snug over his potbelly, and she serene in the soft folds of her lemon yellow jacket. He tilted the painting to the window and stretched out his finger. "See the tiny cracks in the paint? Those are called *craquelure.* Oil paint takes as long as a *century* to dry, so this lady of yours is at least as old as that. Judging by her dress, and if you assume she was painted wearing clothes of the period, I would say much older. And painted by someone who knew what he was doing." He turned his face to Claire, his tired eyes filled with longing and something like awe. "My *God*, where did you get this?"

"I found it in my great-aunt's mobile home underneath the bed. I think she'd been there a long time. My aunt was stationed in Germany after the war ended."

The shopowner looked upward, speculating. "It could be that this little *jewel* went missing during the war. A lot of things lost their way during that time." He handed the painting back to her reverently, reluctantly. "I can't really tell you anything. She's Flemish, perhaps, or Dutch. And I would guess several hundred years old—painted somewhere maybe in the 1600s. I know enough to know when I'm out of my depth. And if you want my opinion, anyone in this *town* would be out of their depth with that. She needs to be appraised by a professional, someone who knows the period *intimately*. Someone who can be shown something and immediately tell you who this lady was, as well as everything from the name of the artist to what he had for breakfast the day he finished the painting—and *then* trace the provenance forward three hundred years."

"The provenance?"

"The history of who owned the painting, how it came to change hands." He smiled apologetically. "Nothing against people who live in *trailer* parks, but I would expect past owners to have been duchesses or earls. The type of people who live in *castles.*" He paused, then chose his words carefully. "There's a time-honored tradition of spoils of war. And sometimes there's a fine line between that and looting."

Claire's head was spinning. Could this painting rightfully belong to someone else? She remembered her great-aunt's diary, with its mention of an inlaid bracelet—probably the same bracelet she had found in the suitcase. "What would you do if you were me?"

Without hesitation, he said, "Go to New York. *Don't* go to a dealer or an art gallery. Take her to Sotheby's or Christie's or Avery's. Have someone tell you who she is, where she comes from, and what she's worth."

"Don't they charge money for that?"

"The big houses don't. Of course, they take a percentage if they sell it. In this case, my hunch is that would amount to a *tidy* little sum."

MYTB$$

∾

Claire arrived back at the office just in time for her monthly "Hold the Gains" meeting with Roland. She knocked on his office door and then pushed it open. Hundreds of staring eyes greeted her. Like Aunt Cady, Roland also had a collection of animals, although in his case it was elephants. The collection dated back to his childhood and had followed him from his parents' home to college to this job, his first. Each Christmas or birthday, someone in the department drew the short straw and was forced to take on the task of finding the group gift—a new elephant unlike the others he already owned. Now they peered at her from bookshelves and the tops of filing cabinets, dozens of elephants in all shapes, sizes and materials. Although Roland boasted that the elephant thing had begun because of his excellent memory, Claire sometimes thought that given his big ears and lumpy body, he felt more at ease surrounded by animal versions of himself.

The elephants weren't the only ones appraising her. Claire repressed a shudder as Roland's eyes slowly traveled from her head to her feet. "Is that a new outfit?" he asked.

She tried to keep things from veering off course by not answering his question. "How did my charts for last month look?"

"That's what I like about you, Claire. Always so business-minded." He pulled a sheaf of paper from a file. "And last month you did your usual excellent job." Roland handed her the charts, created in Excel on his IBM but hand-colored by him with rainbow pens.

Although there were more than a dozen charts, each one actually showed the same piece of information—the number of applications the department had processed, broken down by employee. Roland was enamored of the fact that with just a few clicks of the mouse, the computer could present the same data in many different ways. Each month he printed out pie charts, bar graphs, holograms, scatter diagrams, crisscrossing lines and bell curves. He experimented with 3-D, legends, labels, dual axes and drop shadows. It was Roland's dream to get a color printer so that he wouldn't have to spend hours in his office coloring. At the beginning of each fiscal year, he routinely requested a color printer, claiming he would "utilize it to facilitate improved work process flow." Just as routinely, Ed had denied the request. Now, if Frank's rumor were true, Roland might be able to fulfill his dream.

No matter what chart type Roland used, Claire's bar or pie slice was always slightly larger than her co-workers. Over the years, she had developed the ability to steadily review applications while day-dreaming. And with the exception of today, she had never taken extra time for lunch or over coffee. She had even accumulated 689 hours in her vacation time bank, just under the state-mandated limit of 700 hours.

Claire never knew what she was supposed to say when confronted by Roland's endless sheaf of paper. She flipped through the pages, and after what seemed a long enough silence, she pushed the papers back to him and mumbled, "Thank you."

"You're always pushing the envelope," Roland said. "Do you know how much I appreciate that, Claire? I can always count on you. I wish I could get the others to model your paradigm." Roland spoke incomprehensibly in a vain effort to make other people think he was smart. He invariably had the latest management tome prominently displayed on his desk, and tried out as many of the concepts as Ed permitted. So far, the department had suffered through self-directed work flow, quality circles, self-esteem banks, team-building retreats and re-engineering.

The business end of their meeting presumably at an end, Roland leaned back in his chair, relaxed and expansive. "Did you have a good weekend?" He took one of his collection of elephants—a plastic one about seven inches tall—and began to walk it up and down his desk.

In her mind, Claire saw the woman's painted gaze, felt the ridged brushstrokes under her fingertips. She kept her answer short, hoping that Roland would let her go. "Uh-huh."

"I went to that Rod Stewart concert I told you about. Should have gone with me! You really missed a great show." Roland had offered her a ticket weeks ago under the guise of altruism—he had an extra ticket, it was a sold-out show, perhaps she would like to go.

He had seemed almost angry when she declined. "That guy knows how to rock." For emphasis, he tipped the elephant on its hind legs and made it dance while humming the first few lines of "If You Want My Body." Claire repressed a shudder at the thought of sitting by Roland's side, watching the bobbing bleached crest of the skinny, aging singer as he pelvic-thrust his way through twenty-year-old hits.

She began to push back her chair. Roland had danced the elephant halfway down the desk, until it was now directly behind another elephant—a squat unpainted wood carving. The positioning brought the two elephants' hindquarters into a suggestive proximity. Roland offered her a sideways leer.

"What does this make you think of?"

"It makes me think I'm not going to stay in this meeting," Claire said, surprising both of them. She stood up and reached for the door.

"Wait! Wait! I'm sorry." The dancing elephant dropped onto the desk with a thud.

Claire felt like a teakettle about to boil. "For the last two years I have overlooked your behavior toward me, but that is beyond the limit! Do you realize that what you just did qualifies as sexual harassment? I hear the state has a new head of HR who made her reputation by exposing stuff like that."

"Shh! Shh! Quiet down! You don't know what you're saying! Heck, I didn't know what I was saying!" He was flushed to the tips of his big ears, and Claire guessed he was seeing his promotion slipping away. The sight of him cowering instead of leering sent a thrill of power through her.

"You knew exactly what you were saying."

Roland made a soothing motion with open hands, as if Claire were a dangerous dog. "There's no need to go running off to HR about this. In fact, I was already planning on talking to HR about you in regard to a completely unrelated matter. There's a good possibility of a promotion in this department, and my input on it is pretty important." He gave her a strained, fearful smile. "How would you like to be sitting in this office someday?"

"I don't want to be you, Roland." Claire didn't even want to be herself, but that was too hard to explain to him. "You want me to forget about what you just did? Then give me some time off. I want a week. Starting tomorrow."

"But this is the busy season!" There was no busy season. They both knew Roland was clutching at straws.

"I guess I'll be telling HR about your mating elephants, then."

"All right, all right. You can have a week off."

"Good."

When Claire closed the door, Roland was slumped dejectedly at his desk, his palm resting protectively on the sharp curves of the wooden elephant's butt.

CUNQRT

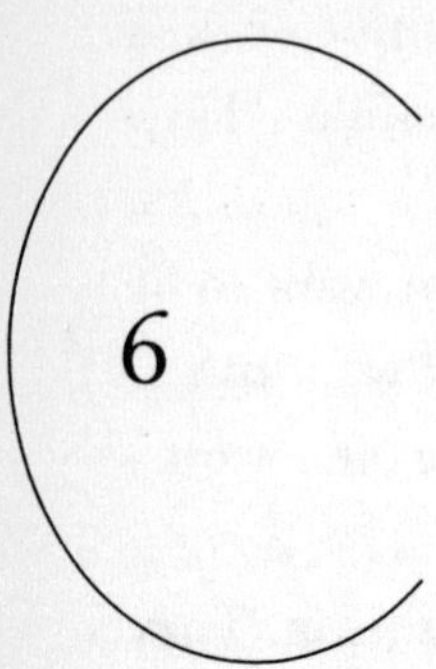

6

Claire ran down the back of one of 35th Avenue's undulating hills, fast enough that she could ignore the autumnal chill still lingering from the night before. Her speed was fueled partly by exhilaration and partly by fear. Only an hour ago, she had booked a flight to New York for the next day, Wednesday. She had half hoped that she might even be able to avoid spending the night, just stay long enough to take a bus from the airport to an auction house, and then bus right back to a waiting plane. That alone had seemed terrifying but possibly manageable. But the airline clerk on the other end had patiently explained that the new low fares required a Saturday night stay. And she had found herself saying yes.

So now Claire was going to New York, a place she knew only from movies and books. It wasn't just the run that was making her heart pound and her palms sweat.

When Claire had proposed the idea last night, Charlie had encouraged her, digging out guidebooks and making lists of things to pack, visit and bring home. But she had not done the one thing that Claire had secretly hoped for—offered to come with her. Charlie loved New York and visited there every few years. But she had just won a part in a Mittleman Jewish Community Center musical, and she could not miss nearly a week's worth of rehearsals.

After she had made her plane reservation, Claire had been excited, thinking that in only a matter of hours she would be doing those things she had read about—studying the exhibits of the Metropolitan Museum of Art, walking through the holding rooms at Ellis Island, applauding a Broadway musical. But now she was frightened by her own daring. She had never been farther east than the Idaho border. By tomorrow night she would be in a city of seven million people, many of them, according to *NYPD Blue*, intent on either conning or killing her.

As she approached the crest of Capitol, she concentrated on keeping her fists pumping. The trick to taking a hill was to forget about the legs and keep the arms pistoning. For two blocks she was helped by another runner who swung in ahead of her, a tall man who landed on the outside edges of his shoes and barely skimmed his feet along the ground. Claire matched him step for step, mimicking both his pronation and his efficient strides.

Once over the top of the hill, Claire began to lengthen her stride. She imagined herself walking briskly down Fifth Avenue, looking right at home in the crowds. With her legs scissoring past each other and the sweetly rotten smell of the wizened roadside blackberries in her nose, she felt fully alive. Maybe she would be okay in New York. People went there all the time. She was an adult, she was strong, she would have Charlie's advice to fall back on. With a surge of energy, she ran faster.

Claire made it to her mom's in record time. Standing outside her apartment, Claire could hear someone inside chatting away. When Jean opened the door, Claire realized the sounds she had heard had come from the twenty-seven-inch Sony that held pride of place in the living room.

A look of alarm passed over her mother's round face. "What are you doing here this time of day?" She was dressed in a purple velour jogging suit that had never been jogged in. "You didn't get laid off, did you?"

"Don't worry, Mom, I'm taking a few days off and was just out for a run. I'll have that job until I die." Claire said it in jest, but she suddenly had a vision of herself at sixty-five, her age-spotted hands bringing down the REJECTED stamp on some twenty-first-century version of ILUV69.

Her mother had already transferred her gaze back to the TV set. A talk show had degenerated to the point where two young girls were toe to toe, screaming at each other, while the audience hooted and booed. "If you stay long enough, you'll have a chance to see your sister."

"Where's the baby?" Claire asked. Her mother, who claimed her bad back had ruled out a full-time job years ago, made a little money under the table watching Susie's toddler, Eric.

"Asleep in the back bedroom. You can take a peek at him if you want."

As she walked down the hall, Claire was lapped by waves of sound, first from the five-inch black-and-white battery-powered Panasonic on the kitchen counter, then from the thirteen-inch Hitachi in her mother's bedroom. At the end of the hall, Claire turned the doorknob stealthily and pushed the door open. Even in here, a TV was on, an old nineteen-inch Zenith that at least was tuned to *Sesame Street*. Eric, who was just over a year old, lay face-down, fast asleep with his knees drawn up under his chest and his overalled butt in the air.

Her mother's whisper startled Claire. The baby had the power to pull even her mother away from her TV show. "Doesn't he have hair just like Top Ramen?"

Claire smiled and reached out to touch the pale kinked waves. Eric sighed and rolled on his side. She pulled her hand back, afraid of waking him. It had been several months since Claire had seen him, and already he looked more like a little boy, not the baby she remembered.

"I cut out the *TV Guide* for the day he was born, to put in his baby book." Jean pulled up a blanket to cover him, patted him so softly that he didn't stir. "You could get you one of these, you know. And you'll be thirty-five next week, so it's not like there's much time left. They have stories all the time on TV about women who wait too long and then figure out their body won't cooperate anymore."

"Evan doesn't feel ready to get married, Mom." Claire surprised herself by adding, "I don't know if I would want to be married to him anyway."

"Married? Who says you have to be married? I didn't have to be married to have you and Susie. And Susie may be as good as married to J. B., but she sure don't have the piece of paper to prove it." Susie had been the product of a liaison with an on-again, off-again truck-driving boyfriend who still occasionally showed up to take Jean out to dinner or to give Susie a birthday present two months after the fact. When she was growing up, Claire had actually envied her sister the certainty of knowing her father, and knowing that he loved her, at least in a small way.

Her mother turned and shuffled back down the hall in too-small metallic gold mules. Claire trailed behind her. In the living room, Jean huffed a little as she bent over and pressed a button on the bottom of the TV, flicking past different images until the opening credits for *A Better Tomorrow* came on.

"The batteries went out on my remote. I have *got* to get to the store today." Jean tapped on the forehead of a rugged-looking man with a stethoscope around his neck. He was holding an anguished conversation with a nurse while they stood inside a supply closet. "His ex-wife is one of the models on *The Price Is Right.*"

Claire was confused. "The doctor's ex-wife?"

"No, honey, the actor's ex-wife. The *character* doesn't know that *his* new wife is really his half-sister, and she has amnesia because of the coma she was in after the car accident that killed his first wife."

To Claire's mother, TV was more than entertainment, it was a family that shared histories and connections. Maury Povich was married to Connie Chung. Marlo Thomas, who had been the spunky star of *That Girl!* years ago, was married to Phil Donahue, who was still important even if he didn't have a talk show anymore. Fred Savage, who had been so wholesome on *The Wonder Years*, might now be seen beating his girlfriend to death on a "fact-based" TV movie of the week.

Watching her mother stare mesmerized at the TV set's manufactured tribulations, Claire felt a surge of gratitude for Charlie. Even before she had met her, Claire had already been distancing herself from these TV sets, this apartment, this way of life that wanted little and expected even less, but moving in with Charlie had speeded up the process.

Now that Claire no longer saw her mother every day, it was hard not to view her the way a stranger would. For one thing, a stranger would never guess that they were related. Claire was tall and thin, while Jean was short and nearly one hundred pounds overweight. Claire had red-gold curls; her mother's hair was currently dyed a frayed, fried blond. Claire seldom wore makeup. Her mother's mouth was a dark red Cupid's bow, outlined and filled in using colors from a makeup kit brought from a TV infomercial. The pitchster had promised that each kit was specially created for each customer. Jean had had Claire take a Polaroid of her to send to the people who custom-blended each order. The result could sometimes be frightening in the blue glow of the TV set—heavy-lidded eyes, lips so dark they were almost black, stripes of maroon blush that added false hollows to Jean's cheeks. Claire's mother looked less a vamp than an overweight vampire.

"I don't really have time to follow the shows anymore, Mom."

When Claire lived at home, her mother had spent every evening's commercial breaks filling her in on the big events of the daytime shows. The weird thing was that Claire had enjoyed it. "One of the reasons I came over was to ask you about Aunt Cady. I started wondering about her when I was cleaning out her trailer. Like, what did she do in the WACs? And did you ever hear anything about a boyfriend she had during the war? A guy named Rudy?"

"By the time I was old enough to pay attention to Aunt Cady, she was already an old maid working at the bank. No makeup and too skinny. Always so serious, with her nose in a book. Men like someone they can have fun with, someone with a little meat on their bones." Jean looked up at the ceiling, thinking. "Maybe I did hear she had a little something going on before I was born, but by the time she came home he was out of the picture."

"Do you know why they never got married? Or what happened to him?"

"Like I said, I wasn't even born when it happened. I'm surprised that anyone would have looked at her twice. Even as a kid, you heard things about what it had been like, you know, about how the women would do anything for a Hershey bar or a cigarette." She swiveled her eyes back to the TV, where two nurses were deep in conversation. They both wore the starched white caps that Claire knew had been out of favor for fifteen years. "Do you know how many women the average man sleeps with in his lifetime?"

"What? What's your source on this?"

"*Geraldo.*"

"The man who put fat from his butt into his forehead?"

"Seven. The answer is seven. Don't you find that interesting?"

"Very." Her mother didn't seem to notice the sarcasm.

TVZTRU

ෙ

The sputtering roar of the unmuffled engine of a car pulling up outside was loud enough to make it difficult to hear the TV.

"There's your sister."

A few seconds later, Susie walked in. She shrugged off her rabbit-fur coat, revealing the yellow-, orange-, and brown-striped polyester uniform of Spud City, where she worked as a prep person. Although still as thin as when she was a teenager, Susie now looked hollowed out and haggard.

"Hey, Claire. What are you doing around the old homestead?" Without waiting for an answer, she turned to their mother. "Is Eric asleep?" Her fingers, tipped with cherry-red nail polish, were busy unpinning her hairnet.

"He just went down for a nap about a half-hour ago."

"Then I'm going to take a shower. I can't stand smelling like grease for one more second." She went off down the hall.

"How are she and J. B. doing?" Claire asked her mother. J. B. didn't seem to have a job, although he sometimes worked as a day laborer doing construction. She remembered the last time she had seen him, on the Fourth of July. The five of them had watched fireworks on TV while eating a sheetcake her mother decorated with strawberries, blueberries, and Cool Whip to resemble an American flag. J. B. had worn a sleeveless denim shirt that showed off his heavily muscled arms, which were tattooed with a dragon, a dancing showgirl and a Harley-Davidson emblem. He and Susie took turns going out into the apartment's courtyard to light up cigarettes, as they had both pledged not to smoke around their son. Claire had liked him for that, and for the way he frequently scooped up Eric for a hug.

"They're still together, which gives her a longer track record than practically anybody else in the family. He's different, but I like him."

Jean stopped talking when Susie walked back into the living

room. She was dressed in tight jeans, a pair of Candie's mules, and a rhinestone-spangled T-shirt that read COUNTRY BLUES. A towel was wrapped around her head like a turban. She sat down in the armchair, unwrapped the towel and began to comb her fingers through her shoulder-length hair, still blond but clearly now with some help. "So, Big Sis, what are you up to these days? How come you're not at work?"

"I came by to ask Mom about something I found in Aunt Cady's trailer."

Her mom turned from the TV to look at her. "I thought you didn't find anything but that diary?" Jean had called Claire the day after her return and had been disappointed by her reply. When she had spoken to her, Claire had found herself neglecting to mention the painting and the troubling baggage it brought with it.

"Well, I did find something. An oil painting of a woman holding a letter. It's only about this big." Claire measured the air in front of her with her hands. "I think Aunt Cady got it when she was in Germany. That's why I've was asking you all those questions, Mom. When I first found it, I knew it was beautiful, but I didn't know if it were real. But I've shown it to a few people, and they think it might be very old. Maybe several hundred years, even. So"—she could feel her heart begin to race again at her audacity—"I'm going to take it to New York. That's what I came over here to tell Mom."

"New York?" Jean echoed. To Claire's surprise, she heard envy in her voice. "The Big Apple?"

Susie dropped the towel in her lap. "I don't understand. Why do you have to go to New York City?"

"I need someone to examine the painting, and that's where the world's experts are."

"You mean you have to find out if it's worth money or not?"

Claire couldn't think of a way to describe all her tangled thoughts about the painting. "That, and how old it is, and who painted it and maybe who the lady in the painting was. Mom, how do you think Aunt Cady came to have it?"

Her mother's answer surprised her. "Things go missing, don't they? And somebody has to find them, right?"

⁂

It wasn't until after Claire left that Jean remembered she hadn't told her about the reporter from the *Medford Mail Tribune* who had called two days before. The paper, he said, was beginning a series of in-depth stories on the recently departed, not to replace obituaries but rather to supplement them. Each story would give readers a glimpse of the real person who lay behind an obituary's brief biographical sketch and list of grieving survivors. The articles would profile the dead through interviews with relatives and close friends, as well as photos of particularly beloved mementos. Jean had told the reporter what little she remembered about her uncle's sister, but as for belongings, she had explained to him that Claire had inherited everything. He had been eager to follow up with her, and requested her phone number and her address, so that he could send a photographer—a *stringer*, he called him—out for pictures. Wouldn't he be surprised, Jean thought now, when he found out that Aunt Cady might actually have had something worth owning instead of just piles and piles of books.

Then the new soap—*Sharing*—came on and she and Susie settled in to watch. And by the time the show was over, Jean had forgotten all about telling Claire about that nice reporter.

⁂

The home office for Kissling Insurance, Inc., was located on the twenty-ninth floor of a downtown office building known locally as

"Big Pink" for its pale copper-colored metal exterior. Patiently, Claire stood waiting in front of the firm's receptionist as she spoke into her telephone headset. She seemed in no particular hurry to finish her conversation. A flock of iridescent-winged starlings flew by the floor-to-ceiling windows. Surrounded by acres of polished dark wood gleaming under recessed lights, Claire felt out of place and unsophisticated. If this was how she felt standing in a Portland insurance firm, then what was she doing going to New York?

The receptionist laughed throatily into the tiny black mike of her headset. "Thank you again. . . . May I help you?"

Without the visual clue of a receiver being put down, it took a second for Claire to realize that this last sentence had been addressed to her.

"I'm here to see Evan Elliott."

"Do you have an appointment with Mr. Elliott, Ms . . . ?" The receptionist arched an eyebrow, clearly not remembering her, even though Claire had been here half a dozen times before to meet Evan for lunch.

"It's Claire Montrose. And no, I don't really have an appointment."

"Then I'll see if he is available. Please have a seat."

She indicated a low-slung leather and chrome armchair. Claire sank into it, her knees higher than her head. The receptionist began a low-voiced conversation, presumably with Evan. From a distance the headset was invisible, giving the impression that she was talking to herself.

"Mr. Elliott will see you now." Continuing her pretense of never having seen Claire before, the receptionist came out from behind her desk to point the way. Claire struggled up from her chair. She was used to being taller than most women. Now she had the slightly disconcerting sensation of being at eye level with the receptionist's red-painted lips, thanks to the woman's four-inch strappy heels.

They were the kind of shoes she and Lori called "fuck-me shoes" if they were in a catty mood.

Claire tapped lightly on Evan's door and then opened it. "Hi, Evan."

Evan looked up from his desk, a frown drawing his brows together. In front of him was a single stack of papers, lined up so neatly that they almost looked bound. "What are you doing here, Claire?"

"I thought I would take you to lunch."

"Lunch? But I brought my lunch." He really looked at her for the first time since she had entered his office. "Since when do you wear jeans to work?"

"I took the day off. In fact"—she took a deep breath—"I took the week off."

"Why?" He looked more put upon than curious.

"Since we got home from my aunt's, I've been showing the painting to people—first to Charlie and then to the guy who owns Eclectica, you know, that shop in Multnomah Village? They both said it was very old, maybe several centuries, and maybe even valuable."

"Right. I'm sure there are a lot of great works of art sitting around under beds in trailer homes across America." For the first time, Claire noticed that the bookshelves behind Evan were dotted with blue stickers from a label maker. She squinted. Under his set of phone books it said "Phone Books."

"They both said the only way to know for sure is to have an expert look at it. So"—she took a deep breath—"I've decided to go to New York for a couple of days. I'm going to get it appraised at Christie's or Avery's or Sotheby's." She found some renewed courage in the way the word *Sotheby's* rolled off her tongue. It sounded rich and exclusive and refined and British.

Evan sat back in his chair and steepled his hands. "You're going to go off on some wild-goose chase, based on nothing more than the opinions of your hundred-and-three-year-old roommate and some guy who runs a junk shop? No, I don't think so."

"What do you mean, you don't think so?" Claire echoed incredulously.

"You're not going to go, that's what I mean." Evan picked up his pen as if it were all settled.

"Are you saying that because of the plane trip? You're worried about it crashing?"

"Of course it's not because of the plane. Statistically, you have an eighty-five percent greater chance of dying in an automobile than an airplane. And that doesn't even factor in for that car of yours." He waved his free hand disparagingly. "No, you're not going because it's a waste—of time, of energy and of money. You're a smart woman, even if you never went to college, so if you think about it even a little I'm sure you'll agree with me."

A wave of heat swept through Claire. Clearly considering the matter settled, Evan wasn't even looking at her anymore. In his tiny, precise handwriting, he made a note in the margin of his paperwork.

She took a soundless step backward on the plush carpet, then another, until her hand was on the doorknob.

"Evan?"

"Hm?" he said, his eyes still on his paperwork.

"I *am* going."

She closed the door on his surprised face. A minute later, Claire found herself shaking behind the wheel of her car.

CC DDAY

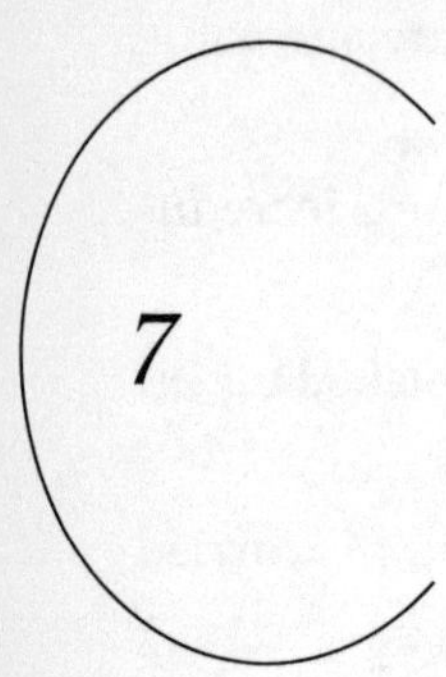

7

Stumbling a little from exhaustion, her bag banging against her hip with every step, Claire emerged from the tube that connected the airplane to the airport. LaGuardia was a huge, ill-lit cavern. Balled-up food wrappers littered the ground around overflowing trash bins. People leaned against NO SMOKING signs, cigarettes in their hands.

On the plane, she had sat next to a woman in her mid-forties who wore her hair in two short blond pigtails, like an aging Olga Korbut. The woman had commandeered the armrest, so that Claire felt boxed in, her knees brushing the seat ahead of her.

As lunch was being served, Claire's seatmate made an announcement. "I've written a book and now I'm going to New York to sell it." They were somewhere over what the pilot said were the Rocky Mountains but what was really only a sea of clouds.

Claire felt a flash of mingled respect and envy. "What's it called?"

"*Freddie the Frog's Spiritual Journey*."

She imagined a green grinning cartoon frog sitting on a lily pad. "So it's a children's book?" She took a bite of her stale turkey sandwich. From the front of the plane came the *tink* of silver on china.

The woman reared back, affronted. "No." She made a little *puh* sound at the stupidness of Claire's question and turned pointedly away to stare out at the clouds.

Later the woman had thawed toward Claire enough to begin chattering on about a recent plane crash in Indiana that had turned every passenger into flesh fragments strewn over a cornfield. "Did you hear about those two hands they found clutching each other? Just the hands?" she asked Claire, oblivious to the angry looks of the other passengers.

Now Claire stood with one foot resting on her suitcase, a safety tip passed along by Charlie, and tried to get her bearings. People streamed around her, as busy and self-possessed as ants. She felt self-consciously tall and pale amid the sea of dark heads that bobbed past her.

Overhead, arrows and signs directed her to limousines, baggage claim areas, rest rooms, food courts, newspaper stands and taxis. This last caught her eye. She'd never been in a taxi and had planned to find a bus to take her into Manhattan. But when in Rome . . .

Outside, Claire took a deep breath, her first official lungful of New York air. It smelled of exhaust with a faint note of disinfectant. Even though it was ten o'clock at night, the sky glowed as if the sun were just about to rise. A long line of yellow taxis snaked its way to the taxi stand, where a matching line of travelers stood waiting. A man with a walkie-talkie waved the first person in line into the first taxi, and the line shuffled forward. That seemed easy enough. Claire joined the end of the line, and tried to affect a posture of boredom. She was relieved to note that her jeans and sweater did not seem terribly out of place.

The man ahead of her turned around and gave her a smile that exposed the jumbled yellow teeth of someone who'd grown up poor. "Want to share a taxi into midtown?"

Claire shook her head without saying anything. The man

shrugged and turned away. Charlie had recommended the Farthingale, describing it as being in the theater district. Claire wasn't sure if that was in midtown or not, and she didn't want to betray her ignorance.

When her turn came she opened the taxi's front door and sat down beside the driver. The driver, a burly man with a beard, gave a grunt of surprise as she sat her bag on top of her feet. Too late, Claire realized her mistake. You were supposed to ride behind the driver, not beside him. Eight hours on a plane had left her muddled.

"Could you take me to the Farthingale Hotel? It's on Forty-fifth between Fifth and Sixth?"

He had already shot out into traffic. "Sure, sure, no problem." His English was heavily accented. The ID card pinned to the sunflap on the passenger side drew her eye. In it, his square, weather-beaten face was without the mustache he now sported.

"Yuri Andropov? Are you from the Soviet Union?"

"No Soviet Union anymore. From Ukraine. See. Ukraine is here." He batted at the air directly above the steering wheel, then moved his hand so that it was over the crackling, squawking radio. "Russia is to the east, here. And Poland to the west. Here." Now both hands were off the wheel. He appeared to be steering solely with his knees. Claire shrank back into her seat. Cars on all sides of them cut back and forth, inches away, without benefit of turn signals, or even, as far as she could tell, a single glance in any mirror. Lanes met, snarled, spun off. Yuri finally dropped his hands to the wheel and Claire could breath again. "Ukraine was rich. Bread basket for Soviet Union."

"Why did you come to America?"

"Independence from Russia was 1991 year. First, we were happy. But things don't change, really. Communists, socialists, they are there still. To open even bank account is bribe after bribe. I work in mines. In six months, I was not paid. So I come here." He turned to look at her, again neglecting the traffic. "Where you live, huh?"

"I'm from Portland, Oregon."

Yuri gave her a blank look as the taxi narrowly missed a black limousine with tinted windows sliding into the lane ahead of them.

"It's above California. On the other coast." Claire found herself imitating him, patting the air above the plastic dash that shone as if it had been polished. "I'm just here to visit."

"You have boyfriend?"

"Not really." Too late, Claire understood Yuri might have an interest in the answer, had read something into her accidentally slipping into the seat beside him.

"I am forty-four years old. Good man. I am in health training, yes?"

"Health training?" Claire echoed.

"I have renounced from meat products utterly. My hand don't touch the sugar basin and salt cellar. I lift the dumbbells on the biceps." He lifted his hands from the steering wheel again, grasped them and shook them above his head like a wining boxer. The taxi began to drift to the side. At the last possible second he dropped his hands to the wheel again. "I engage in jogging also. It is known that jogging is coaching the lungs, heart and vessels excellently. Muscles on my legs tight as the rope. "

Claire patted her bag, on more familiar ground. "I run. I even brought my running shoes for this trip."

"See? We are alike each other. My handshake isn't flabby; my smile isn't guilty. I am good man." Yuri grabbed her hand and placed it on his abdomen. "Stomach muscles strong as oak's board. I am calm, restrained and indulgent to the people's weaknesses. We go to West Virginia tonight and get married, okay?"

"What are you talking about?" Claire tried to pull her hand away, but he gripped it tighter.

"Feel," he said, raising her hand higher. "Feel how my heart intensely beat. I am now falling in the precipice. The question is about the precipice of love."

Claire wrenched her hand away. "There is no question. I am not in love with you." She was relieved when he slowly put both hands back on the wheel.

"No West Virginia?" Yuri's tone was more wistful now, and his eyes were back on the road and not on her. She was relieved to see that they still seemed to be driving into the city.

"No. The Farthingale."

"Too bad." He sighed. "Thus we must decide to turn up from the precipice."

"Yes, we must," Claire agreed.

OL4LUV

*

Even at eleven at night, the circular lobby of the Farthingale was crowded with travelers who wheeled, dragged and kicked suitcases back and forth, the sounds echoing under the high ceiling. A babble of languages washed over Claire as she took her place in yet another line. But the clerk at the front desk, while cheerfully agreeing that she had a reservation, told her that there wasn't a single room left in the hotel.

"But I reserved it on my credit card!"

"Don't worry, ma'am, we've taken the hold off your card. And you can come back tomorrow. It's only tonight that we're overbooked. We've already made arrangements for you at the Hotel Ford. It's just two blocks from here—right across from the *New York Times* building."

Claire shouldered her bag again. What had once seemed an admirably restrained number of items now weighed as much as a bag of cement. She pushed open the brass-bound glass door and walked out into the night. Alert for any sign of danger, she found the street deserted. She walked a block in the wrong direction, past shuttered delis and camera stores with metal pulldown blinds, before finally realizing she must turn back.

In Portland each building was clearly separated from the next, but here the buildings presented a seamless facade. She finally found the address she was looking for in tiny gold leaf numbers on a pair of dirty glass doors. One of the doors was held together with silver duct tape. Inside, three threadbare and dirty carpeted stairs led up to the lobby. Taking advantage of the shelter, an old woman stood at the bottom of the stairs, blowing on her clenched fists. At her feet were a cluster of tattered shopping bags. Being careful not to make eye contact, Claire edged past her and into the lobby, which was decorated in seventies harvest gold and burnt orange. Between her and the front desk were three more transients, young men in stained clothing. A young Chinese man was trying to shoo them outside.

Claire desperately wanted to go someplace else, but where could she go? If the Farthingale was sold out, other hotels probably were, too. And if she went back outside she would be all alone on the street with the three transients, who were finally leaving the hotel. If it was just for one night, Claire decided, she could probably survive here. Behind the bulletproof glass that surrounded the front counter, a bored Chinese woman watched her, smoking a cigarette. For the seventy-dollar charge, Claire signed a hundred-dollar traveler's check and pushed it through the cupped slot.

"ID." The woman looked at her, unsmiling. It was hard for Claire to understand her through the circular silver grate.

"What?"

"Two pieces ID."

Claire had never used a traveler's check before, but this certainly seemed a far cry from the simple matching of signatures the American Express paperwork had promised. She slipped the woman her driver's license and a credit card, and with a sullen expression the woman copied every piece of information from the two cards onto the check. She finally slid back Claire's ID, along with sixteen crumpled ones, two quarters and two dimes.

"I thought it was seventy dollars," Claire protested.

"Tax. Tax nineteen percent." The woman exhaled a cloud of white smoke that completely filled the space between her and the glass.

Claire was filled with a humming nervous exhaustion, too tired to argue, too tired to care if she was being duped. Flushed from his success with the transients, the young man bounded over to take the key the young woman slid to him and then the bag from Claire's slack hand.

"Show to your room," he said.

The elevator smelled of urine, a thought Claire carefully denied when it entered her mind. It had been inexpertly recarpeted with what looked like a garish polyester blanket—a huge red and black plaid pattern, the material already matted and pilled. The carpet been cut slightly larger than the floor, so that the edges curled up against the scarred wooden walls.

They exited into a dimly lit hallway carpeted with the same material as the elevator. Claire picked her way around the bubbles of air that had been trapped underneath. Finally, the bellboy turned the key in the lock of a room at the end of the hall. He opened the door and motioned her ahead of him.

The room was tiny, but he gamely went through the motions, waving one arm around the darkened room as if he were showing her a grand suite, even opening the doors to the tiny bathroom and minuscule closet. None of the lights seemed to be working, but his smile only grew wider each time he flicked a switch and was met with no response. Finally one worked, and he grinned at her, white teeth under flat eyes. "Mood lighting!" he announced cheerfully. He turned on the TV and began to flip through the snowy channels until he found an ice skating competition. Satisfied, he stepped back to regard the oddly fluorescent colors. Behind his head a huge insect that Claire guessed must be a cockroach was crawling up the wall. She was relieved when he left her alone.

It was only after he was gone that she noticed the old newspapers lying in a corner, the toilet that never stopped running, and the sink that gushed forth brown water, even after five minutes. She decided against brushing her teeth and took out Aunt Cady's diary instead. But she read only a page or two before falling asleep.

June 22, 1945

Al and Rudy have become friends, which has surprised me a little. Maybe I didn't really know who Al was in high school, or maybe it's more that I still don't know Rudy, not really. Al, like Rudy, is a fixer who knows how much everything is worth on the open market, not the black market exactly, but certainly a gray one. Al's taught himself all the useful words in German, like "chocolate" and "girl" and "liquor" and "gold" and "gun." He's told me that all the Nazi paraphernalia, banned now, will be worth money someday, so he's busy collecting it up. The Germans, who of course were only members of the Party because they were forced to be, have been happy to trade SS rings and flags bearing the broken cross for something really useful, like bread.

I remember Al from my social studies class, where he didn't seem that bright. He just sat in the back passing notes to his friends. Whereas I was good in school and have never fit in in the real world. I know boundaries of countries that don't exist any more. My A's in social studies and typing didn't prepare me for much except to work for Harold.

Al has managed to get Rudy assigned to the same post, and today I got to see the place they spend their time guarding, the storeroom where the Army keeps everything we've seized. It's considered a plum assignment, since Al and Rudy don't do much behind the closed door except play with an ivory and ebony chess set that was confiscated from one of the Nazi party leaders. If the brass stops by, of course they jump to attention.

While I knew theoretically about what was in the storehouse—I've been typing up the records for weeks—it was still simply amazing to see it all. Pictures leaning in stacks against the walls, sacks full of coins and jewelry, complete sets of silver and china lined up on tops of furniture or stacked on the floor, vases, linens, ornaments, clocks and watches, crystal goblets, silk sheets. There was everything from children's toys to books to statues.

Harold wanted to pick out a few pictures for his office, and I went with him. Al nodded at me, but Rudy and I were careful not to even make eye contact. While the only ban is on officers dating enlisted women, Rudy likes his secrets.

Harold selected two landscapes. He asked me my opinion. I thought they were both boring and told him they were exquisite, especially the one with the cow. Rudy and Al saluted while Harold walked out with them. When I was looking at the list today, I noticed that neither of the pictures seems to be on there, so I wonder if they will ever be returned.

Harold has acquired a "source," which sounds better than a "spy," his red-headed Elvira, who has two fat little cheeks above her fur collar. Clearly she had more than acorn soup to eat during the last months of the war. Her official purpose is to report on the populace's mood, if any coups are afoot, that sort of thing. Which explains why her stipend is triple what I make. I know because I type up the invoices.

In the middle of the night the heat went out. Claire woke to the sounds of the city, of traffic and sirens and people shouting on the street below. It was then that she realized that the air conditioner did not fit within the window, leaving a two-inch gap through which all the forty-degree air in New York City was attempting to enter her room.

1DRKNYT

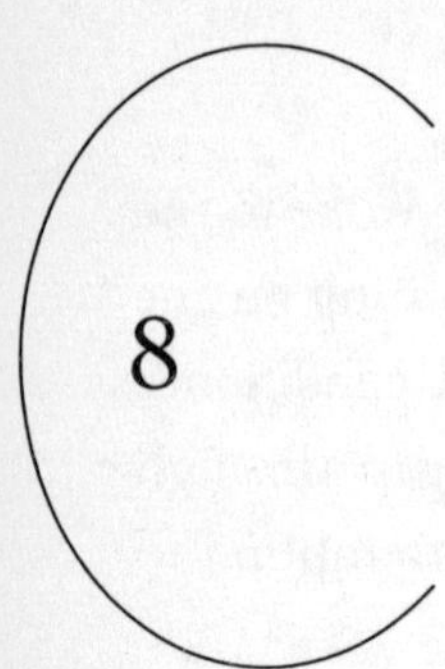

8

In the morning, Claire persuaded a clerk at the Farthingale to hold her bags until she could check in. She had already burned her bridges by checking out of the Ford, which had looked even more frightening in daylight.

For breakfast, she walked to a diner on the corner, carrying her backpack with the painting inside. The sight of the tall buildings that lined the street, faced in glass and steel and stone, squeezed her heart. Far above her, the sky was a bright, cloudless blue, but the sun had not yet penetrated the concrete canyons. Claire zipped up the collar on her Polartec jacket. Streams of cars and bright yellow taxis filled the street, none of them, as far as she could tell, using turn signals or obeying stoplights. Even when the WALK signal came on, she was forced to half run across the street. Outside the diner, a skinny black homeless man was opening the door for patrons. Claire squeezed by him nervously, seeing too late the Styrofoam cup he held ready to catch whatever was given for this service.

She sat at the long red ribbon of counter that rippled in and out to form several promontories. The two men across from her were speaking in German. They were smoking cigarettes, a fact that would normally have annoyed Claire, but here seemed simply part of the ambiance of the city. One of the men ordered a latte. It looked good so she followed suit, even though it bore no resemblance to the lattes served in Portland. It was served in an oversized coffee cup and lacked a heap of foam on the top. Even so, it tasted heavenly.

She left a tip for the waitress, using Charlie's suggested method of an amount double the sales tax. On the way out the door, Claire was careful to make her good luck offering, dropping four quarters into the white cup with teeth marks around the rim.

ග෧

Avery's was on the corner of 61st Street and Park Avenue, or, Claire had calculated over breakfast, just twenty blocks away. Charlie had told her that even though it was 150 years old, Avery's was considered a relative upstart when compared to Sotheby's and Christie's. Claire hoped they wouldn't be as snooty as she could easily imagine the other two being.

Walking there seemed like the easiest choice. Charlie's tiny map, cut from page 56 of Fodor's *Guide to Manhattan on $75 a Day*, showed the city laid out in an uncomplicated grid. Claire need only walk in a straight line, make a few ninety-degree turns, and she would easily reach her destination. It would be a good way to get her exercise, and was certainly preferable to alternative means of transportation. Taxis would be too expensive. Buses would probably follow some arcane route. The subway system was too intimidating. Claire was afraid of climbing down underneath the city. She'd seen too many movies where people were assaulted on an empty subway car rattling through the darkness, or were pushed onto the third rail by a recently released mental patient. And there was another, more likely possibility—what if she boarded the wrong train and ended up in the Bronx? Walking was the best choice.

It soon became clear that what passed for blocks in New York stretched for what seemed a quarter-mile. The blocks that ran east to west were twice as long as the blocks that ran north to south, making them seem even longer by comparison. The other women she saw, clearly natives used to the hikes needed to get from one place to the next, were dressed all in black except for white athletic shoes and socks. Claire's outfit of cream sweater, tan pants and a Polartec jacket patterned with moss green leaves was more exotic than she had intended. On her feet were beige Aerosole flats, which she was beginning to wish were her Nikes.

At least the city offered plenty of distractions. Yellow taxis tore through the street. White steam wafted mysteriously from manholes. A rat looked at her from its perch on a garbage bin. A woman sold jewelry from a tiny table and a man offered books spread out on a blanket. At every corner, Claire was stranded curbside as she waited obediently for DON'T WALK signs to change while packs of fast-moving natives surged past her.

Claire felt intensely alive, aware of every sensation in a way she never was in Portland. The wind pressed gently against her back, scudding bits of paper in little wind devils that mirrored her thoughts. What would happen at Avery's? Maybe Evan was right and they would laugh at her, tell her it was a paint-by-numbers job. To take her mind off her nervousness, she used her old running trick and picked a person to mimic. First it was a young woman in a short black dress, black tights and lime green Doc Martens with white topstitching. She walked fast, keeping her hips in a straight line, elbows pistoning. By the time she entered an office building two blocks later, Claire had her slightly pigeon-toed stride down flat. In succession, she learned the smooth shuffle of a man wearing a black hat and earlocks, the hitching stride of an older woman, the gentle sway of an Indian mother in a bright orange sari. Her game occupied her mind so well that Claire was a little surprised when she arrived at Avery's.

From the outside, the auction house was luxuriously understated, a pale gray-colored stucco building with an arched doorway set in gleaming bronze that was echoed by smaller arched windows. An American flag flew over the front display window, which was divided into nine squares like a shadow box, each showing a catalog for an upcoming auction.

Inside, a uniformed security guard was talking to a woman who leaned from the half-door of a coat check filled with the gloss and shine of leather and fur. To the right was a set of granite stairs, to the left an elevator.

Claire tried to look confident as she approached the guard. "Where do I go if I have something I want to have appraised?"

"And you have an appointment with . . . ?"

Claire flushed. She should have realized that despite what the antique dealer had said, she just couldn't waltz in off the street and expect to be seen. This was the kind of place that sultans and queens and people with old family money went to. Not someone who had a painting that had spent the last fifty years under the bed in a trailer park in White City, Oregon.

"I—I don't have one," she said, already turning to go.

The guard held up a restraining hand, a smile transforming him from a faceless man in a uniform to a good-looking young man in his twenties. "That's okay. You don't have to have one. You might have to wait a few minutes, that's all. Just go on up the stairs and tell someone at the front counter what you have. They'll get someone out to take a look at it for you."

The granite stairs, trimmed in shining oak, weren't steep at all, but still Claire could feel the pulse in her throat as she reached the top. Across a long pale distance of flat carpeting stood the front counter. It was shaped like a cube, with the corner of the room forming two sides and a chevron of highly polished wood making up the other. The fortyish woman who sat behind the desk kept herself busy with paperwork even after Claire was standing in front of her. She wore a suit in soft gray wool flannel. There was nothing about the suit that drew attention to itself—no trim, no extra-wide collar, no gilt buttons—but Claire knew immediately that it had cost at least a thousand dollars.

In addition to calculating the worth of the receptionist's suit, the wait gave Claire plenty of time to study the thick, glossy auction catalogues displayed on the desk—English antiques, Impressionist paintings, jewelry. It reminded her of a very upscale clothing store she had wandered into accidentally once in downtown Portland. The whole atmosphere was designed to weed out the kind of people who didn't belong.

Finally the woman looked up and gave Claire a cool, professional smile. "May I help you?" Her accent was British.

"Um, yes, well, I have a painting and I was wondering if I could have someone evaluate it." Claire felt both underdressed and stupid.

"Do you have an appointment?"

She was getting used to this. "No." With an effort, she erased the quiver from her voice. "The security man downstairs said I didn't have to have one." The scent of the flowers that filled a huge vase on the edge of the counter was making her dizzy. Had it been only two days since she sat in her gray burlap cubicle and approved a florist's vanity plate—BO-K? What was she doing here?

"I could see if one of our painting experts is available to take a look at it. You would have to wait."

There was no invitation in her flat voice, but Claire decided she hadn't come three thousand miles for nothing. "I don't mind."

"What type of painting is it? We have specialists in every area: Old Masters, Impressionists, American, modern, contemporary, Latin American."

Claire thought about slipping her backpack from her shoulder to show the woman, but the woman's long narrow upper lip would probably curl at this proof of her commonness. "I really don't know much about it. It's a little painting of a woman with a letter. Someone I showed it to thought it was at least a hundred years old."

This fact did not impress the woman behind the counter. She probably dealt with paintings every day that were centuries old. "One of our generalists will need to examine it and make an aesthetic determination. Please have a seat."

Claire sat down on one end of a blue-striped sectional sofa that ran along two sides of the room. Behind her, a large French-paned window revealed the brightening day and the tall white building opposite. Her stomach felt in free fall. She slipped off her backpack and put it on her lap.

The room was a hub of subdued activity. People bustled in and out with books and brown-paper-wrapped packages. Two young women, both wearing pearls and black velvet headbands, walked carefully through the lobby carrying a large painting of a man on a horse. The elevator doors opened to reveal an elderly woman with diamonds in her ears and on her fingers, accompanied by a dapper Continental-looking man. She requested an armful of catalogs for upcoming sales, but Claire noticed it was the man who paid.

"I understand you have a painting." The voice was unhurried and deep.

Claire turned. The speaker was a man in his mid-thirties, dressed in a black single-breasted suit cut close to his body. His shirt was midnight blue, and his tie was the color of eggplant. The cut and unusual colors all said "money" in an understated way. Above a triangular-shaped face, his dark blond hair was cropped close, and his eyes were the green of cat's-eye marbles. Claire got to her feet.

"I'm Troy Nowell." His palm was cool and dry as they shook hands, and she worried that hers was not.

"Claire. Claire Montrose. I appreciate your seeing me without an appointment. Here, um, let me get the painting . . ." She began to unzip her backpack under the receptionist's fish-eye gaze. With the tap of a finger on the back of her hand, Troy stilled her.

"No, no, let's wait until we're in the viewing room."

The words *viewing room* were an incongruous reminder of her grandmother's funeral. As she followed Troy down a narrow hall, Claire remembered how the funeral home had displayed her in an open casket in what it had also called a viewing room. Grandma Montrose, kept thin and ultimately killed off by her three-pack-a-day habit, had been buried in her old Hormel Girl uniform. In the pink and white satin she had looked like a shriveled drum majorette.

As Troy strode ahead of Claire, she noted his height—a few inches over six feet—and the way he walked from the pelvis, padding down the hall in expensive-looking ebony loafers. The hallway was lined with a series of doors set close together, and he opened the last door on the left, revealing a small, utilitarian room far removed from the thick carpet and polished mahogany of the lobby. It held two plain wooden chairs and a small table. The acoustic tile ceiling was low enough to seem oppressive. The room looked more suited to a police interrogation than appraising fine art.

Troy pulled a chair out for her, then sat down in his own. They were so close their knees grazed until Claire inched back her chair. In such tight quarters she was aware of everything, of the dampness at the small of her back, of a curl that was hanging right in front of her eyes, of the green gaze appraising her. She ran her tongue over her teeth, hoping that the peppermint flavor of her toothpaste was still holding out.

"So you've been transporting a painting in a backpack?"

Claire pushed the curl of hair back impatiently. "It *is* wrapped in bubble wrap." She was getting tired of feeling stupid. "You sound like the receptionist looked."

"Did Maggie get to you?" He gave her a conspiratorial smile.

"She's a snob and terribly inefficient, but they consider her a treasure. It's that British accent. And her father's money. Her father is Lord Cornaby-Jones. He's one of the landed gentry, which allows her to dress in the way they desire all Avery's employees to dress, in a manner reflecting our passage through finishing schools, riding academies and debutante balls."

Claire detected an edge of bitterness. "And did you?"

"Pardon?"

"Did you pass through riding academies and debutante balls?"

His voice lost some of its crisp precision. "Not hardly. My father was a garbage man in Jersey. Of course, I don't say anything about that here. If pressed, I'll admit he was in the waste management business." He sat back in his chair, resuming his businesslike demeanor. "So, has this painting been in your family long?"

Claire imagined a line of semi-royals, one passing it down to another. She tried to match Troy's precise, expensive-sounding way of speaking. "Since the war, I believe. When my great-aunt died she left me her estate, which included this painting."

"And this was—where?"

"In White City, Oregon. But I live in Portland."

"Oregon, hmm?" he echoed, mispronouncing Oregon so that it ended in *gone* instead of *gun*. "Well, let's have a look." From his jacket pocket he produced a pair of white cotton gloves and pulled them on, smoothing them over his long fingers.

Claire unzipped the backpack and pulled out the painting. With her fingernail, she caught an edge of tape, peeled it back from the bubble wrap, and finally unfolded it. She looked up as she bared the painting.

Troy's face went as still as a mask. Following his gaze, she looked down at the painting, at the woman who stared back at her, revealing nothing in her gaze except that she had her own secrets. Claire rotated the painting to face him. Viewing it upside down freed her to see the care with which it had been painted. What appeared to be a single color, like the woman's yellow jacket, was instead created from minutely different tones, tiny overlapping lozenges of paint that reflected the influence of light and shadow. Even the white wall showed each subtle change of light intensity and tone through almost innumerable variations of colors.

Troy was so quiet she could hear his breathing. Finally he stretched out his white-gloved hands and picked up the painting with just his fingertips. He tilted it to the overhead light, and then away. His breathing was not any faster, but on some level she was aware that it was deeper. The silence and his closeness gave the moment an intimacy that heightened every one of Claire's senses.

Still without speaking, he switched on a lamp that had a round magnifying glass attached to it. It was as if he were alone with the woman in the painting, talking to her without words, asking her what mysteries she held close.

While Troy methodically examined every centimeter of the painting, Claire focused for the first time on the fine white cracks that ran through the paint, an effect that softened and blurred the image at close range, but that at a distance of more than three feet was nearly invisible. Along the white wall, the cracks showed black where untold years of dust had collected. What had the man at the antique store called them? Craquelure?

Except for his breathing, Troy continued to be absolutely silent, his concentration so intense that Claire was free to study him. No wedding ring, she noted. And even though every inch looked well-cared for, there was nothing effeminate about him. The first, catlike impression she had had of him was heightened by his complete stillness and self-absorption, as watchful as a cat observing something he desired.

Troy flicked off the switch of the magnifying lamp, then turned on another, smaller lamp. Still without speaking, he reached back and clicked off the overhead lights. The room went dark except for an odd purple glow emanating from the lamp. Claire realized it was a black light, like one she remembered from grade school, the mysterious glow that lit up a friend's older brother's room filled with specially designed psychedelic posters. When she turned her eyes from the light to the painting, she inhaled in surprise. Part of her painting, in the right-hand corner next to the painted window, was glowing faintly purple!

"What does that mean?" Influenced by the intimacy of the darkened room, her voice came out in a whisper.

"It's an addition made after the original painting was finished. Sometimes if a painting becomes damaged, a restorer will try to touch it up." Troy finally tore his gaze from the painting and looked at her, a half-ghost, the hollows under his cheekbones glowing purple in the light. "You said you showed this to someone in Portland? Who was that?"

"A man who owned a store that sold antiques. He didn't know much about paintings, though."

"And have you shown it to anyone else in New York?"

"I was also thinking about bringing it to Sotheby's or maybe Christie's." Claire felt disloyal mentioning Avery's greatest rivals. "Mostly because I like the way Sotheby's sounds when you say it. It sounds so rich and refined and British."

Troy snorted. "Sotheby was just a book salesman who decided to use an auction to force people to stop dawdling and buy in a few hours. He was one step up from a tinker."

He reached out, his arm brushing past Claire's, and flicked off the switch for the black light. For a half-second they sat in complete darkness. The warmth of his breath crossed her face as he reached back for the light switch. Something inside of her felt as if it were coming undone, but when the overhead light went on Troy's face was impassive as ever.

"Tell me more about how your great-aunt acquired this painting."

"She was in a woman's branch of the Army, stationed in Europe as a clerk right after the war. I think she may have gotten the painting from a man who was also in the Army."

"And when was this?"

"She was there until the end of 1945."

"And stationed—where?"

"Munich."

Troy was quiet for a long time. "There are a number of striking things about this painting. Its small size. The light coming from a window on the left. A solitary woman with broad-spaced eyes. An ermine-trimmed yellow jacket. Then there are the lion's-head finials on the chair, and the crumpled Turkish carpet on the table."

"Do you know what it is?"

He picked up the painting again, tilting it toward him and then away. "Have you ever heard of a seventeenth-century Dutch painter, Vermeer, Jan Vermeer?"

"Didn't they have a big show of his paintings in the National Gallery a couple of years ago?" Claire remembered reading about the curator, the years of effort spent assembling a show only to have it closed first by a government shutdown and then by the fiercest snowstorm in a century. A thrill went through her. "Is this one of his paintings?"

An expression she couldn't name flickered across Troy's face. "There are many parallels with his general style, yes." His voice was careful.

"But?" Claire prompted.

"But I'm afraid what you have here is known as a pastiche."

"A pastiche?"

"A forgery. A forgery in the manner of Vermeer, combining all the elements he is known for—northern light, yellow satin jacket, even a woman reading a letter. It's a compilation of every Vermeer cliché, all simmered together to make a single painting." He turned the painting back so that again the woman looked Claire in the eye, her gaze steady and enigmatic. "I'm sorry. I know you've come a very long way."

"Then if it has all those things, how do you know it isn't a Vermeer?"

"It *is* good to find parallels. But there are wholesale borrowings here, just changed a bit. Vermeer already painted something very similar to this scene, called *Woman Reading a Letter at an Open Window.* And the way she looks at you is lifted straight from one of his most famous paintings, *Girl with a Pearl Earring.*"

Claire looked down at the woman's liquid eyes. They refused to become a flat dead layer of paint on canvas. "But don't painters have certain mannerisms or ways of doing things that would show up in painting after painting?"

"That's a very good question. And you are absolutely correct. A good forger takes advantage of that. You see, he doesn't copy a work in toto. Instead, he might take tracing paper and sketch out four or five elements of different paintings of, say, Rembrandt, and then mix them together. The result is a copy that looks like the real thing. And that's what our friend has done here. And not that long ago. I'd guess somewhere in the last hundred years, when the market for Vermeers began to improve. Certainly it's not the three hundred and fifty it would need to be to be a real Vermeer."

"But the man I showed it to in Portland said it was very old. He said those tiny cracks only happen in old paintings."

"As paint dries over many years, it does crack like this. But craquelure can be faked fairly easily."

Claire remembered the way a corner of the painting had glowed under a black light. "What about the repainting? Doesn't that mean it has to be old? Why would someone bother to patch up a brand-new painting?"

"An experienced forger knows that a painting doesn't go through three centuries unscathed. So he takes what he has created, finds a place that won't matter much if it's ripped or torn—like the background—damages it and then repairs it. His little sacrifice makes it that much more likely that people will be fooled."

"But how can you just look at it and tell that it's not a real Vermeer?" Claire didn't understand why she was so disappointed, but she was. When she looked at the painting, she had imagined its creator painting his true love, not some back-alley forger out to make a quick buck.

"Do you know why they employ me here?" The question was rhetorical, and Troy's gaze was unfocused, looking at something he saw with his mind's eye. "For my aesthetic sense. I am paid to *see*, and to communicate to others what I see. It's more than education, more than experience. Sometimes I think you have to be born with it. I know when something is accomplished or merely workmanlike. I can look at a painting and feel who painted it. Was it from the master or an apprentice? Or did a master lay down the main strokes and then leave someone else to fill it in? Or is it simply a daub done by a nobody aping his betters?" He turned his green eyes to Claire again. "Fakes lack soul. Like this painting. It is simply not alive."

Claire dropped her gaze to the painting, to the woman who held unknown words in her hands. Were they a lover's praises or his rejection? Did they bring news of a fortune or the sorrow of a death? "How do you know you're right if all you're going on is a feeling?"

Instead of being offended, Troy looked thoughtful. "It's much more than that. It's difficult to explain to someone who hasn't spent the last fifteen years learning how to truly see." Troy looked intently at the painting, then traced his gloved hand in the air above the woman's body. "Here. Look at the folds of her dress. They're unnaturally stiff. And her hands lack Vermeer's delicacy. The whole thing simply rings false. You could find better examples of Vermeer in Dutch airport souvenir shops."

Claire winced. "Are you sure?"

"I'm sorry to disappoint you. Frankly, I spend a lot of my time looking at junk. People believe in miracles, that they have priceless items which just happen to be lying around in the attic. They've read about how someone found the draft of George Washington's inaugural address under a sofa, or heard about the million-dollar fourteenth-century wine jug someone was using as an umbrella stand. But of course that's why the media loves those stories—because they *are* so rare."

Claire turned from Troy's intense green gaze, looked down again at the woman who seemed caught in time. "I really didn't bring her here wanting money. I just wanted know who she was, who painted her, what he was thinking about when he did. She just seemed so, so—so real somehow. Like she could step out of the boundaries of the frame."

Troy gave her a smile that somehow connected them, breaking through the cool reserve he wore every bit as much as his expensive suit. "Very poetically put." He lifted the painting from the table. "This certainly isn't something Avery's would be interested in offering at auction. It's too clearly a knockoff. But if you leave it with me I might be able to get some money for it through a private sale as a curiosity."

The young woman's painted eyes still steadily returned Claire's gaze. "No, that's all right," Claire said, surprising herself. She realized she didn't care who had created the painting or when. Despite what Troy said, the woman was alive to Claire. The secret of her letter still intrigued her. And if the painting ended up over Charlie's fireplace instead of in a museum, would that really matter?

"Are you certain? I'd hate to see you come all the way to New York and then have nothing to show for it. I might"—Troy hesitated—

"I might be able to get as much as five or ten thousand for it."

Given her state salary, five or ten thousand sounded like a lot of money. Claire was tempted until she looked back down at the painting. "No, no, I want to keep it. Even if it's a fake, there's something about it—about her—that I really like."

For the briefest instant, Troy's lips seemed to tighten, but then his face relaxed into a smile and he nodded. "Think about what I've said. Give me the number where you're staying, and I'll ask around a bit before you leave New York. Who knows, there may be heightened interest because of the show last year."

STAY2ND

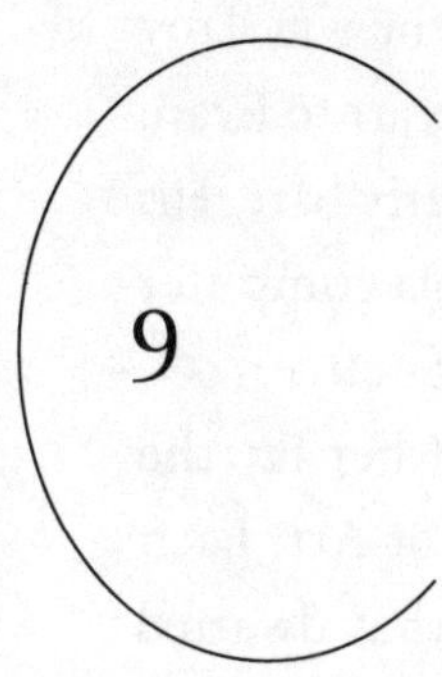

9

In the shelter of Avery's doorway, Claire took the page from the *Guide to Manhattan.* She was only about two dozen blocks from the Metropolitan Museum of Art. Aware of the painting bouncing lightly against her back with each step, she set off.

In some ways, Claire was relieved that she didn't have to deal with all the complications that would have ensued if Troy had said the painting were real. Now it was simply hers to enjoy. When she had first seen it, its beauty had stolen her breath. If it were an imitation of something else, did that make it less beautiful?

And could only an original be beautiful? Were there degrees of falsehood? Was something more or less of a fake—and thus more or less beautiful—if it wasn't an exact copy but made up of familiar elements combined in new ways? Although perhaps to a trained eye her painting wasn't beautiful at all. Troy had talked about a stiffness, a lack of life, a falseness, all things that she had been unable to detect but that he had seen as clearly as he had seen Claire—if not more clearly.

Claire's thoughts kept coming back to Troy. She had never met anyone like him before—smart, sophisticated, beautiful in a way that was entirely masculine. His kind couldn't exist in Portland, or probably anywhere outside New York City. Everything, from the way Troy made his living to the way he dressed, was in sharp contrast to Evan. Evan cared little for art. The walls of his house were nearly bare. His state-of-the-art security system was there to protect his computer and stereo system, and because it was statistically cost-effective.

She rounded the corner onto 81st Street. Ahead of her lay the sprawling stone edifice of the Metropolitan Museum of Art. Each entrance door was bracketed by pairs of fluted pillars that dwarfed the people clustered on the sweeping outdoor staircase. Claire's heart gave a little bounce, reminding her that despite the disappointment of the painting, she was here in New York City, doing just fine on her own, thank you, and about to enter a place she had been reading about for years.

Inside the magnificent openness of the Great Hall a grade school class in blue plaid uniforms raced around her, testing the acoustics. The space was big enough to muffle even their squeals. After checking her jacket and backpack, she climbed the broad central stairway that led to the rooms of European paintings. She walked quickly past the canvases, her eyes skimming over portraits, allegories, religious subjects. Troy had mentioned that the Met had several Vermeers and she wanted to see what the person who had painted—or copied—her painting had been trying to imitate. His careful way of seeing things must have rubbed off, for Claire found herself noticing the colors in each painting and how the paint itself had been applied, sometimes in tiny dabs, sometimes in broad daubs a quarter-inch thick.

The rooms of the gallery flowed from one to the next, each with white painted walls and pale hardwood floors that showed no sign of the thousands of feet that must have scuffed over them. Claire passed couples and an occasional knot of people speaking softly in what she guessed was Japanese, German, French, Italian. For the most part, though, the Met was relatively uncrowded on a Thursday afternoon in October.

Then she saw it. A painting, only a little more than a foot square, nearly lost amid the much larger ones that surrounded it.

In the painting, a young woman, evidently asleep, sat at a table. Her eyes were closed and her head rested on one hand. Her black hair was drawn back, emphasizing the widow's peak that accented her pale oval face. Claire's heart skidded. The table in front of the woman was covered with a bunched oriental carpet in deep shades of red and blue and cream. On top of the carpet rested a bowl of fruit and a white curving jug with a brass top. She had seen both the carpet and the jug before. They were identical to the ones in the little painting in the backpack she had checked downstairs.

Claire moved closer. On the right side of the painting, part of a chair was visible, with brass buttons on its dark back and lions' heads at the tops of the posts. The chair, too, was a mate to the one in Aunt Cady's painting.

Her gaze dropped to the inscription under the painting. *"Girl Asleep at a Table," c. 1657, oil on canvas, Jan Vermeer, Dutch, 1632–1675. Bequest of Benjamin Altman.* She was a foot away from the real thing, but still, despite what Troy had said, she couldn't tell the difference between this painting and the one she had checked downstairs.

"Hmmm." It wasn't until the man walking by her stopped that Claire realized she had made a sound in the back of her throat. Before turning his dark eyes to the painting, he offered her a smile. One of his teeth had been broken and then mended with a flash of white. With his dark curly hair and a gold hoop in one ear, he looked like a pirate, only one dressed in an old Pendleton instead of a white ruffled shirt. When he spoke, he had the flattened vowels of a native New Yorker.

"Some people say she's a still life masquerading as a portrait. That she's simply an excuse for painting light and color."

Claire considered the woman in the painting. Even in repose, her face contained an inner radiance. "Are you saying she doesn't seem real? To me she looks like she could open her eyes at any second." Claire could almost see the dark blue eyes (somehow she knew they were blue) regarding them calmly.

"Maybe you're right. Maybe I've seen her too often to really see her." His dark eyes were level with Claire's. He shook her hand with one that was cool and slightly callused. "Dante Bonner."

"Claire. Claire Montrose. Are you an artist?"

"Not in the same class as Vermeer. But I majored in art history at college."

Which meant she had glibly offered her opinion to a man who had spent years studying painters. "I'm really interested in Vermeer, but I don't know much about him."

"There's not a lot *to* know. He died young and penniless in Delft, leaving eleven children. He owed such a huge bill to the baker that after his death it had to be paid in paintings. That's about it. Did he always live in Delft? Where did he learn to paint? Nobody knows. Nobody even knows what this painting means. Some experts think this woman is drunk, others that she's sleeping. Some people insist that she is the lady of the house. Or no, that she's a maid stealing a siesta. And some people say the woman is depressed because she has lost at love."

"Sometimes a cigar *is* simply a cigar," Claire said, happy that she had thought of something halfway intelligent to say. "You *do* know a lot about Vermeer."

"Unfortunately, I've just told you about everything there is to know. No one even knows how many paintings he painted."

"Does the Met have any more?" She felt sophisticated, casually referring to the museum in the diminutive.

"Four more, which is an amazing number when you consider we know of fewer than forty that he painted. Would you like me to show them to you?"

She nodded, then allowed herself a small private smile. For the second time in as many hours, Claire was following a gorgeous man.

Dante's first stop was a much larger painting. It showed a woman in a white dress posed theatrically, her foot resting on a globe. Behind her was a painting of Christ on the cross. Claire saw nothing in this painting that reminded her of the one she had in her backpack downstairs, which pointed out just how little she knew about art.

Dante said, "I'll start with the Vermeer I like the least. It's called *Allegory of the Faith*, and was probably a commissioned painting. Pretty much everything in the painting is a symbol."

"You mean like the apple and the crushed snake?" They lay on the black-and-white-tiled marble floor.

"You got it. That's why this painting doesn't work. Vermeer did his best work when he painted mysteries, not allegories."

"Mysteries?" Claire echoed, thinking of the woman in her painting, her enigmatic expression, the letter containing unknown news.

"Think of the first painting we looked at, *Girl Asleep at a Table*. It's a common genre theme, but no one remembers other paintings like it. What makes it different? I think it's that other artists of the day always spelled out what everything meant. Another artist would paint an empty jug of wine, so everyone would know the woman was drunk. Or children gone wild so the viewer would know it's about a housewife neglecting her duties. Instead, Vermeer painted a sleeping beauty and left the viewer to figure out what it meant." Dante's rough voice was oddly soothing. "The interesting thing is that when Vermeer first painted her, there was a man waiting for her in the doorway. Later he painted him out."

"How do they know that?"

"You can X-ray a painting to see the underlayers, and with Vermeer, there are always changes to the underlayers." He turned to her, and Claire saw that his irises were flecked with gold. "Am I boring you?"

"No, this is fascinating!" Claire protested, afraid he might disappear. She was enjoying seeing things through the eyes of an artist.

"Let me know if you change your mind. Here's a painting that's more typical of Vermeer—*Portrait of a Young Lady.*"

Against a nearly black background was a three-quarter view of a girl's head and shoulders. She appeared to be in her early teens. Her dark hair was pulled back from her face, her shoulders covered with a white satin shawl. A pearl earring glinted at her lobe. Her expression was calm, with a hint of a smile. With thin lips and seemingly lashless eyes, she was no beauty, yet she had been portrayed with a serene self-possession that Claire found appealing. The small painting was itself astonishingly delicate, a complex play of light and rich shadows.

Surreptitiously, Claire also examined Dante as he examined the painting, his thick lashes and generous mouth. He spoke softly, keeping his eyes fastened on the small portrait. "This girl could be one of his daughters. There's no way of knowing. But he was so poor and worked so slowly that he probably couldn't afford a professional model."

The next painting Dante showed Claire was *Lady Playing a Lute*. In it, a young woman played a bowl-shaped stringed instrument. Her head was turned to the side, her expression a half-smile. Diffuse golden light poured into the room through the leaded window on the left of the painting, glinting off the woman's earring and the yellow satin of her fur-trimmed jacket.

That jacket! Claire thought. It seemed to be the same jacket as the woman in her painting was wearing, although not as much of it was visible. And again there was the chair with the lions' heads on the posts. What had Troy said? That her painting was a pastiche of every known Vermeer cliché?

She looked again at the woman's face, at her high forehead and wide-set eyes. "This looks like the same person in the last portrait, only a few years older," Claire ventured.

"But *Portrait of a Young Lady* was probably painted a year or two *after Lady Playing a Lute*. It could be a family resemblance. This could be Vermeer's wife, and the other one his daughter."

Dante took Claire's hand and led her a few more steps, then released her fingers as easily as he had taken them. "I've saved the best for last. *Young Woman with a Water Jug*." At first, Claire had difficulty paying attention to the picture, her mind still on the light pressure of Dante's fingers.

In the painting, a woman stood with one hand on the frame of an open window. The other rested on a brass pitcher set in a matching shallow basin. She wore a starched and pleated white headdress attached to a capelike collar. Dante pulled a small black plastic oval from inside his jacket, surprising Claire. He flicked it open to reveal two black-framed clear circles—tiny magnifying glasses—and bent forward to squint at the canvas.

Claire wondered if he were allowed to get so close, even though he wasn't actually touching the painting. But when a guard walked by, he took in Dante's actions without even breaking stride. She relaxed enough to look at the same spot where Dante was focused, at the underside of the brass basin. It was a mosaic of tiny chips of colors reflecting the carpet on which it rested.

Dante's voice was a near whisper. "It all seems so simple, but when you look closely, you realize you can't find the edges of anything. And look how much light is in the map behind the woman, and then compare that to the blue haze underneath it. Even the wall is more like a rainbow than pure white. There's pink-white, yellow-white, blue-white, purple-white. But he makes it seem like one color."

"Is that why you like Vermeer so much?" Part of Claire was listening, but another part was wondering how she could keep the conversation going. She was absurdly conscious of her heart beating, of her mouth pushing out each breath. She knew it was silly to lust after a stranger, but the combination of his looks and intelligence was proving irresistible.

Dante straightened up and slipped his magnifying glass back into his pocket.

"That, and I guess I like all the mysteries—knowing so little about his personal life, or who taught him to paint, or whether he used the camera obscura."

"What's that?"

"It was a kind of early camera. You took a completely dark room and admitted only a pinhole of light. A box with a lens captured the image of a scene on ground glass. Some artists used it to trace the projected image. There's no way to tell for sure if he used it, but many of Vermeer's paintings have optical effects like those of a camera. See what he did here?" Dante pointed to the woman's dark skirt silhouetted against the white wall. "He accentuated the contrasts of light and dark, like a camera would. And everything he paints has blurred edges, like they're slightly out of focus. And many of his paintings, especially his later ones, are marked with circles of confusion."

"Circles of confusion? What are those?" Claire was beginning to feel more than a little confused herself. She had never looked at anything so closely before.

"Highlights that are slightly out of focus, the way you often see them in photographs. See this luminous spot? It's a circle of confusion." Dante pointed to the liquid white dot that sparkled on the plump curve of the woman's lower lip. He turned his attention back to Claire. "I'm afraid that's it for the Vermeers. I've probably bored you with my lecture."

"Not at all," Claire said, not wanting the conversation to end. A way to prolong it suddenly occurred to her. On top of Charlie's list of "must see" sights had been the Met's sculpture garden. "I really enjoyed it. It was like having my own private tour guide." She took a deep breath. "Can I thank you by buying you a glass of wine on the rooftop garden? I've never been up there, but I hear the view is incredible."

Dante hesitated before answering, and Claire could feel a flush crawling up her neck. But then he said, "I think I'd like that."

Claire made a quick decision. "I need to get my stuff from the front desk."

"I'll save us a good spot."

After retrieving her backpack, Claire entered the elevator and waited for it to groan skyward, amazed at her own daring. Last week she had been vetting LUVBABY, now here she was at the greatest museum in the world, about to have a glass of wine with a fascinating man. A bead of sweat traced the length of her spine, and she shivered.

Just as Charlie had promised, the view from the rooftop was breathtaking. The museum rested on the eastern edge of Central Park, which cut a green swath through the city's brownstones and highrises. The avenues bounding the park squared it off like great garden walls. Viewed from this vantage point, New York City was gorgeous, the litter and crowds and homeless people invisible. And for the first time since she had left Oregon, Claire could see the full sweep of sky. Belying the fall chill in the air, the sky was a clear blue with scudding white puffy clouds.

Dante was waiting on a bench, watching her with a half-smile, a glass of red wine in each hand.

"That's not fair!" Claire protested. "I was going to treat you!"

"You can buy next time."

Claire accepted the glass of wine from him and took a sip. To cover her nervousness she studied the bronze sculpture facing them. It was of a nude woman who stood on tiptoe, her arms raised shoulder-high, fingers spread. She was larger than life, with a rounded stomach and full breasts. The sculpture was sensual rather than sexual, but even so Claire felt awkward facing her breasts and belly.

Dante saved her by asking her a few questions about what she did. He seemed gratifyingly amused by her descriptions of bizarre license plate requests.

"What drew you to painting?" she asked.

"The magic of it." He took a sip from his glass. "How do you take a stick with hairs on it, rub it in colored dirt, wipe it on a piece of cloth wrapped around some wood—and make something that didn't exist before?" Dante looked away as if embarrassed, turning his face to the sun. "You're lucky to have such beautiful weather for your visit."

"Could you tell right away that I was a tourist?" Even though she wasn't dressed in black, Claire had secretly hoped she fit in.

"No real New Yorker would put up with a guided tour from a stranger who accosted her in front of a painting. But you had such a look of wonder on your face that I thought you would enjoy it."

"I did enjoy it, very much. In fact," Claire took a deep breath, "I had a special reason for wanting to know more. I came to New York because I inherited a painting, and I wanted to find out more about it. Someone at Avery's told me it was a Vermeer imitation, a"—she searched for the word Troy had used—"a pastiche. In those paintings you just showed me I saw a lot of the same things it has: a white pitcher with a brass top, an Oriental carpet—even a chair with those lions' heads on the top."

Dante straightened up. "Really? So where is it now? Locked up in the safe at your hotel?"

"Actually, it's right here. In my backpack." She patted her lap. Dante's eyes opened wider, but at least he didn't curl his lip the way the receptionist at Avery's had. "Would you like to look at it?"

When he nodded, Claire unzipped the backpack and undid the bubble wrap. After having spent the last hour scrutinizing real Vermeers, Claire was surprised to find that her own painting had lost none of its power over her. The woman still intrigued her, with her parted lips, calm gaze and mysterious letter.

"May I?" She wondered if she saw a quiver in his outstretched hands as he gently lifted it close to his face. He was quiet for a long time, and when he spoke, his voice was reverential, pitched so low that Claire wondered if it were meant only for his own ears. "We have an oil painting, about fifteen by fourteen inches." He slipped the magnifying lens from his pocket again and began to examine the surface, inch by inch, exactly as Troy had two hours before. "The support is a plain-weave linen. The frame seems of a more recent period. The paint surface is slightly abraded. Very free brushwork." He lifted his eyes to her. "My God, where did you get this? And why do you think it's a forgery?"

Dante listened intently as she quickly summarized for him Aunt Cady's death, the suitcase with its Nazi memorabilia, and what Troy had told her about the painting.

"What reason did this guy at Avery's have for telling you it was a forgery?"

Claire tried to remember what had made him so sure. "He said that's what he does for a living, evaluate things. He said it was awkwardly painted and lifeless." At this, Dante shook his head but didn't interrupt. "And he said it was a compilation of every Vermeer cliché. That's why he called it a pastiche."

"But there's a lot of repetition in Vermeer. He was poor, so he used the same objects over and over again. I don't know that I would call this a pastiche. But on the other hand, I don't know that I would call it a Vermeer, either. That's a big leap to take simply because everyone has Vermeer on their mind these days. Let's forget what that guy told you, and assume for a moment that it didn't begin life as a fake. To me, it looks genuine, even old enough to be an Old Master, that is, a painting before 1800. Not a lot of painting was going on then. The way she's dressed, the things in the room, make me think the painter was Dutch."

"So it *could* be a Vermeer." Claire realized she was holding her breath.

Dante traced a finger an inch above the surface of the painting. "I'm leaning in a different direction than your friend at Avery's. The jacket, the white pitcher, this chair with the lions' heads, the carpet—it *could* be a Vermeer. But there are literally hundreds of genre paintings—paintings of the upper middle class's daily life—with one or more of those elements. Just off the top of my head, I can think of Jan Steen, Nicolaes Maes, Pieter de Hoogh, Gabriel Metsu. There were probably half a dozen other Dutch painters who were painting at the same time. It was the fashion to paint peaceful interior scenes with one or more figures. And not only that, painters all borrowed subject matter from each another. Instead of Vermeer, or a person forging Vermeer, the person who painted this might have simply been influenced by Vermeer."

Claire was impressed. "You know a lot." She felt more at ease now that his focus had been transferred from her to the painting.

"I told you I majored in art history. Plus, it interests me." He turned his attention back to the painting. "You have to remember that the loose jacket and those chairs reflect a certain period in history. They aren't unique to Vermeer. To her"—he pointed at the young woman—"her jacket isn't a costume, it's only a jacket. Everyone owns a chair like the one she has, or has the same white pitcher. And everyone she knows has a Turkish carpet—on the floor certainly, but maybe hanging as a wall decoration or used as a tablecloth. The more I think about it, the more likely it is that this is a painting by one of Vermeer's contemporaries, which would make it worth a few thousand dollars, instead of fifteen or twenty million."

"Million?" echoed Claire. The word came out with more emphasis than she had intended.

"Million. Of course, that's only a guess. No one's sold a Vermeer on the open market for decades. But there's only the slightest chance this is a Vermeer, even though it might not be a forgery. That guy at Avery's may be right, but he should have done more research. I'll tell you what—I'll research the archives here, look at every known seventeenth-century Dutch painting. Then I can tell you what this probably is—and what it probably isn't. But in order to really do that, I need to be able to examine it very carefully." Dante's fingers tightened slightly on the edges of the frame. "I suppose there's no chance you'd let me borrow it for a day or two? I'd take good care of it."

Uneasiness lapped at Claire. Who was this man, anyway? She had met him only an hour ago and now he was trying to walk off with something that made him stammer. She reached out and took the painting from him. "No, sorry, I don't think so. I wouldn't feel right parting with her."

"If I were in your place I would say the same thing. Can I take a few pictures of her, then? I have a camera downstairs."

While Dante went down to the coat check to retrieve his camera, Claire thought about the two men she had met that morning. Holding the painting, she walked over to look over the city once more, but this time she didn't see what was in front of her. Who was telling the truth? Troy, with his story that it was a forgery, or Dante, with his story that it was probably old but not very valuable? Was each of them telling her what they believed—or was one of them lying?

If Dante were right, that meant Troy was wrong. Could Troy have deliberately lied to her when he told her the painting was a pastiche?

Claire thought back to Avery's viewing room, where they had sat knee to knee and he had told her the painting was an imitation Vermeer. Was that why he been so insistent that he could help her out by selling the painting for a nominal amount? Avery's didn't seem the kind of place where people cared about small sums of money. Maybe the buyer Troy had had in mind was himself—with the thought that he could turn right around and sell the painting for a fantastic sum.

Just then she saw Dante step out on the wooden deck. His face tightened with anxiety until he spotted her. "For a minute I thought you had disappeared." He laid the painting on a bench, then quickly snapped a dozen photos. "If you tell me where you're staying, I'll give you a call and let you know what I find out."

"I'm at the Farthingale until Sunday morning."

AMYSTREE

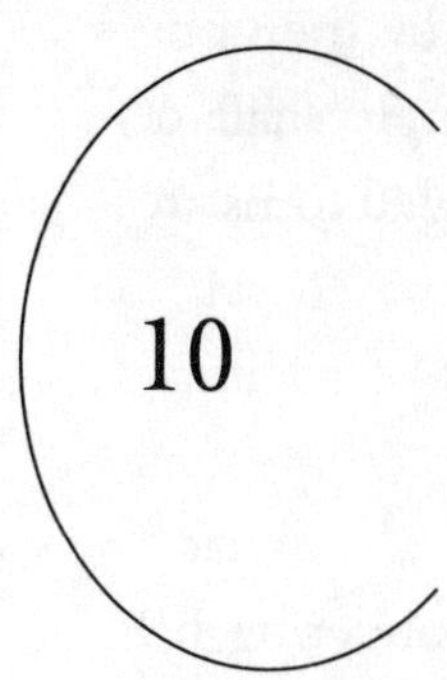

10

After Claire had turned down Dante's request to keep her painting, he hadn't even stayed long enough for her to buy him another glass of wine. Instead, as soon as he finished taking photographs of the painting, he had abruptly asked her what time it was, and then said he was expected someplace else.

Claire chanced a bus back to her hotel, figuring she couldn't get too lost if she could see out the windows and watch the street signs. When she'd asked the driver if the bus went as far as 42nd Street, he mutely gestured at the coin drop. When she repeated the question, he repeated his silent gesture, which she took to mean yes. It was like having a conversation with the Ghost of Christmas Past. There weren't many people on the bus, so she put her bag on an outside seat and then leaned her head against the window. Exhaustion slipped over her like a soft quilt.

Back in her hotel room, Claire ate a chocolate PowerBar and then curled up on the bed. In her dream, the woman in her painting turned to Claire, opened her mouth and began to explain everything in a low melodious voice. Claire strained to make out the words, until she finally realized the woman was speaking Dutch.

She woke to the ringing of the phone. For a long moment, she was confused by the flowered blue polyester coverlet, by the stone buildings pressing up against her window, by the single shaft of slanting light that pierced the room. Finally, she managed to locate the phone on a small table by the bed.

She fumbled the receiver to her ear. "Hello?"

"Is this Claire Montrose?" A man's voice.

"Uh-huh."

"This is Troy. Troy Nowell from Avery's. I was wondering if I could take you out to dinner tomorrow evening?"

Claire sat up, pushed her hair off her face. "If you wanted to talk to me about the painting, I haven't changed my mind about selling it." Especially not after talking to Dante.

Troy laughed. "You come right to the point, don't you? No, I don't want to talk to you about the painting. At least, that's not all I want to talk about. I also want to talk to you about *you*. I've been thinking about you all afternoon. I've never met anyone quite like you before."

A flush began at her throat. Maybe he was telling the truth. Or maybe he was just trying to find another way to convince her to let him buy her painting for next to nothing. But would it hurt if she let him buy her dinner, let herself live an entirely different life for one evening?

"Try being from Oregon. This whole city is full of things I've never met the likes of. But if you promise not to pester me to sell you the painting, I'll go to dinner with you." Clothes, she thought. She had no clothes to wear to such an excursion. What in the world was she going to wear?

They arranged to meet in the hotel lobby at eight-thirty the next evening. In Portland, most of the restaurants would be emptying out at such an hour, but Claire knew that in New York people dined fashionably late.

After she put down the phone, Claire hurried over to the closet where she had hung up the things from her suitcase. Two pairs of jeans, a pair of leggings, an ivory fisherman's sweater hand-knit by Charlie. The nearest thing she had to a dress was a nightgown. She had a momentary vision of Troy in his Armani and herself in her flannel, then shook her head. This was one emergency that clearly called for the use of a credit card.

She took out her little map again. Charlie had told her about a discount place called Filene's, with one store near Wall Street and another uptown—not far, in fact, from the Met. She decided to take advantage of her newfound familiarity with the bus system to take one to Filene's. If she had time afterward, she would walk over to the American Museum of Natural History, which Charlie had said was not to be missed.

Before she left, though, Claire had to do something about the painting. She no longer felt comfortable with it in her backpack, not in the jostling crowds of people, not leaning back against a bus seat. She didn't want to leave it out in the open, but then again, where could she hide it? Claire looked around the room. There were few choices, all of them obvious, and most of them unsuited to a fragile painting. Slipping it between the mattress and box spring, for example, was definitely out. She could tape it in its bubble wrapping to the underside of a dresser drawer, the favorite hiding place of a thousand movies, but she didn't have any tape. The closet contained only a few hangers. The TV was bolted to a black metal stand. She stepped into the bathroom, but there were no possibilities there, either. It was all white ceramic without even a cupboard or medicine chest. She turned back to survey the room again, her glance falling on the table and chair that sat beside the window. The chair was upholstered in blue vinyl. She tipped it on its side. The base was covered with dusty netting, held in places by tacks. Claire went to get her Swiss Army knife from her backpack.

ᔓᔕ

Filene's was crowded with bargain hunters, many of them, to judge by their accents, native New Yorkers. On the lower level, Claire finally found what she was looking for, outfits she would never have an opportunity to wear in Portland. The racks were crammed with satin, velvet and silk garments, many of them bugle-beaded or sequined. The colors were head-turning—black, scarlet, neon green, shocking pink, silver lamé—and the styles ran the gamut—from palazzo pants to see-through minidresses.

Claire fingered through the overstuffed rack, occasionally picking up an item that had slipped to the floor. Her confidence was beginning to plummet. Troy had instructed her to wear something "nice," but what did that mean? She was clearly out of her element. She didn't have the right personality to carry off any of these outfits, let alone make intelligent conversation with Troy. And what would she talk about? The latest obscene license plate request she had turned down? Dante had found her stories funny, but she couldn't imagine having the same conversation with the more patrician Troy.

"Looking for anything in particular?"

Claire looked up. The speaker was what she had already realized was a rarity in Filene's: a salesclerk. A young black woman with a name tag that read "deShauna," she had a hundred tiny braids framing her high cheekbones.

"I need something to wear to dinner. I'm visiting here, and someone I met asked me out to dinner tomorrow night. I have a feeling it's someplace pretty nice. The only trouble is that I didn't pack anything more fancy than Levi's."

"Do you know what restaurant?"

"Cri du Coeur." Claire said the French words in a careful imitation of Troy's flawless-sounding accent.

"Cri du Coeur?" DeShauna stepped back and gave Claire an

appraising look. "Girl, you must run in better circles than I do. I've read about that place in *People*. You have to be somebody special just to get in the door."

"That's just the trouble. Even if I was at home, the dressiest thing I have is an awful bridesmaid's dress that was supposed to be seafoam green but turned out to be the color of Comet cleanser."

"Come on back to the dressing room. We'll see what we can do."

First deShauna brought Claire an outfit that consisted of a black vinyl jacket, black satin hot pants and a black bustier. Dutifully, she climbed into it, although she knew it was a mistake. The price tag, though was the real shocker—$299, marked down from $1,700.

"I don't think this is really me," she said to deShauna when she returned to check on her progress. "I look like a hooker."

"But an *expensive* hooker," the young woman said, and Claire had to laugh.

Next deShauna brought Claire a floor-length black knit dress. On the hanger it looked conservative enough, but when she pulled it over her head she found it had diamond-shaped cutouts that began at the navel and gradually got bigger as they approached the neckline. They both agreed that the dress had definitely been designed for a woman with implants. "Which I see a lot of, believe me. When they're seventy-five and lying in their coffin, those old tits will still be standing straight up."

The next outfit that deShauna handed through the door was a floor-length satin dress. At first Claire thought it was cream-colored, but then she realized it was the same color as the flesh of a peach. It had a sweetheart-shaped bodice, with shoulders and sleeves of sheer netting. The sleeves were so close-fitting that she had to hold her fingers together while she slipped her hands through. She had a flash of Marilyn Monroe being sewn into her dress before she went on stage to breathe her way through "Happy Birthday, Mr. President" to Jack Kennedy.

After she had pulled the dress down over her hips, Claire stepped back to face the mirror. From a dozen darts that nipped in the waist, the dress flowed down over the curves of her hips and legs and then widened just enough to allow for walking. The subtle peach color complemented the red-gold of her hair. Looking at her own reflection, Claire felt beautiful, sexy and voluptuous—not words she normally associated with herself. She felt like Cinderella.

Her fairy godmother, played by deShauna, tapped on the door, then pushed it open. "Mmm-mmm-mmm. Don't you look nice." She became professional, plucking at the shoulders to straighten the seams, buttoning a tiny back button Claire had overlooked. "That netting is sexy without looking too obvious."

"Without looking too obvious?" Claire echoed. "To successfully wear this dress I'm going to have to completely forget about underwear."

"All you need is a strapless bra and a pair of those pantyhose with the built-in panty. That's not much of a sacrifice for looking gorgeous."

Claire hesitated. The dress *was* gorgeous—but who was she kidding? This wasn't the kind of dress someone like her could wear. Its real owner was meant to be a movie star straight out of the glossy pages of a magazine. "I'm from Portland, Oregon, and nobody there wears dresses like this."

"But, honey, you're not *in* Portland." She saw Claire hesitating and playfully pushed her shoulder. "And if you don't wear a dress like this to Cri du Coeur, they probably won't even let you in."

After parting with $149 for the dress (marked down from $899), plus another $30 for some strappy shoes, $7 for pantyhose, and $16 for something called a strapless demi-bra that basically put her breasts on a shelf, Claire left Filene's with her backpack and her arms filled with packages. The day was slowly changing into dusk. She looked at her watch. She had a little more than an hour and a half if she wanted to see the American Museum of Natural History. This was, of course, not nearly enough to see what *Fodor's* said was a million and a half square feet of exhibits. Her time in New York was slipping through her fingers like water. Tomorrow she planned to explore the tip of Manhattan, take the boat to the Statue of Liberty and Ellis Island. There were a million places she had yet to see. Who knew if she would ever be in uptown Manhattan again? She began to walk a little faster.

In the fading light, the five pink granite stories of the American Museum of Natural History seemed all towers and turrets, a fairy-tale castle. With only an hour or so until closing time, people were beginning to stream out, laughing and talking. Claire felt like a salmon swimming upstream as she made her way to the entrance. Like the Met, the main hall was a marble-floored, monumental soaring space, only this one featured an exhibit of a long-necked dinosaur mother, complete with a smaller version of herself that was still large enough to make Claire feel tiny and insignificant. She craned her neck back, back, back to look at the towering mother barosaurus—like a giraffe, only with a tail nearly as long as its neck—which dwarfed the chamber's Corinthian columns.

She checked her bags except for her backpack, hoping that she might be able to surreptitiously eat another PowerBar while viewing the exhibits. There clearly wasn't enough time to see more than a single section, so she randomly selected the Ackley Hall of African Mammals. When she entered the hall, Claire took an involuntary step back. A battle-scarred bull elephant challenged her with ears extended, trunk probing the air. He stood in the center of the hall on an elevated platform, and behind him was clustered a herd of excited elephants, all shown in full alarm. A young bull had wheeled around to protect the rear of the herd. The elephants were life-size, and so lifelike that Claire could almost hear them trumpeting, feel the ground shake beneath her feet.

She was admiring the meticulously re-created texture of their skin when she belatedly realized that the elephants weren't just life-size, but were taken from life. They were stuffed, a tribute to the art of taxidermy and a time when people felt justified in killing something, no matter how magnificent, in order to show it to someone else. For the first time in two days Claire thought of Roland, her boss at the License Plate Division. With his penchant for elephants, he would probably love this display.

All around the elephants, embedded in walls of dark polished marble, dioramas beckoned. In the darkened hall, each stood out in a blaze of internal sunshine. The dioramas were like windows into other worlds, other times. They reminded Claire of an old movie she had seen on TV about a scientist who had invented a time machine. Through its porthole he could examine the time and place in which he had landed before deciding to disembark.

The nearest diorama showed a family of mountain gorillas foraging for food. The dominant male stood erect, beating his chest, while an infant and several other gorillas sat munching leaves. Sheathed in moss, a massive tree trunk lay rotting in the center of the scene.

As she peered at one diorama and then the next, Claire realized she was totally alone. Since it was so close to closing time, she supposed whatever visitors remained were upstairs gawking at the dinosaur bones. There wasn't a guard in sight, but then again, there was no need for a guard when the dioramas were covered by plate glass. She looked around, then took a vanilla PowerBar from her backpack. Without much success, she tried to manage a discreet nibble, but the PowerBar's taffy-like texture demanded an energetic bite.

Still chewing, Claire moved to the next diorama, half filled with what looked like real sand. The blazing artificial sun cast just enough light into the dim hallway to allow her to read the small print of the guide she had picked up at the museum's entrance. According to it, the dioramas were also called habitat groups, and the idea was to show plants and animals in their native habitat against a realistically painted background. Plants, flowers, rocks, dirt and trees—down to the bark, broken twigs and leaves—had been duplicated or, in some cases, shipped wholesale from Africa. The results were works of art.

As she walked through empty branching hallways that smelled faintly of mothballs, Claire was accompanied by the sound of her own footsteps. She moved from diorama to diorama, one showing broad grasslands at high noon, the next a deep jungle dripping with rain, a third a harsh desert at sunset.

She was wondering how the curators had created the strings of glistening saliva that hung from a hyena's mouth when the faint sound of another set of footsteps startled her. She turned her head, but the hall branched in such a way that she could see only a few feet in any direction. The sound seemed to have stopped. Claire began to move forward again, but she found it hard to pay attention to the exhibits. Was it her imagination, or did she hear a faint echo of footsteps joining hers? The dimness no longer seemed just a clever way of drawing attention to the exhibits. Instead it took on a sinister cast.

She abandoned the dioramas completely and began to hunt for an exit sign. The darkened halls had made so many twists and turns that she was no longer sure where she was in relationship to the rest of the building. The one thing that was clear was that there *were* footsteps following her. Claire whirled around and caught a glimpse of a man in the room she had just left. He wore a raincoat and had the bill of a baseball cap pulled over his eyes, and the way he moved made her think he was young and agile.

It was impossible to see clearly in the dim hallway, but every time she looked behind her—and she couldn't help glancing back every few seconds—he was making no pretense of looking at the exhibits. At the same time, she wasn't completely sure he was following her, since he didn't seem to be coming any closer. She could see nothing of his shadowed face, but the third or fourth time she turned around she caught the flash of the whites of his eyes as he stared directly at her.

Claire thought of Charlie's warnings about New York. Never count your money in a public place. Don't get in a gypsy cab (which had turned out to be an unlicensed cab instead of a cab driven by a fortuneteller). Never engage in a game of chance on the street. And, most important, don't allow yourself to be alone in a dark and isolated spot with a stranger. The last one had really been a warning about strolling the streets of Manhattan at night, but to Claire the darkened recesses of the American Museum of Natural History were beginning to feel equally dangerous.

The hallway branched and turned, and she chose paths without pausing to think, hoping to lose him in the maze, or to come upon a guard or at least an exit. She wondered what would happen if she screamed.

Finally, the welcome green glow of an exit sign lit the far end of a chamber. She turned. The man was closer than he had been, but still absolutely silent. Claire gave up all pretense of not being frightened and began to run. Next to her was a rolling barricade of canvas and wood pretending unsuccessfully to be a wall. As she passed it, she grabbed one end, swung it around and pushed it back as hard as she could. She heard the man give a little grunt of surprise, but she was too afraid to look behind her to see if it had really hit him.

With a final burst of effort, Claire ran out of the hall and nearly into the arms of a plump guard who was watching the last of the departing visitors.

"Whoa, little lady!"

"Someone was chasing me!" She tried to catch her breath.

"Someone was what?" he said, not even bothering to turn to the door she had just run out of. Claire looked behind her, but the door had closed and didn't open again.

"A man was just chasing me in the Hall of African Mammals."

He gave the sigh of the continually put-upon. "I'll go take a look."

Claire hovered at the exit, not daring to follow. But when the guard reappeared five minutes later, he said, "There's no one there, ma'am."

"It was a man in a raincoat with a baseball cap pulled over his eyes. He must have left by another way."

"Could be. But I didn't see anyone. Maybe it was just another visitor in a hurry. It is closing time now, you know." He looked pointedly at his watch.

"He was *following* me."

"I'll put a note in my report." By the tone of his voice, Claire knew he would do no such thing.

She retrieved her packages from the coat room and then followed on the heels of a family of five out to the sidewalk. It was full dark. She certainly didn't feel safe waiting for a bus, especially encumbered as she was. The father of the family stepped to the curb, raised his arm the way she had seen on a thousand movies and TV shows, and just like on screen, a yellow cab pulled up immediately. Claire followed suit while she still felt brave. As her taxi was pulling away, she turned back in time to see the silhouette of a man wearing a baseball cap emerge from the museum. He was scanning the street, but he didn't seem to see her.

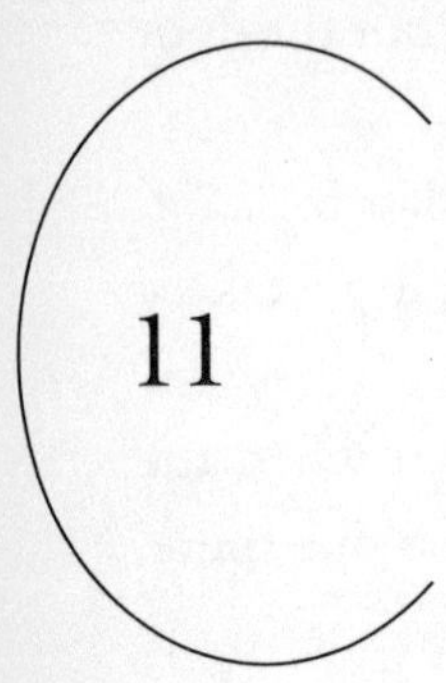

11

Claire woke up in a big bed with white sheets, momentarily confused by the anonymity of her surroundings. In the cool morning light, her fears of being followed the night before seemed groundless, the product of an overstimulated imagination. Just as the guard had suggested, the man in the baseball cap must have simply been a last-minute visitor, hurrying, as she had been, to finish viewing the exhibit before the museum closed for the night. He had probably seen her walking faster and faster and felt spurred on by her speed. By the time she had finished getting dressed, Claire had molded the incident into an amusing story she could tell Lori or Charlie when she got home.

She looked out the window. New York City didn't seem to have as much weather as Portland did, but the day looked promising. When she craned her head back she could just see a sliver of washed blue sky. Tonight she would be going out with Troy Nowell of Avery's auction house, but today she hoped to cram in a few more of the sights. In two more days she had to go home. It was hard to believe she had dreaded coming here.

Claire took a bus as far as she could to Manhattan's tip, then walked to Battery Park. A beggar at a subway entrance stood up to hold his Big Gulp cup in front of her face. "It's money time!" He shook the coins on the bottom to remind her of what he meant. "It's money time now!" She averted her eyes and detoured around him without speaking, relieved when she heard him start in on the person behind her.

Her breakfast was a stale pastry and weak coffee in a blue and white paper cup while she waited in line for the next ferry to the Statue of Liberty and Ellis Island. Pigeons pecked at every crumb that fell. Three black teenagers performed a tumbling routine for the waiting crowd, and when one of them passed the hat, Claire contributed a dollar.

She managed to snag a seat on the top deck of the ferry. As it slowly chugged away from the city, she thrilled at the sight of the gloriously crowded Manhattan skyline punctuated by the narrow twin towers of the World Trade Center. All around her video cameras whirred.

She elected not to climb the Statue of Liberty and instead continued on to Ellis Island. The glass display cases were filled with the artifacts immigrants had carefully selected to bring to the new country—wooden toys, Bibles, jewelry, lace petticoats, clocks, snuffboxes, ivory carvings, swords, tortoiseshell hair ornaments, wedding dresses and silver spoons. And photos, always photos, of the old country and the people left behind. The display that moved Claire the most was a preserved fragment of wall covered with layers of graffiti in three dozen different languages. The accompanying text explained that people had come to Ellis Island from all over the world, only to find themselves spending hours or days waiting in lines, or even weeks in quarantine. A potter's field on the island held the graves of those who had died within view of their hearts' desire.

Claire's knowledge of her own family history was limited, extending only about as far back as Grandma Montrose. According to her mother, they were "Heinz 57," without enough of any one type of blood in their veins to have inherited traditional foods, costumes or holidays. The one person who might have been able to tell her more about her past, Claire realized, was Aunt Cady.

It was early afternoon when she returned to the city. She walked among the bustling gray suits on Wall Street and past the pillars of the Stock Exchange, familiar from a thousand photographs. She ate a late lunch at a Tex-Mex restaurant, where she had a pork chop, fried okra and the best milk gravy and mashed potatoes she had ever tasted. Afterward, she lost herself on the narrow winding streets of Greenwich Village, window-shopping stores that sold bizarre clothing no one in Portland would ever wear. The art galleries were also from another planet, many displaying items that didn't seem to Claire to be art at all, like a blackboard that had a sentence written on it in chalk, "Fair wind follows the sailor," or another gallery that featured a half-dozen pig embryos floating in a brine-filled aquarium. Three hundred and fifty years from now, would someone still regard these as art, the way Claire looked at her painting now and still thought it beautiful? When she found herself on a familiar street—Fifth Avenue—she realized that the sky was nearly dark. She looked at her watch. Five o'clock. Troy was picking her up at eight-thirty. It was time to go back to her hotel and attempt to transform herself into the type of woman who would not look out of place at Cri du Coeur.

༄

"You look stunning."

"Thank you." Standing in the hotel lobby, Claire examined Troy's face and decided that he meant it. Before his arrival, while people dressed in sneakers and jeans eddied around her, she had felt as out of place as a yellow fantail among goldfish. Now she had become part of a matching set. Troy was dressed in another dark, elegantly cut suit, this one with a faint chalk stripe. He took her arm and the crowd of tourists parted before them. She heard them whispering to each other, hazarding names from the gossip columns. As they stepped into the night, Claire glimpsed her reflection in the lobby doors. With her hair caught up into a mass of ringlets, eyes enhanced by eyeliner and mascara, and of course the camouflage of the dress, she looked nothing like herself. Once again she thought of Cinderella.

Her carriage turned out to be a long black limousine, idling at the curb. A uniformed driver leaned against it, wearing a black cap on his short-cropped orange hair. He held the door as Troy handed her inside and then slid next to her on the leather seat. A fine tremble washed over her as the driver got inside.

"Are you cold? I'll ask John to turn up the heat."

Troy leaned forward to tap on the glass, but Claire laid a hand on his arm. "I'm not cold. Just a little nervous."

"Nervous? Why?" His eyes were guileless, as if he really didn't see the incongruity of them sitting side by side.

"This isn't the kind of thing I normally wear." She fingered the slippery fabric of the dress. "And this isn't the kind of car I normally ride in. If I were at home right now, I would just be finishing work." The state's list of vulgar words, her REJECTED stamp, the day's highlight the peanut butter cup cajoled from the secretary's secret stash—all that seemed to belong to someone else. Outside her tinted window, the muffled world slid by. "My job's so boring. Your work is much more glamorous."

Troy snorted. "Glamorous? All day, every day, I deal with people who treat me with much less respect than they would a waiter. If your family name didn't appear on Mrs. Astor's List of the Four Hundred, or if you can't lay claim to a relative who's a prince or at least a baron, then you simply don't matter to them." In the enfolding darkness of the car, Claire heard the edge of bitterness in his voice. "They'll come into Avery's with something beautiful—or half a dozen somethings—but they have no appreciation for what they have. They want to get rid of a Tintoretto because it no longer matches their loveseat. Or they need a little cash because they've overspent again, so they bring in an ancestral portrait that's been in their family for three hundred years and hope it will fetch a few hundred thousand. Or they gather up everything they have on their walls, from Old Masters to paintings of big-eyed children, and haul it all in. It's all the same to them—a piece of canvas held in a frame."

"I can see where that would be really frustrating," Claire agreed, thinking Troy's frustrations still sounded glamorous. The limousine pulled up outside the restaurant and Claire waited for someone to open her door as if she had been born to this life.

Everything in Cri du Coeur was white and gold—from the starched white damask tablecloths to the gold-armed chandeliers ending in frosted white glass tulips. Claire was relieved to see that her dress, which had looked so over the top in the hotel lobby, fit right in here. With sidelong glances, Claire appraised the women they passed as the maitre d' escorted them to their table. One woman wore a dark suit with a fluidly draped jacket and a skirt briefer than Claire's running shorts. Another woman sported black leather pants topped with a jacket made of curly white fake fur. A third with cropped red hair wore a floor-length electric blue dress, complete with a small train that she had looped over the back of her chair.

In the center of the room was a table that held a group of laughing people, including an actor famous for his rugged face and turquoise blue eyes. Claire was shocked when he gave her a quick once-over and a smile! It was as if she had stepped onto a movie set or into a particularly vivid dream. She was so befuddled that she didn't notice the maitre d' pulling out her chair and sat down instead in the one opposite. Troy slid into the offered chair as smoothly as if he had expected it. Claire blushed, hoping no one had seen her faux pas. The nearest person, a woman in a green jacket with straight black hair cut in a way that made Claire think of Cleopatra, was completely absorbed in her own conversation.

Troy slid the menu from her hands. "I'll order for us both, if you'd like." What Claire had glimpsed of the prices, even in elaborate calligraphy, had seemed outrageous. A cup of coffee was eleven dollars! For that you should get lifetime refills.

Despite its name, Cri du Coeur didn't serve purely French food, but a range of items that spanned the globe. For starters, they shared a plate of a half-dozen Cajun-style oysters, accompanied by a bottle of white wine. The flavors of sea and spice unfurled in Claire's mouth.

"I've been thinking about your painting," Troy said as he refilled her glass. "Clearly it's a forgery, but who really painted it?"

After her afternoon with Dante, Claire felt on firmer ground challenging Troy's opinion. "How could you tell right away that it was a forgery?"

"I knew it from the second you peeled back that—what was that, anyway? Bubble wrap? There are two ways to uncover a forgery. One's scientific. If I were a scientist, I could put your painting under, say, an optical emission spectrograph pigment analyzer, and I'm sure the results would allow me to be able to point to a graph and tell you that your painting couldn't have been painted by Vermeer. But the other way, the way I'm paid to use, is the product of a trained eye. Or maybe it's in the gut. I actually felt nauseous when I first saw your painting."

Claire, the woman with a dozen dictionaries lined up across her desk at work, couldn't resist a chance to show off that she too knew something. "You mean you felt nauseated. If you're nauseous, it means you cause nausea."

Troy narrowed his eyes for a split second, then shook his head and laughed. "All right, I felt nauseated. Whatever. I just knew. And that can't be taught. It's aesthetics. When I look at a painting I evaluate it subconsciously. Every painter has a dozen little personal mannerisms, from the way he loaded his brush with paint to the light he liked to work in. Even if a forgery tries to copy something exactly, he can't. Because he is *copying*, not creating, whatever he produces lacks the freedom of an original. Five years ago, Avery's went against my advice and bought a painting. It was supposedly a masterpiece, a Botticelli showing an angel hovering over the Madonna and the Christ Child. The first time I saw it I knew it was wrong. But they bought it, and it went under the hammer and sold for a very good price."

"Then what happened?" Claire took a sip of her second glass of wine. Or was it her third?

"A year later, they were forced to buy it back, very quietly. An analysis of the paint had turned up Prussian blue—which wasn't invented until 1704. That's almost three hundred years too late." Troy suddenly shook his head. Then he leaned forward to squeeze her hand. "I'm sorry! I've been lecturing, not having a conversation."

"No, no, I'm really interested." Claire took another sip of wine. It had been years since she had had more than two glasses of anything, but she was finding she liked the way it enhanced what already seemed a waking dream. In a few more days she would be back at work rejecting 6ULDV8 for the umpteenth time, but for now she planned on enjoying herself.

The waiter cleared their plates and brought the next course, a surprisingly delicate white bean soup. After Troy had an animated conversation with the sommelier, all about noses and legs, another bottle of wine was brought to the table, tasted and approved of. The woman at the table opposite Claire unbuttoned yet another inch of her lime-green jacket. She was clearly not wearing anything underneath it, and she laughed and swished her black hair, as shiny as patent leather, while she toyed with the collar.

Troy continued. "So the question is—if Vermeer didn't paint your Vermeer, then who did? And I'm beginning to wonder if you might have a real curiosity on your hands—a 'Vermeer' painted by Han Van Meegeren. Didn't you say that you thought your aunt acquired this painting during World War II?" He pronounced it "awnt" the way only rich people did in Portland.

"As far as I can tell, she got it during the war, put it under her bed, and then left it there. Who was Van Mee—, Van Meeg—?" Her tongue stumbled over the unfamiliar name.

Over the soup, Troy told Claire the story of Han van Meegeren, a 1930s Dutch painter whose own work had fallen out of fashion with the critics. Angry at their inability to recognize his genius, he had turned his talents to forgery—specifically seventeenth-century Dutch masterpieces. He was successful beyond his wildest flights of fancy. The same critics who had once called his own paintings shallow and sentimental now greeted the discovery of one after another of Van Meegeren's newly created "Vermeers" with reverence.

Troy explained the painstaking steps Van Meegeren took to make sure his paintings would meet all academic and scientific tests. First, Van Meegeren needed genuinely old canvases, stretched on old wood stretchers and held in place with 300-year-old tacks. So he bought minor seventeenth-century paintings at second-rate antique stores and then scraped off the images. To ensure the authenticity of the smallest details in the backgrounds of his paintings, he also bought seventeenth-century household objects: pewter plates, candlesticks, fabrics, jugs.

But by choosing Vermeer, Troy explained, Van Meegeren had set himself a puzzle. Vermeer was famous for his blues, yellows and whites. Even Van Gogh had praised Vermeer's use of those colors. Unfortunately for Van Meegeren, they were precisely the three colors whose manufacture had changed the most over three centuries. Van Meegeren knew he couldn't just go out and buy tubes of paint, because tiny samples would be put under a microscope and give the game away immediately. He had to make his own paint the way painters did centuries before—from plants, resins and minerals. To get one special shade of blue Vermeer was known for, Van Meegeren was forced to spend thousands of dollars on lapis lazuli and then grind the semiprecious stone by hand, as Vermeer had done. If he had ground it mechanically, the microscope would have revealed that all the paint particles were the same size.

The main course arrived—veal in some kind of brown sauce the waiter had called a reduction, accompanied by garlic-infused potatoes. It tasted a lot like potatoes and gravy to Claire. Troy barely touched it before he put his fork down and continued his explanation of Van Meegeren's clever approach to forgery.

Van Meegeren knew that an occasional bristle from his paintbrush would be left in the paint and thus might be lifted out and examined. So he made his own paintbrushes from badger hair shaving brushes, because Vermeer painted only with badger hair brushes.

All these measures were only just the beginning. Van Meegeren also had to find a way to make the paint prematurely hard, because oil paint normally took a century to dry completely. New synthetic chemicals were just coming on the market, and he found one that would make the paint dry quickly—but would still soften at the touch of mineral alcohol, the standard test to reveal a true Old Master.

Van Meegeren spent months painting his first "Vermeer," and then when he finished he baked it in a specially constructed oven to help dry and crack the paint. He knew it was impossible for a 300-year-old painting to be in perfect condition, so as a final step, he damaged the canvas with a number of unimportant abrasions and one small tear. Then he carried out some deliberately bumbling repairs before tacking the canvas onto the wood of the old stretcher, using the same old tacks. His last step was to plant the painting where it could be "discovered" by an eager critic.

Claire tried to imagine this man, this Van Meegeren, painting the face of the woman in her painting, not 350 years ago but 50. She said, "All that must have taken him years. There must have been a lot of trial and error and starting over again. How or why did he invest so much time and money when he had no idea if in the end people would believe they were really Vermeers?"

"He'd had some experience, though. When he was in art school, one of his professors believed the only good ways were the old ways, so he had taught all his students to paint using the same methods the Old Masters had. And when Van Meegeren first began to create his forgeries, he sold some of the less believable forgeries to unscrupulous dealers who didn't mind looking the other way."

"So you think the painting I have is a Van—fake by this man?" The waiter had brought their fourth course and a third bottle of wine, and Claire's lips were going numb. With great care, she sank her fork into the thin sheet of Parmesan cheese that lay on top of her artichoke and avocado salad. The woman at the next table got up to answer a tiny cell phone she drew from her purse. The entire dining room took notice, their eyes on the leopardskin shorts and the legs that unfolded endlessly from beneath the table.

Troy nodded. "There's a good chance it could be. His early Vermeer forgeries were genre paintings, paintings of—"

"—the upper middle class's daily life," Claire interrupted, remembering what Dante had told her.

Troy shot her a curious look before continuing. "Like your painting, Van Meegeren's first forgeries were clearly based on other well-known works by Vermeer. But then he took a gamble. He knew that if it paid off he would not only get revenge against those critics who had rejected him, but that he would also become very, very rich."

Troy explained that art historians had long speculated that in his youth Vermeer might have spent some time painting in Italy. So Van Meegeren set out to create a Vermeer like no one had seen before—a religious Vermeer with Italian overtones.

"Ironically, twenty years later a religious painting that everyone had thought was Italian turned out to be a Vermeer. And it's nearly an exact copy of a painting by a Florentine artist. So does that make Vermeer a forger? The only difference between what Van Meegeren and Vermeer did is that Vermeer signed the imitation with his own name." Troy seemed completely alive, green eyes snapping, hands cutting through the air. Claire could tell he admired the forger's cleverness. "Now all Van Meegeren needed to do was to completely take in one critic—in this case a half-blind old guy in his eighties. Once he had reeled him in, the critic did all the work to convince the rest of the world. An unknown masterwork by Vermeer had been found—by his one and only connoisseur's eye. A Dutch museum bought it for an incredible sum, and hundreds of thousands of people lined up in the streets to see it. All this time, Van Meegeren was busy making more paintings while living the high life on the Riviera—and developing a taste for cocaine."

"So how do people know all this?" Claire asked. "Why aren't we still looking at his paintings and thinking, you know, thinking they are really Vermeers?" While she was still following what Troy said, it was getting harder to articulate her own thoughts.

"Because Van Meegeren got greedy and sold paintings to Hitler's general, Göring. Both Hitler and Göring were fanatical art collectors, but Göring had better taste. After the war, the Allies found a 'Vermeer' in Göring's castle and traced it back to Van Meegeren. Then they discovered he had sold other 'Vermeers' to Göring. He was arrested and charged with collaborating with the enemy by selling Dutch national treasures to the Nazis. After weeks in prison, he broke down and admitted that the paintings he had sold Göring were not really Vermeers. In fact, he, Han Van Meegeren, had painted them."

"What happened then?" Claire's mind was whirling. Vermeers that were not Vermeers but that did end up having a little bit of truth in them.

"They laughed at him. Finally, to prove his point, he offered to create another 'Vermeer' right in front of their eyes. They brought canvas and paints to his cell, and he began to paint. When the authorities finally realized he was telling the truth, they dropped the collaboration charge."

"Did they let him go?" Claire became aware of Troy's knees grazing hers under the table.

"Are you kidding? Everyone was angry at being taken in by this bad painter with a drug habit. Instead they accused him of forgery. He died in prison. Just before he died, he told his daughter that there was another of his Vermeers that had never been discovered. I think he was talking about your painting. He could have sold it to Göring or another collector."

Claire tried to picture this, tried to see an embittered man creating the woman in her painting, not from love, but from a desire for revenge. Tried and failed. "But if that's true, then how did my Aunt Cady get it?"

"The art market during World War II was very, well, I guess the best word would be fluid. When there's a war on, things tend to get discarded or bartered or left behind. Your aunt could have run across the painting and picked it up. She might not even have known it was supposed to be a Vermeer."

"But what makes you think it's a Van Meegeren?" Claire still didn't understand why Troy was so certain.

"Four reasons." Troy spread out his fingers and began to tick them off. "One, my gut reaction to it as a forgery. Two, the complete lack of documentary evidence that Vermeer ever painted a painting that matches this description. Three, while your painting is a pastiche, it's a very accomplished one—just like the ones Van Meegeren did before he turned his hand to religious forgeries. And four, the time period in which it appeared—just when Han Van Meegeren was known to be churning out fakes."

The waiter had brought two slices of lemon meringue tart. Claire should have been full, but the sharp tartness of the lemon filling, enlivened by tiny pieces of zest, contrasted marvelously with the cloud of meringue. She ate every bite, then scraped her fork across the china to get a last lingering crumb of pie crust.

Troy had been watching her with a smile. "Would you like some of mine?" he asked, already turning his fork to cut off a piece for her. He leaned closer and slid the fork between her lips, then turned the fork aside, wiping his thumb across her upper lip to catch an errant crumb. His touch made her shiver. She wished she hadn't drunk so much. When she tried to think of Evan, his pale face seemed as insubstantial as a ghost's.

"You make a lot of noises when you eat," Troy observed.

"I do?" Claire felt her face begin to flush. God, she had drunk too much!

"These little moans of happiness. Don't worry, I like that in a woman. Someone who knows how to enjoy herself." He gave her a cat's sleepy smile, eyes half-closed.

Claire had had too much wine to keep her guard up, had even forgotten that she was supposed to be wary. Now she couldn't tell whether she still needed to be. Troy hadn't mentioned buying her painting at all. Was her painting really a Van Meegeren forgery? Thoughts formed and then slipped away.

She excused herself to go to the ladies' room. The walk down the long narrow room seemed endless, and her feet were so far away. Colors were brighter and bits of conversation floated past her. When she pushed open the door, she was surprised to see an old woman sitting in a plastic chair next to the sink, a basket of small white towels at her feet. Claire wasn't sure what protocol demanded of her, but her bladder was so full that she just gave the woman a swift smile and went into one of the stalls. With exaggerated care, she gathered up her dress and sat down. She pressed her fingers into her numb cheeks. How much had she had to drink tonight? There had been three bottles of wine—or was it four? Enough so that everything was slightly out of focus. She finished, flushed the toilet and went back out into the main part of the rest room.

"Am I supposed to tip you?" Claire had decided that she was no longer capable of pretending that she really lived this kind of life.

"Most people give me a dollar." The woman's voice had a trace of an accent, perhaps Russian, reminding Claire a little of the Ukrainian taxi driver who had picked her up at the airport—was that just two days ago? They regarded each other in the mirror. In her white-collared black polyester uniform, with her legs planted wide, the old woman presented a complete contrast to Claire. "You look like beautiful bride."

"Um, thank you." Claire fumbled for a dollar in the beaded purse she had also purchased at Filene's. She finally found one and exchanged it for a towel.

"I am half Gypsy. For another ten dollar I read your palm."

Claire wondered if the management knew about this money-making sideline. "I'm sorry, but I need to get back."

She was still holding the towel, uncertain of where to put it. The woman reached out, first taking and discarding the towel into another basket half hidden by her chair, and then grabbing Claire's palm and turning it over. Her fingers were surprisingly soft. Without even seeming to look at Claire's palm, she rattled off, "I see danger and opportunity, great wealth and true love. But only if you follow your heart."

Her heart? What was that supposed to mean? Claire felt that she had to give the woman something. She managed to find a five-dollar bill, dropped it into the woman's lap and left before she could demand more.

Troy was waiting for her just outside the door. He put his arm around her. She was grateful for the support. Unaccustomed to heels, her feet were having difficulty setting a straight course. In the car, he drew her to him without speaking and tried to kiss her. His mouth tasted of wine and lemon. Although desire washed over her like a wave, Claire put her hand on his chest.

"What about him?" she whispered. She imagined the driver's flat, acne-scarred face watching them in the mirror.

"Who? The driver? Forget about John." Troy took her hand, turned it over and kissed the palm. "He's there to drive. He's not paying any attention." He pulled her to him again, only this time she let him kiss her.

The car came to a stop, and outside the window, made dreamlike by the tinted glass, she recognized the outline of the Farthingale. "Can I come up to your room?" Troy murmured in her ear. Part of her could imagine them strolling through the lobby, hips bumping together, their arms around each other and the crowds parting before them. But the spell had been broken. She couldn't imagine them lying down together in her small room, couldn't even picture them on the elevator. And was it her he wanted—or just to be in the same room again with the painting? Claire shook her head. "I'm sorry, I just can't."

"Why not?" Troy's green eyes narrowed a bit. "Do you have a boyfriend?"

She nodded in agreement, but instead of picturing Evan, Claire found herself thinking of the painter she had met, Dante with his pirate's grin.

∾

In her room, she went to her hiding place and pulled out the painting. The woman regarded her with her mysterious, serene expression. Who was she? A patchwork cribbed from other Vermeers, created by a failed painter fifty years before in the hopes of making a fortune? Or had Vermeer himself captured her image, magically creating an arrested moment of stillness in what must have been a chaotic household overrun with children?

The woman's face revealed nothing and everything. Whoever she was, Claire decided, she had been painted with passion.

She put the painting down and went into the bathroom, where she regarded herself in the full-length mirror. The lighting in here was bright and harsh, not really the kind meant to be softly reflected by satin. Her face held none of the inner stillness of the woman in the painting. Her eyes were wide, her lips a little swollen from kissing, her hair a wild halo half sprung from her pins. Still, part of her approved of this woman in the mirror, this other version of Claire Montrose. If nothing else, this trip to New York had revealed to her a new side of herself, a woman who could talk about art and turn a movie star's head and make her way around a city of seven million people on her own. She carefully removed the dress and hung it up, but she was too full of unexpelled energy to sleep. Finally she took Aunt Cady's diary from her suitcase and began to read.

June 20, 1945

Rudy has a room he rents from an old lady at the edge of town. He keeps things in it. Me, for instance. There are simply times when we have to be alone. He pays for it in cigarettes, and the woman he rents it from is glad of the occasional American dollar he tosses her way. We went there last night to be alone, never minding the holes in the roof. We took a bath together. He has hair on his chest and belly, which seems unusual for a blond man. I played with it as it dried from the heat of the fire, combed it with my fingers until it was the shape of a butterfly. Afterward he showed me how underneath a piece of oilcloth he keeps pistols and rifles, cameras and binoculars still in their carrying cases, an antique ornamental sword. His pride and joy is a newly acquired motorbike, an almost brand-new German Zündapp. Everything he has is expensive and beautiful, the best in the world.

I see it all around me. People take what they want, just pop through a hole in the side of a house and survey the ruins. If they don't take it, someone else will, so what's the point of leaving it? If no one took it, it would be ruined by the weather. Even the ambulance drivers and medics and nurses did their own share of appropriating, took things from men who lay wounded on stretchers, and then neglected to return them.

Still, it doesn't seem right to me. Rudy does not regard it as stealing, and it's true that he says he bought a lot of what he has. Although how much he paid and whether the seller ever really owned it are other matters. He says all the occupying forces are looting. The army does look the other way. We're permitted to mail home captured enemy equipment provided there is no "military need" for it. Technically we're not supposed to send home things that come from German homes or public buildings, but no one seems to care. At least, no one enforces it. To prove his point, Rudy brought up the Reverend Joiner, who sends home more than anyone. Rudy has a friend, an officer, who will scribble his signature on a package without looking inside. An officer's signature means that a package will arrive home intact, unexamined.

He tells me I shouldn't worry about such things, that

worrying will give me wrinkles and ruin my beautiful face. No one has ever accused me of being beautiful before. Of course, Rudy is much more beautiful than me, as a man is sometimes beautiful. His eyes are such a pale blue they are almost silver. He reminds me that mine are blue, too, but it's an ordinary, washed-out blue, nothing like his.

July 2, 1945

Rudy was drunk when he came to pick me up last night, drunk and amorous. My body has need of him always, so when we were out walking and found an abandoned house I didn't protest when he pulled me in after him. The house was remarkably intact, looking as if whoever had lived here had fled less than 30 minutes before. Rudy systematically went through the cupboards in search of something useful—i.e., something edible, drinkable, burnable. He found some noodles in the cupboard, and then gave a cry of triumph when he discovered three bottles of wine stashed underneath a loose floorboard behind the stove. I cooked for us. Although it wasn't much of a meal, the wine made it go down easier. It was as if we were already married, in our own home with nice things. We hadn't even finished eating before he took me into the bedroom. He pulled me into bed with him, just as we were, with our dirty uniforms and muddy boots. The sheets were fine and smooth and cool beneath us.

Afterward, it all began to be spoiled. I was lying beside him, and we were laughing at something, I don't even remember what. I felt almost giddy, imagining us a year from now, lying at home on our own sheets on our own bed. I was smoking a cigarette and for once so was Rudy. When he was done he threw the butt onto the carpet. I didn't really notice what he had done until the smell of smoke began to fill the room. I got up and found my shoe and pounded it on the place where smoke was curling from the rug. There was enough moonlight to see that it had left a burn mark in the middle of the fine deep pile.

"Maybe it can be mended," I told him. The carpet was an oriental pattern, so it could have been rewoven without the new patch standing out.

He laughed and called me a Miss Priss. "You don't get it, do you? These people are the enemy. They don't deserve all this. Look around you. Think these people should be living the good life when so many of our boys are dead?"

There was an armoire by the bed, old and cavernous, standing on carved legs. He got out of bed and shook my clothes off a chair, then picked it up by the back. He planted his feet like a baseball player, pivoted, then swung the legs at the armoire's mirror, shattering it. I felt little pieces of glass prick my face.

"See," he said, panting, happy somehow, "it doesn't matter. It's what these people deserve." He unfolded his pocket knife and stuck it high up in one of the silk draperies, then brought it down with a sickening tearing sound, the beautiful old cloth parting before the shine of his blade. He slashed and slashed again until the silk hung in strips.

I was crying, in shock that things had changed in only a few minutes. Where was the man I loved? He picked up a ceramic figure from the bedside table and hurled it against the wall, then turned to me with a smile.

"Don't you get it?" he said. "It's all ours now. We can do what we want." That was the frightening thing for me, because I think that was the real reason, not what they had done to our boys. But that he could do what he wanted.

I've never dated at home. I knew what they said about me behind my back. Plain. Too serious. Born to be an old maid. Rudy, I thought, was different. He was serious, too. He was a man, not a boy. But now I wonder if he just liked the challenge. Or because I help keep the records.

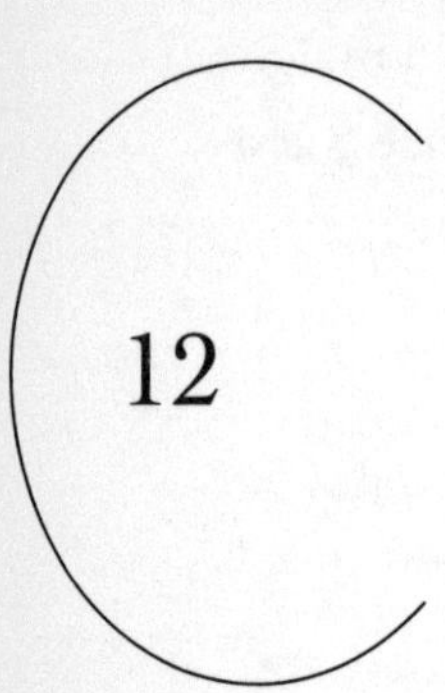

12

Each of Claire's teeth was covered with a little mitten. She ran her tongue over them and was immediately sorry. Her face was pressed into the bed, her cheek slashed with pain. Without opening her eyes, she rolled onto her back and ran her fingertips across her face. She found not a cut, but a deep crease from where she had fallen asleep on top of Aunt Cady's diary.

In the shower, she rubbed her face with both hands as she thought about how she had acted the night before. Wobbling around in high heels, so drunk that she needed Troy's assistance to get into the car, then letting him kiss and paw her in front of the driver. She must have looked pathetic. And what about Evan? Even if she was no longer sure about their relationship, was her heart so fickle? Claire stayed under the spray for a long time, as if the water could strip away her memory of the night before.

With the sour taste scrubbed from her mouth and her hair still damp, Claire was walking through the hotel lobby when someone called her name. It was Dante, the painter she had met at the Met, wearing a heavy fisherman's sweater and faded Levi's. At the sight of his high-cheekboned face, something inside her shifted, catching her heart off-balance.

"Dante! What are you doing here?"

"Waiting for you. I tried to call you last night, but you were never in. I figured if I came over early this morning and waited that eventually you'd walk past."

"That guy from Avery's took me out to dinner." Claire couldn't resist adding, "To Cri du Coeur."

Dante raised an eyebrow. "Sounds like you've been sampling the best of our fair city." Claire wondered what it would have been like if he had been the one sitting across from her the night before. But Dante was all business, next saying, "I have to know—is your painting in a safe place?"

She thought of the hiding place she had finally settled on. "Yes."

"Good. We need to talk. Where were you headed?"

"There's a Starbucks up the block. I didn't get much sleep last"—she changed course, trying to make it sound better—"I stayed up too late, reading."

"Uh-huh. Yeah." He gave a little nod and Claire realized he didn't believe her. "How about letting me buy you some espresso made by people who've been drinking the stuff for fifty years, not the last five?"

"That does sound good."

She followed him outside, where he raised his hand to hail a taxi. "I know an Italian place in the West Village where they make a double cappuccino strong enough to make the dead get up and walk."

"Is that what you are—Italian? With a name like Dante, I should have guessed." A taxi pulled up at the curb, and Dante gave the driver quick instructions before settling down beside Claire.

"Only three-quarters. My grandfather was German, which is

where the Bonner came in. But for all practical purposes I was raised one hundred percent Italian."

The taxi jostled through streams of traffic, then turned onto a winding cobblestone street. They passed a parked refrigerated truck, its back door open to show rows of pale pig carcasses swaying from hooks. A man in blue coveralls walked up the ramp that led to the back of the truck and threw a carcass over his shoulder, the slit in its belly gaping open like a long mouth. Claire swallowed hard and resolved to give up bacon. A few blocks later, the taxi pulled to a stop and Dante paid the driver.

"Is this Little Italy?" The narrow winding street was crowded with young people window-shopping a gallery selling huge canvases with a single splash of paint, or bargaining for jewelry, scarves and T-shirts at a makeshift market that had sprung up in a vacant lot.

"That's another area of the city. The real Italians pulled up stakes there long ago. For that matter, there aren't that many left here. It was a lot different thirty years ago. I grew up in an apartment a couple of blocks from here, and there were times you heard more Italian than English when you walked down the street."

"Does your family still live here?"

"No. My father runs the family business now. He and my mom live on Long Island in something a hell of a lot bigger than the apartment I grew up in."

As Dante spoke, he opened the door to a restaurant with a white-tiled floor and the silver gleam of a pressed tin ceiling. With its red-and-white-checked tablecloths, it was a world away from the trendy scene outside. An ancient waiter in a battered black suit seated them at a table near the espresso machine, an imposing chrome apparatus resting on a green-veined marble countertop. Dante waved off menus and ordered cappuccinos and cannoli for both of them.

Claire watched as a white-jacketed barman placed a heavy white cup under a spout and slowly pulled down one of the long levers. A hiss, and the cup was half filled with oily black espresso. The mouth-watering scent of freshly roasted coffee filled the café. The barman drew down another cup, then poured milk into a second pitcher, held it up to a another spout, long and thin, and depressed still another lever. He swirled the pitcher under the jet of steam until it grew into a cloud of foam. The frothed milk went into the heavy mugs, and finally a shaker of shaved chocolate was tapped over the finished cappuccinos.

"Now tell me if that doesn't beat Starbucks," Dante said after the waiter brought their order to them.

Claire took an appreciative sip and nodded her head in agreement. It would be easy to spend the day here in this big leather booth, watching the old men in buttoned-up sweaters and non-power suspenders playing dominoes under the ceiling fans. She took a bite of her cannoli, enjoying the fresh custard and crisp pastry, then chased it with another sip of frothy cappuccino. "This is really good. Thanks for bringing me here."

"I wanted someplace quiet where we could talk without a waiter trying to hurry us along. Since you first showed me your painting, I haven't been able to think of anything else." He pulled a stack of photos from an envelope and placed them in the center of the table. Even reproduced, the painted woman's calm gaze drew both their eyes. "We need to answer two questions. Who painted this and how did your aunt happen to get it? And more and more, I think the answer to the first question may well be Vermeer."

Claire found it hard to take a breath. What if her painting really were a Vermeer? Then, like a cascade of cold water, she remembered Troy's equal certainty that her painting was not 300 years old, but 50, and painted by someone named Van Meegeren. And Troy was paid for his opinion, whereas Dante was just a former art history major. "Why do you think it's a Vermeer?" Claire kept her voice carefully neutral.

"First, there's the subject of the painting." Dante explained that a woman with a letter was a common theme in seventeenth-century Dutch genre paintings. Vermeer himself had made six known paintings of a woman either reading, writing or receiving a letter. "Unlike other painters of his day, though, he left it up to the viewer to guess the content of the letter and the lady's reaction to it." Dante took a final sip of cappuccino, then signaled to the waiter to bring him a fresh cup.

"The other day, you told me you liked Vermeer because he painted mysteries."

"Exactly. Just like the mystery in this painting. And look at all the details—the same things you noticed when I met you. Because Vermeer never made much money when he was alive, he probably painted in his own home, not a studio. He used the same everyday items over and over again. Take this jacket, for example." Dante tapped on the lemony glow of the photograph. "A jacket just like the one in your painting—ermine-trimmed, yellow satin—appears in six Vermeer paintings. When he died at forty-three, a lady's yellow satin jacket was in the inventory of his possessions."

Dante ticked off the other visual clues in Claire's painting that pointed to Vermeer. Her painting had a Turkish carpet. In nine Vermeers there was a Turkish carpet, often bunched in folds and used as a tablecloth. Her painting showed a leather-backed, brass-studded chair with lion's-head finials—as did eleven other Vermeers. There were pearl earrings in eight other Vermeers, white ceramic wine pitchers in six.

"But even those things weren't what convinced me. They are all typical household goods of the period. When I was looking through the archives I even saw an identical yellow jacket—right down to the ermine trim—in another seventeenth-century Dutch painting. Only this one was by Gerhard Ter Borch." Dante leaned forward in his chair, his dark eyes boring into Claire. "Then I looked at the windows in your painting. Vermeer almost always shows a window on the left-hand side of his paintings, either a set of plain leaded glass or a set with stained glass—probably the two sets of windows in his home. This"—he tapped his finger on one of the photographs—"is identical to one of those two sets."

"But shouldn't all of those things make you suspicious?" Claire asked, her mind on what Troy had told her the night before. "You're telling me that everything in this painting points to Vermeer. Isn't anything that perfect likely to be a forgery?"

Dante shook his head. "That's ridiculous! You can't say that because the painting is so clearly a Vermeer then of course it can't be a Vermeer. I take it that guy from Avery's has told you the story of Han Van Meegeren. Did he actually show you any photos of Van Meegeren's paintings?"

Claire had to shake her head.

"I can see why he didn't. Anyone would be able to see in a glance that these paintings were not Vermeers. Most forgers can fool only a single generation. Fifty years ago, there was nearly mass hysteria in the art world when these new 'Vermeers' were discovered. Now they look ridiculous. All the subjects look the same. They have long faces, hollow cheeks and hooded deep-set eyes. Kind of like a third-rate Marlene Dietrich. And nothing like your lady." They both looked down at the perfect oval face, her parted lips, before Dante continued, "Plus, there's no record of a painting like this in the known Vermeer forgeries. I spent a lot of time looking through the museum's archives yesterday. In the Dissius auction of 1671, a Vermeer came under the gavel that was described as 'A woman with a letter standing at an open window, very nicely painted.' And a few years later, there are records showing that Jacob Crammer Simonz had three Vermeers—the *Geographer,* the *Lacemaker*, and something called *A Woman with a Letter*, now lost. I think that this"—he tapped the stack of photographs—"is that lost painting."

The waiter brought fresh cappuccinos. Speaking Italian, he

directed what sounded like a question to Dante. Claire had the uncomfortable feeling he was asking about her. Dante answered him in a rapid slur of consonants and vowels. The waiter laughed and shuffled away.

"You speak Italian?" Claire asked the obvious question.

"Kitchen Italian mostly. My grandmothers both kept to the old ways and I spent a lot of time with them when I was a kid." Claire had a mental picture of an iron pot bubbling on the back of the stove while a black-dressed, white-haired woman strung laundry on a line that stretched over the alley. The picture was so clear that it took her a moment to realize it came direct from one of the *Godfather* movies—was it *Godfather II*?

Claire held the fresh mug to her collarbone, enjoying the feeling of warmth from the heavy ceramic. "I wish I had an ethnic background. I'm a mutt. I always thought it would be great to have holidays where you talked about the old country in another language while wearing a special costume and eating traditional foods. I don't even know who my father was. He got my mom pregnant and was long gone before I was even born. I only recently realized that Aunt Cady was probably the only one in the family who would have known about our family tree."

"So what was your great-aunt like?" Dante turned his mug to catch the foam that clung to the sides.

"I hadn't seen her for probably twenty years." Claire thought back to the family picnic when she was fifteen, and Aunt Cady had advised her to live in the real world. "I think she was lonely. Judging by what she had in her trailer, she spent her time reading. Even though I don't think she had touched this painting for years, I think she kept it because it reminded her of a time when she was young and in love, right after the war."

"Where was she stationed?"

"First she was in London, and then when the war ended in

Europe, she went to Munich. She was a clerk, and I guess the idea was to free up a man to fight against the Japanese."

"I wonder if she ever met my grandfather. He was stationed outside of Munich just after the war. He was born in Germany and came over here as a child. He never lost his accent, but he was proud to be an American. He came from a family of weavers, and when the war broke out he tried to enlist right away. But what did the Army want with a fifty-year-old tapestry expert? He pestered them until finally, near the end of the war, they gave in and assigned him to the Monuments, Fine Arts and Architecture Division."

Claire imagined a group of artists advanced into battle wearing smocks and waving paintbrushes. "What was that?"

"MFA&A was part of the Army. Its job was to protect the art that had survived the war and return it to its rightful owners. My grandfather spent a year working for them in a place called Berchtesgaden, just outside Munich." Dante rolled the *r* of "Berchtesgaden" in the back of his throat in a way that reminded her of Charlie. Clearly his grandfather had taught him as well as his grandmothers. Claire realized she was enjoying herself.

"So he tracked down missing tapestries?"

"That and a little bit of everything else. A lot of tapestries didn't make it through the war. They were too heavy to carry and too bulky to hide. Not like jewelry, which can be slipped into a pocket. And as the war went on and on, beauty became more of an abstract concept. He said it wasn't unusual for refugees to saw apart a Gobelin tapestry and use it for blankets."

Between sips of cappuccino, Dante painted a picture of a country in chaos. Jewelry and silver were hidden and then forgotten about. Art vanished into the hands of neighbors, refugees, the secret police, soldiers on both sides, and people who simply saw an opportunity and grabbed it. Things were available for the taking, even more so after Germany lost the war.

"My grandfather said the Russian DPs were the easiest to work with because they always crossed themselves when they saw pictures of the Madonna, and did not dare touch religious works. And when they broke into museums they usually limited themselves to taking the more useful costumes."

"So your grandfather traced art back to its original owners?"

"He spent most of his time there worrying about what to do with Göring's estate."

"Göring!" Claire started. "My roommate is seventy-eight, and originally from Germany. She's Jewish, and they tried to bribe their way out with an old family painting that was supposed to be a Rembrandt. But the person who took their painting gave them papers that were no good and they were arrested. Charlie lost her whole family in the camps." Claire thought of the little boy whose name Charlie never uttered. It was as if she could not bear to pull him into the world again. "She told me they traded the painting to someone who worked for Göring."

Dante tapped his heavy white mug with his index finger. "My guess would be that whoever gave them false papers did it without Göring's knowledge. Hitler was never too particular about the provenance of his art, but Göring wasn't a thief. Of course, he didn't have to be. People were eager to do him favors, and it was known he collected art. He especially liked early German and Dutch Old Masters." They both glanced at the photos of Claire's painting, clearly something that would have interested Göring. "Sometimes he bought things for ridiculously low prices. More often they were given as 'gifts' that were really bribes—like the deal your roommate tried to make. He let several art collectors smuggle out their collections in return for a prize painting or two. They say that by 1940, he had the most important art collection in Europe."

Dante told Claire about Göring's collection, which bordered on obsession. The walls of his estate were hung so thickly with hundreds of paintings that their frames touched. He lounged on 500-year-old hand-carved furniture, walked on rare tapestries, ate off plates made from silver and gold. "He had a vase filled with diamonds, and while he was thinking he liked to pour them from hand to hand. By the end of the war, he was wearing red velvet robes covered with jewels."

"He sounds a little crazy."

Dante nodded. "Probably more than a little. But he was a crazy man with excellent taste. My grandfather used to get all worked up when he told me about what happened to all those beautiful things."

"What happened? Were they bombed?"

Dante explained that at the end of the war, a worried Göring packed a train full of his precious art and then tried to find a safe place for it. First it went to Berlin, but the Soviet army threatened it. Then the train tried and failed to make it to his county home near Berchtesgaden. When the Americans and the French swept in, they found an abandoned train on a railway siding. They didn't know what they had until Göring's art adviser gave himself up.

"My grandfather made it to Unterstein—the little spot where most of the train cars ended up—too late. He said from a distance it was as if the people were streams of ants. When he got closer, the streams of ants turned into people fighting to get into cars and then fighting to get out of them again, only this time with their arms full. Children were running between people's feet, grabbing what fell. The station was littered with broken bottles of wine, enormous paintings, statues that had turned out to be too heavy to carry. He cried when he told me about how he found a group of men tearing up a tapestry because it was too big to carry in one piece. He chased them off by giving them some food and wine he had found in one car." Dante shook his head. "Even after all that looting, there were still more than six hundred paintings left on the train. But a lot of Göring's collection had vanished."

"Wasn't Göring hanged after the war?"

Dante shook his head. "Two hours before he was supposed to be hanged, he committed suicide by swallowing cyanide capsules he had smuggled into his cell. His ashes were thrown into the last incinerator in Dachau."

They were both silent for a minute.

Claire set down her mug. "Did they ever find the stuff that disappeared from the train?"

"My grandfather spent a year dressed in lederhosen roaming the villages around Berchtesgaden, attempting to recover items from reluctant locals."

"Did he succeed?"

"Only to a degree. He also had to cope with our own soldiers, who weren't any better. You probably remember the story about the guy from Kentucky."

"Was that the one who sent home a bunch of things that had been hidden?"

Dante nodded. "Treasures from a cathedral stored for safekeeping in a cave. One of the items he helped himself to was a fourteenth-century painting of the Christ child. He knew that it must be valuable because it had these big emeralds and rubies set around the frame. I don't know how he thought he was going to turn up with a six-hundred-year-old painting and pass it off as something that had been in his family all along."

"I don't remember what happened to him." When Claire had read about the case, she had never guessed that it might someday be of personal interest to her.

"He died not long ago. There was a lot of controversy when the German government bought the painting back from his family for several million dollars. Last I heard, the IRS was slapping his estate for back taxes. And they were considering criminal charges. But now that he's dead, who knows what will happen? At least he didn't pry the jewels out of the frame. During the war, the average soldier didn't care too much about art. My grandfather used to cry when he told me about what he had seen over there. Soldiers smashed or shot at sculptures. People used Renaissance Limoges enamels as plates and then threw them away. If a soldier did have an appreciation for art, he simply took what he liked and sent it home through the military field post."

"Aunt Cady mentioned something like that in her diary."

Dante sat forward. "Your aunt kept a diary when she was stationed in Germany?"

Claire nodded. "I was reading parts of it last night."

"Where is it now? In your hotel room?"

"Actually, I have it right here in my backpack. Before you hijacked me, I was planning on reading it while I had my coffee."

"Would you mind if I looked at it? It might tell us exactly where that painting came from."

Claire wasn't sure how she felt about it. Was it right to share Aunt Cady's musings, her fears, her desires, with a stranger? Claire had a connection to the woman, memories that helped her understand her attraction to Rudy. She didn't want Dante to judge her aunt.

He was still looking at her expectantly, so she showed him what she thought were the relevant parts—the day Aunt Cady had met Rudy, the description of the warehouse that Rudy had been set to guard. Dante eventually took the diary from her hands and read to her.

July 17, 1945

A radiant summer day. The German housewives have been busy, dusting, wiping and scrubbing. When you go outside you hear the sounds of carpet-beating, sweeping, hammering. Munich is being cleaned up. Children look washed again. Everywhere you see refugees on their way home, family groups with little handcarts piled high with sacks, boxes, suitcases. Many of the carts are pulled by women or boys with ropes over their shoulders, followed by children or a grandfather pushing the cart from behind. Atop almost all the carts either children or very old people sit huddled among the baggage. These old ones, whether men or women, look awful—gray, emaciated, already half dead, listless bundles of bones.

This morning I saw a garbage truck belonging to the city of Munich. On it were six coffins, one of which the driver used as a seat. The garbagemen were having their breakfast up there. The sun sparkled off the beer bottles they raised to their mouths.

After breakfast, Frau Lehman, our cook, told me about what happened to her younger sister. Last year, when she was seventeen years old, her leg was torn off by shrapnel when she got caught outside during a bombing raid. She bled to death. Her parents buried her in their garden behind some red currant bushes. For a coffin they used their broom cupboard.

Tried to extract from her the German word for dream. By paraphrasing it in various ways such as "a movie in the head," "seeing pictures with one's eyes closed," and "not-real things taking place in one's sleep," I finally succeeded. *Traume.* It sounds a lot like the English word "trauma."

I dreamed about Rudy last night. I dreamed we had just finished making love and I was lying on my back with my eyes closed. I opened them, only a little bit, and he was watching me with a look, his eyes flat and his face expressionless. He didn't say anything, just watched me, but for some reason when I woke up I was frightened.

"Dante!" A man in his mid-fifties had entered the café and now came straight to their table, waddling a little because he was extremely fat. His bulldog face was split by a grin.

"Hello, Uncle Alfonso."

He turned to give Claire a frankly appraising glance from eyes nearly buried in folds of flesh. "So who's this you have with you? Have you been keeping something from the family?" His growling voice gave a special emphasis to the word "family."

"I'm Claire. Claire Montrose." She held out her hand. "I only met Dante a few days ago, at the Met."

His grip was soft, but with a surprising underlying firmness. He gave Claire's hand an extra squeeze before releasing it. "The Metropolitan Museum of Art?" He curled his lip when he said the word *art*, then appealed to Dante. "When are you going to join the business? Family is family."

Dante's answer was soft, but Claire saw a pulse in his jaw. "I like what I do, Uncle Alfonso. You know I'm not cut out for all that."

"You should give up this nonsense. Stop being afraid of getting your hands dirty."

Claire, who felt as if she had stepped onto a movie set, was finally putting it all together. What was all this talk about the family business? Dante was Italian, wasn't he? And wasn't New York home to the five families, the mob bosses who ruled the Mafia?

She shook her head, realizing she was letting fantasy overtake her.

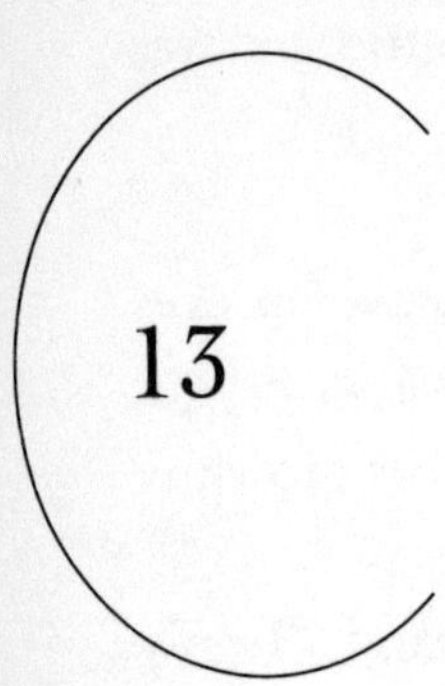

13

Claire sat on the bed in her hotel room and laced up her Nikes, the new ones with an extra-cushioned midsole. They were embarrassingly white, with a brilliant aqua stripe. Anyone looking at them would think she had never run before.

It was still early, just after seven on Sunday, but it seemed wrong to be sleeping away her last day in New York City. In twenty-four hours she would be back in the Custom Plate Department, listening to Frank describe his weekend in excruciating detail.

When she had returned to her hotel room, after having spent most of the day with Dante, Troy had called. He was all apologies for his behavior the night before, calling himself boorish. And partly it was Troy's use of the word *boorish*—a word that no one she knew would ever use—that had made Claire relent and agree to let him take her out to breakfast before she left. But she had decided she would go as Claire Montrose, not some woman in a too-sexy dress. It was too much work to be anyone but herself.

To Claire's surprise, Fifth Avenue was practically deserted. Seven-fifteen in the morning on an October Sunday, and the greatest city in the world looked almost unpopulated. The pavement was wet from an overnight shower, but the clouds had retreated and were now scudding high overhead. She braced her hands against a wall and began to stretch out her legs. Rather than rinsing the air, the rain had released all the smells of the city, so that the stink of garbage and gasoline and urine and the perfumey scent of a basement laundry hung all mixed together in the air, acrid and steamy.

Claire had read that the portion of the brain responsible for processing smells was one of the more primitive parts, making it the sense that aroused the most emotions. The same article had talked about what smells people associated with their childhoods, saying that people over fifty associated being a kid with natural scents, like bread baking or the sweetish smell of manure, while anyone younger than fifty thought of childhood when they smelled artificial smells, like the scent of crayons or Play-Doh. For Claire it happened when she smelled a particular kind of cheap plastic—a reminder of a doll that had miraculously materialized under the Christmas tree straight from the pages of the Sears Wish Book. Or sometimes at work when she ripped open a freshly printed pack of forms she would be back in fifth grade again, sniffing the milky scent of mimeograph paper.

She hit the button on her black rubber wristwatch and set off. New York didn't look so unconquerable when seen at this hour, in this place. Without the streams of honking cars and sidewalks full of rushing people, Claire was free to glory in the buildings that stretched up to the sky and the wide wet street that ran between them as straight as a ruler. She felt a surge of energy rise from her belly to her chest, a wordless joy at life's possibilities. It was hard to believe that a single phone call from her mother had led her here.

As she ran, she passed an old couple in their Sunday best, speaking what she thought was French. Taking no chances on the overcast sky, they shared the shelter of an oversized black umbrella. The doorway of a sub shop held a bundle of rags that proved to be a sleeping human being. A Lycraed woman Rollerbladed past Claire, her taut figure belied by her middle-aged face. While the gutter held scraps of paper and an occasional pile of dog droppings, Claire thought the city was remarkably clean. People had obediently filled the street-corner wastebaskets with paper cups and candy wrappers and discarded yellow and black Playbills left over from the night before.

Claire settled into an easy pace. On these flat streets she could run forever, at least until she ruined her knees by pounding on pavement. She thought about Troy and Dante. Her last meeting with Dante had ended awkwardly, with her promising to call him when she got back to Portland, promising to think about lending him the painting so he could arrange to have it tested, while thinking to herself she didn't know what she would do. She needed more time to think, to weigh the various opinions Troy and Dante had offered her.

The two men were so different. Dante clearly wanted her painting, while Troy claimed to want her. But Claire wondered how much Troy's fascination, too, lay not in her but in a foot-square painting of a woman with a letter in her hands and an unreadable expression on her face.

࿐

Troy surprised Claire by showing up minus a limousine or even a car. They walked a few blocks to a deli he suggested, which was again a surprise. The people who filled it were mostly tourists, and Troy, in his dark, fashionably cut suit, stood out among them like a swan among seagulls.

Over bagels, cream cheese and lox, they spent more than an hour exchanging stories. Or, more accurately, Troy regaled her with tales about some of Avery's famous clients. A rock musician who snorted cocaine off the viewing room's table. An actor who bought an abstract painting for several million only to hang it upside down. She told a few stories of her own about Custom Plates, but mostly she just listened, aware of the minutes slipping by. She was Cinderella watching the clock edge toward midnight, and tomorrow the drudgery would begin again.

Finally she said, "I really have to get back to my hotel if I'm going to make it to the airport on time."

"No—is it that late?" Troy looked at his watch. "Damn—I forgot I had promised to call someone this morning. Would you excuse me for a moment?"

Claire studied him as he used a phone in the lobby. He was so different from any other man she had ever known. Then she amended that. So different from the men in Portland, at least. Dante was in many ways like Troy. Both were strikingly handsome. And both were smart. Only Troy moved through the upper strata of New York City's society—while Dante looked as if he might know the city's underbelly.

Claire watched as Troy punched a series of numbers into the pay phone, listened, punched in some more numbers, then finally hung up. Voice mail hell, she guessed. She was familiar with it herself from work. Every day, it seemed, she was forced to listen to a woman's voice—complete with a false note of sadness—saying, "I'm sorry. That is not a valid option or password," when Claire had been trying for neither, but simply to leave a message for another state employee. The thought of state employees reminded her that she had one more task to fulfill before she boarded the plane. She was ordering a dozen bagels from the man behind the counter when Troy rejoined her.

"Don't trust plane food?"

"There's an unwritten social contract at work that anyone who goes on vacation has to return with an edible souvenir. It was either this or some of those big pretzels they sell on the street."

Troy pulled a face. "They keep those pretzels stacked up to the rafters in warehouses in Jersey, with the rats running over them."

"Guess I made the right choice, then."

"Maybe you should break the rule and see what happens. It doesn't sound like you like the people you work with all that much."

"Oh, most of them are all right," Claire said, thinking of Lori. With some effort, she pushed away a mental picture of sitting in Roland's office tomorrow, surrounded by elephants and the miasma of his sullen lust.

As they left the deli, Troy took her free hand. "I wish you had more time here. Promise me you'll come back."

"I want to," she said, but it was Dante's face that flashed into her mind. In a few days her adventures here would seem like a dream.

"What are you thinking about?" Troy was examining her with a half-smile.

"Just that I don't want to go home." They had slowed to a walk and now were standing outside an apartment building. The glass doors revealed floors of black and white marble. Between two elevators was a huge arrangement of colorful flowers. Only a few inches away from them, but on the other side of the glass, the doorman sat reading a tabloid, seemingly oblivious to their presence.

"That's the only thing you're thinking?" Troy didn't give her time to answer, just took her chin in his hand and gave her a kiss. To anchor her in the world, Claire kept her eyes open, so that she saw the edge of Troy's face, a slice of the sidewalk on which they stood, the doorman's expressionless eyes watching them.

After a second, Claire stepped back. "I don't know, Troy," she said, not spelling out what she didn't know. "I have to go now or I'll miss my plane." Already, though, Troy seemed insubstantial, like a character in a movie who was so real on-screen but faded away by the time you walked to your car.

"Call me," he said, and she nodded without speaking, then walked the last block to the hotel.

As she pulled open the hotel's heavy brass-bound glass door, Claire was nearly bowled over by a man in a dark overcoat wearing a hat pulled low. His flat, acne-scarred face registered nothing, even when she fell to one knee.

At the touch of her key, the door to Claire's hotel room swung open. She let out a startled gasp. A whirlwind had been through it, leaving nothing untouched. The mattress was upended, her suitcase emptied out and flung on top of the heap of her clothes, all the drawers pulled free from the dresser.

The upholstered chair that had stood next to the bed was now turned on its side. The netting on the bottom had been roughly torn away. Claire's breath hung suspended. She was staring into an empty cavity that had once held her painting.

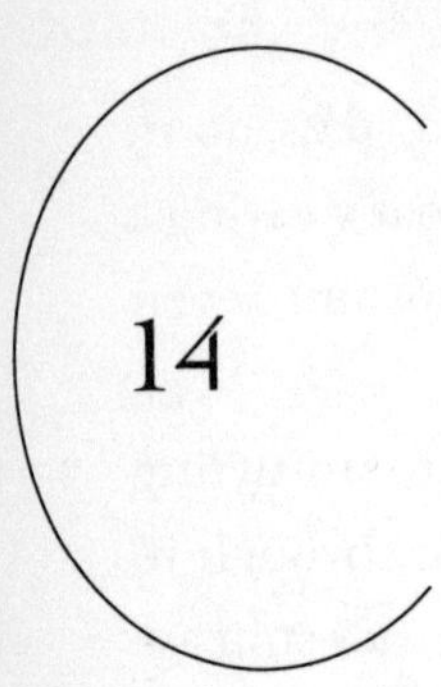

14

Long before the taxi driver pulled to a stop at La Guardia, Claire had a ten and a twenty ready, clutched in damp fingers. She had spent the entire trip peering over the edge of the back seat trying to examine the drivers of the cars that swarmed around them—an impossible task. Her taxi driver, a dark-skinned man who had not said a single word during their trip, seemed to take her behavior in stride. Perhaps he was used to ferrying refugees from one calamity to another. While the taxi was still sighing to a stop, Claire thrust the money into his hand and was out the door. Underneath her buttoned-up—and, luckily, loose-fitting—jacket, she wore her backpack backward across her chest, the painting as strange and stiff as a bulletproof vest. But at least she still had it—for now.

The destruction of her hotel room had stunned Claire. The search had been hasty but thorough. Whoever had hunted through the room had found each hiding place she had, only a few hours before, considered and rejected. They had tossed aside the mattress, overturned drawers, emptied out her suitcase and slit the lining. Even the bottom of the upholstered chair had been ripped open, the place where Claire had come so close to hiding the painting. She was lucky that their eyes hadn't fallen, as hers had, on the brown bulk of the air conditioner, set high in the window. It was here that she had lifted the painting the night before, taping it into place on the back, and it was here that, as she stood on her tiptoes, her searching fingers found again the reassuring give of the bubble wrap that still held the painting secure.

Claire had righted the chair and stood on it to free the painting. Only when it was in her hands did the tightness in her chest loosen a little. The bubble wrap revealed little lozenges of paint—a red fragment of carpet, a circle of cream-colored wall, a single blue eye, oddly magnified.

Only belatedly did it occur to her that whoever had done this could still be nearby. Balanced on the chair, the painting clutched to her chest, Claire eyed the closed bathroom door. Was that a faint sound? She caught her breath and strained to listen. Silence. Had she conjured the sound into being? Her eyes fell on the telephone. She could call the front desk, ask them to send someone up. Probably it would be the liveried young man whom she had passed a few minutes ago, surveying the lobby with his hands clasped in front of him. It seemed likely that he would become distracted by the mess. She could imagine him asking pointed questions about the destruction of her room, pulling out a calculator to add up the charges against her Visa card, not even looking up when the true perpetrator burst out of the bathroom, gun in hand.

There! That was definitely a sound. But now she realized what it was. A choking moan followed by a thump.

"Is there someone in there?" Claire called out. The only answer was another moan, louder this time. She hurriedly laid the painting in one of the empty drawers that had been abandoned on the carpet and covered it with the tossed-aside quilt. Taking a deep breath, she put her hand on the knob and pushed. The door gave only a few inches before it struck something waist-high made of silver metal.

Claire realized the door was jammed against the maid's cart. She shouldered her way in. In the middle of the floor was the maid herself, trussed up in a torn sheet. She lay amid a heap of canisters and bottles of various cleansers, efficiently hogtied, wrists to ankles, with a strip of white cloth over her eyes and another across her open mouth. As frantic as a bug on its back, she was straining without success against her bonds, the effort accompanied by the groans Claire had been hearing.

"It's okay!" Without planning to, Claire found herself whispering. "This is my room." The maid stopped struggling, and her head thumped softly on the floor, producing the same noise Claire had heard earlier.

The knots were pulled too tight for Claire's fingers to pick them free. She hurried to her backpack and returned with a Swiss Army knife. With great care, she slid the blade in between the woman's cheek and the white cloth, and cut away the blindfold. The woman's eyes, the pupils so dark they were nearly invisible, strained to focus on Claire before her body relaxed a little. Claire then cut the gag and pulled a wadded white washcloth from the other woman's mouth. The maid took long, shuddering breaths and worked her mouth, occasionally mumbling to herself in Spanish. Claire finished cutting her free, and the woman sat up and leaned against the white bathtub, rubbing the angry red marks on her wrists.

"Do you need a hospital?" Claire's best Spanish was rewarded with a blank look. She tried speaking more slowly. The woman shook her head, but Claire didn't know if it was because she still didn't understand her or because she was all right. She tried combining parts of a few more sentences from her Spanish tape. "Who has searched my suitcase?"

The woman's answer was in a Puerto Rican Spanish Claire could only haltingly follow. "I didn't see. I came in to clean the room. He was in the closet. Came behind me. He said I must close my eyes."

"Did he have a weapon?" The dire words from her "Let's Learn Spanish!" tape—*hospital, search, weapon*—were actually coming in handy.

"A gun, maybe. I felt something in my back."

Claire didn't completely understand, until the woman stood up and put a trembling finger between Claire's shoulder blades, miming the barrel of a gun—or perhaps only the tip of a finger.

"But a man, yes? Not a woman." The maid nodded, flexing her fingers as they slowly regained their color. "Was he tall or short?"

"I never saw him. All I know is that he was taller than me."

Claire realized how useless this single piece of information was. The girl—for looking at her more closely, Claire realized she was about eighteen—was also tiny, probably no more than five feet tall. Any man would be taller than her.

"He left when he started beeping."

"What?" Claire didn't follow her words until the woman pointed at the beeper she wore on her belt. She could remember when a beeper was a status symbol, meant you were a surgeon or something. Now anyone could wear one, including a maid and a robber. "And you're not hurt?"

"No." The woman looked up at Claire. "You must have something he wants. He kept asking where you were."

Those words had been enough to push Claire into action. At any moment the man could return. She had scooped her things into her mutilated suitcase, slipped the painting into her backpack, put her backpack on so that it lay across her chest, and left the hotel via the staircase.

Now Claire sat in 16A, a window seat in economy class. The plane was floating somewhere over the Midwest, but she didn't have time to be distracted by the patchwork of green and tan fields threaded with placid rivers that lay below them. Instead she was trying to decide if any of the other passengers on the plane looked suspicious.

In the airport she had seen a man who looked like Dante from a distance, but on closer inspection he was ten years older and twenty pounds heavier. And twice she had thought she caught sight of Troy, but instead each man had turned out to be a bored businessman in a crisp expensive suit, with a cellular phone in one hand and a calfskin briefcase in the other.

The plane was full, and the economy-class seats were arranged so that Flybees could pack in as many people as possible. Before coming to work for the state, Lori had been a stewardess. What had Lori told her Flybees was known as? Greyhound of the sky? Even when she stood in the half-crouch necessary to avoid banging her head on the overhead bin, Claire found she couldn't see everyone. Her seatmates, a young couple in love with being in love, didn't look up from their nibbles and kisses.

She didn't even know who she was looking for. Dante? Troy? The acne-scarred man who had nearly knocked her down outside her hotel? A man in a baseball cap, like the man who had chased her through the American Museum of Natural History? A stranger who would refuse to meet her eyes? She tried to remember who she had told about this flight. Charlie, of course. But Claire also had a vague memory of telling Dante about the good deal she had gotten on the ticket price. And hadn't Troy asked her—perhaps, in retrospect, a shade too casually?—about her flight before he left her this morning?

But then again, Troy had been with her while her room was being broken into. Which made Dante a more likely culprit. Claire remembered the intensity with which he had talked about the painting, and the way his mouth had softened when he looked at it, like someone anticipating a kiss. She had actually felt a flash of jealousy of the painted woman. Dante had desired the painting for itself, not for the money it might represent.

But what if Dante were right? What if the painting was worth a fortune twenty times over? That would be enough to tempt any man to steal it, no matter if it were beautiful or not. And if Dante were right, that meant that Troy was wrong. Had Troy deliberately lied to her when he told her the painting was a pastiche? That would explain why he had asked her to sell it to him in Avery's viewing room. But if he had really planned on cheating her, why had he stopped asking her to let him sell it for her?

Her thoughts chased themselves, doubled back and came to the same dead ends. What had Dante called the hallmark of Vermeer's technique? Circles of confusion? For Claire, the question of who was trying to take the painting from her was beginning to overshadow the question of who had actually painted it.

She slid back down into her seat as a new thought occurred to her. Even if all the other passengers on this plane were what they appeared—travelers in search of a cheap fare—there was nothing to stop the hunter from following her to Portland. It would be easy enough to track her down. Claire winced a little, realizing it could be as simple as looking up her name in the phone book.

The painting, it was clear, wouldn't be safe stashed away at home. Whoever was after this painting was serious about it, and Charlie, despite her "Self-Defense for Seniors" classes, would be no match for whoever had neatly hogtied the maid this morning. Claire gave the painting a gentle pat through her jacket as she thought about where to hide it. It needed to be someplace she could get to fairly easily, but also a place others wouldn't be able to easily access. It had to be safe from the elements and from accidental discovery. Nothing seemed quite right, but she finally settled on an idea.

Still, she needed to warn Charlie. Her eyes focused on the phone set into the back of the seat ahead of her. There was a groove for a charge card, and the tiny print detailed outrageous charges. But Charlie—who had left Germany fifty years ago but still had a Teutonic sense of punctuality—would be awaiting Claire's homecoming. Claire's stomach rumbled a little at the thought of something warm and homemade—maybe a roast and mashed potatoes? Hiding the painting was going to delay her at least an hour. She reached for her Visa card.

The phone rang once, twice. Claire looked at her watch, frowning as she calculated the time in Portland. She knew Charlie's schedule as well as her own, and on a Sunday night at 7:15, the older woman would be settled down with a glass of red wine in front of *60 Minutes.* Charlie enjoyed the fact that most of the age-spotted hosts were nearly as old as she was, yet they still kept busy exposing evil and wrongdoing.

After the fourth ring, the answering machine clicked on. Charlie's recorded voice sounded crackly and insubstantial as she repeated their phone number—she thought that by not saying their names she kept them safe from anyone who might take advantage of women on their own—and instructions to leave a message at the tone. As she waited for the beep, Claire decided that Charlie must be at the nearby Hoot Owl Market, otherwise known as the Korean Food Museum, since the other customers only stopped in for beer and cigarettes. But Charlie and the owner, with his handwritten and completely unconvincing sign warning PROPERTEES UNDER SURVALLANCE, had gradually become good friends. They traded recipes—his for Korean barbecue, hers for sauerbraten—and he had even prevailed upon her to try kimchi. Over time, Charlie had persuaded him to stock real vanilla extract, ultrafine sugar and marzipan alongside cheap plastic lighters and twelve-dollar bags of Huggies. And that was where Charlie probably was now—at the Hoot Owl, asking Mike (as the owner styled himself in America) just how old the eggs really were.

The beep sounded. "Charlie—it's me. I'll be home about an hour later than I thought. Something has come up that I need to take care of. And I also wanted to warn you to be careful about, about"—suddenly Claire thought of eavesdroppers, of her voice echoing in the empty living room for anyone to hear—"about talking to people you don't know, okay? And I'll see you real soon." Claire ended with the words that were easier to say to Charlie than her own mother. "I love you."

She slid the phone back into its slot and tried to relax. Her thoughts were too skittery to allow her to focus on the book she had packed five days ago. It was a nonfiction account of how the world would soon be destroyed by plagues unleashed by the overuse of antibiotics. Claire found it hard to worry about the planet's long-term survival when her own in the short term seemed to be in jeopardy. The man across the aisle pushed the bell for the stewardess, who returned a few minutes later with a copy of *The New York Times.* Claire pressed her own call button.

"Do you have any more copies of the *Times*?" The woman's makeup was effectively a mask, making her look like a sister to the other stewardesses on board, even though they came from varied racial backgrounds. Lori had told Claire that in stew school they had spent more time learning makeup application than safety procedures.

"Sorry. I just gave out the last one."

"What other newspapers do you have?"

"*The Wall Street Journal* and the *Oregonian.*"

Claire didn't have the energy to read *WSJ*, with its conservative editorials that always made her so angry that she found herself talking out loud to the paper. "I'll take the *Oregonian.*"

She started with the Metro section, figuring that most of the front section would be world news a day old, cribbed from the *Times* she had been reading every day in New York. So the plane was already circling Portland before she read the front page.

Woman Killed by Car Bomb Identified

A woman killed Friday in southwest Portland when her car exploded has been identified as Sonia Wallin, 37. Police say the bomb appears to have been detonated when she turned the ignition. Wallin was killed instantly. Her car, an older-model Mazda 323, was destroyed.

A Multnomah Village neighbor, who did not want to be identified, said that Wallin was the mother of two girls, ages 7 and 9. The children were at school at the time of the explosion. They are now being cared for by a relative. Neighbors said that Wallin had been divorced for less than a year, and that her ex-husband, Richard Wallin, a former mill worker, was rumored to have been angry over the divorce.

A police spokesman declined to say whether Richard Wallin was a suspect in his ex-wife's death, saying only that he was a "person of interest."

Claire's eardrums filled with the sound of her own heart beating fast and hard. From her daily runs, she knew every car in the streets around her neighborhood. And she could think of only one other Mazda 323 in Multnomah Village besides her own. The one she passed every morning on the way to work. The one where the woman behind the wheel was like a Latina reflection of Claire, with her hand stretched out in a wave as they drove past each other. The neighbor's Mazda 323 that was exactly like Claire's—only hers had been parked at the airport for the past five days.

QS10ALL

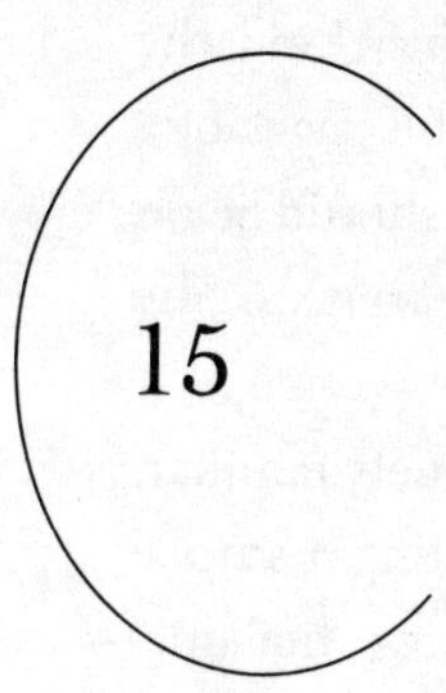

15

Claire sat in her car, parked just off Broadway Boulevard, her eyes on her office building. The seventeen-story building was dark except for the first floor and two or three scattered offices where someone had come in to catch up over the weekend. She counted up to the thirteenth floor, but it was dark. Claire didn't know what she was looking for, but she watched the building anyway. In the darkened interior of the car, her breathing sounded loud and a little fast. Her throat was tight and her hands were slick on the hard plastic of the steering wheel.

Maybe the man who had followed her through the American Museum of Natural History had been just another visitor in a hurry. It was even possible that the man who had broken into her hotel room had just been looking for traveler's checks to steal. But there was no way to chalk up her neighbor, blown to bits on what should have been just another Friday, to Claire's overactive imagination. Until now, she had thought someone was after the painting. Now she didn't know what to think. Why would someone want to kill her? And why would they risk blowing up the painting along with her?

She looked at her watch. Thirty minutes had passed since she had arrived. During that time, no one had entered or left the building. The security guard was still in the same position behind the front desk, slouched in his chair and slowly turning the pages of a paperback. To all appearances, everything was just as it should be on a Sunday evening, but Claire no longer trusted appearances. She took a deep breath and got out of her car.

The guard, a big guy in his mid-twenties, looked vaguely familiar. Claire realized she had seen him a time or two, sneaking a smoke outside the back entrance to the building. "Good evening, ma'am." His voice reminded her of whoever had done the voice-overs on *Dragnet*, old-fashionedly polite and a little world-weary.

"Hi. I'm Claire Montrose. I work on thirteen. In the specialty license plate division. I need to get up to my office for a second. I accidentally left something behind."

"You'll need to sign in." The security guard—his name tag read BRUCE—pushed a clipboard toward her. "Then just use your ID badge to get the elevator to take you to your floor."

"That's the thing, see? I drove all the way over here and then realized I left my badge in my other coat." This was true, as far as it went. Claire's badge was in the pocket of the black raincoat she wore to work and had left at home five days before.

"Sorry, ma'am. The rules are pretty strict. Can't let you in without your badge."

"I can show you all my other ID. I've got two with pictures," Claire said, before realizing this would mean having to unzip her jacket, revealing the backpack she now wore across her chest. Bruce would probably decide he had a terrorist action on his hands and tackle her.

"Oh, *I* know who you are. I see you every Monday. You come in right at seven-thirty just when I'm getting off work—and you're always in a hurry." He shrugged. "But that doesn't matter. The rules say I can't let you in without your badge."

Maybe she could kill him with kindness. "Wow, if you're still here on Monday morning, you must really work a long shift."

"Seven-thirty to seven-thirty. Twelve-hour shift, three days a week. The rest of the time I go to school. Criminology."

"Do you work the whole twelve hours by yourself?" Claire put on an interested expression even though she felt like reaching across the counter and shaking him. The back of her neck itched. Was someone watching her even now, just as she had been watching the lobby only minutes before?

"They don't really need more than one person. I'm just here to check people in and out, but it's the computer that decides where they can go. The whole thing practically runs itself. Having someone here is just—what do they call it? A system redundancy."

"But can't you override the system? Just to let me up on my floor? I promise it won't take more than five minutes. All I want to do is"—What did she want to do, anyway? She hadn't thought this thing through, and now she was paying for it. Her glance fell on the Stephen King paperback tucked underneath the overhang of the counter—"is get a book I left up there. I forgot to take it home on Friday, and it's been driving me crazy thinking about it. I need to see how it turns out. I can't wait until tomorrow."

"Well, just this once," Bruce said. "But you'd *better* be back here in ten minutes." He came out from behind the desk, almost but not quite smiling, clearly enjoying the power of saying yes or no. Closer to, he looked no more than twenty-three, his pressed white polyester shirt concealing both thick muscle and a layer of baby fat. His belt sagged under the weight of several key rings and various holsters. One held a flashlight, another a walkie-talkie, the third she guessed contained a pair of handcuffs. Bruce pressed the button for the elevator. When it arrived he leaned in, pulled his ID off his shirt, flashed it over the sensor and pressed the button for thirteen. "You've got ten minutes," he said as the doors were closing between him and Claire.

On the plane, Claire had considered and rejected any number of places to hide the painting. In the movies, people hid things in airport lockers, but then again, in the movies that always turned out to be a bad idea. Finally, she hit on the idea of her office. After hours, her floor was accessible only to people holding a state-issued ID card, providing a built-in first wall of defense. But where to hide the painting once she got to work? She had considered tucking it in a filing cabinet or slipping it behind a bookcase. Maybe hiding it in the storage room full of boxes of forty-year-old motor vehicle records that Roland spoke vaguely about someday putting on microfiche.

But then Claire had remembered the additional phone lines that had been installed two months before. The workman had stood on a ladder in the middle of the hallway. He had pushed up on one corner of an acoustic ceiling tile, then turned it at an angle and slid it between the silver metal struts that held it in place. One by one, he popped out an entire row. Then he had climbed up even farther to stand at the top of the ladder, so that he was visible only from the waist down, the top half of his body swallowed up by the ceiling, and strung the phone wire over the next row of intact ceiling tiles. The tiles certainly weren't strong enough to hold a person, but if they were strong enough to hold a bundle of phone wires, Claire thought they could easily hold a painting for a day or two. At least until she figured out what was going on.

The elevator doors opened into a darkness broken only by the lights of the city sparkling in the windows and the green glow of the exit sign. For a few minutes, she watched the empty streets below, reassured to see no one following her in the building, no one loitering on a corner. Claire felt along the wall for a light switch. The office, which in the daylight was as familiar to her and as unremarkable as her own bedroom, was now filled with mysterious objects that threw themselves in her path. She tripped over the rolling stepstool the secretary used to get to the tops of the filing cabinets, stumbled into a chair that bruised her hip. Finally she found the switch. Under the artificial light, the flat orange carpeting looked particularly garish. She looked at her watch. Seven minutes left—not just to hide the painting, but also to try entering a name into the state's computer and see what popped up on the screen.

൭

She made it back to Bruce with fifteen seconds to spare.

"Thanks again!" she called, already pushing open the door to the outside.

"Did you find your book?"

"Yup, and I'm really looking forward to seeing how it turns out!" She waved it vigorously in his direction, hoping she was moving too fast for him to read the title, *The New American Dictionary of Slang.*

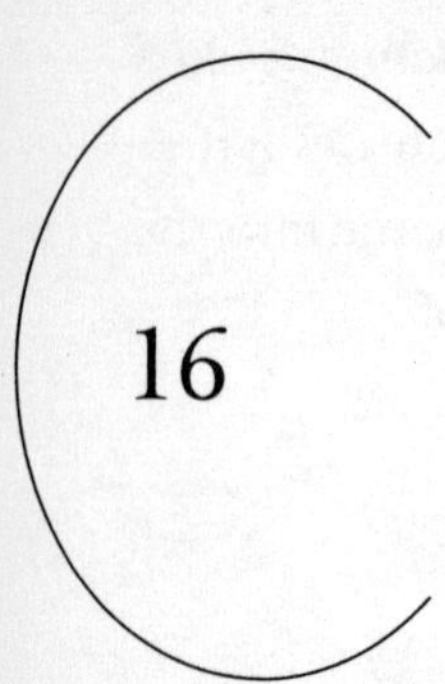

16

When she pulled up in front of the house she shared with Charlie, Claire felt something ease inside her. She was home. Fishing her key from her coat pocket, she stepped onto the porch. Duke's huge dish—Charlie's inexpensive version of a burglar alarm—shone faintly in the streetlight. Usually it was full of dry kibble, but tonight it was empty. One of the neighborhood mutts must have discovered the stash. Then Claire's left foot slipped on something, and she realized that the shadows had obscured the dark pebbles littering the porch. Belatedly, she began to look around her, and she didn't like what she found. Why was the porch light not on? Why was the house dark?

She put her key into the lock and turned it without hearing the tumblers click. The door was already unlocked. "Charlie?" she called, meaning her voice to carry to the back of the house. It came out in a near-whisper. "Charlie?" The word was more like a thought.

She took a step into the darkened house. Slowly, she reached out for the light switch, half fearing that another, rougher hand would clamp down on her own.

The light revealed devastation. Everything that had been neat and orderly was now ripped, battered, strewn, broken, sliced, crushed and thrown. It was all too familiar—the mess of her hotel room, only on a bigger scale.

With an effort, Claire made her voice bigger. "Charlie?" she called out into the dark house, already knowing it was futile. "Charlie?"

Only silence answered her.

The minute she had crossed the threshold, some part of her had known there was no point in calling Charlie's name. There was no one to answer. But did that really mean Charlie wasn't here? What if Charlie were here—but dead?

An iron band closed around Claire's chest. Could whoever had trashed the house have also killed Charlie? It seemed all too possible. A tiny old lady in pink tennis shoes wouldn't pose much of an obstacle. Claire was frightened by how easily she could picture her best friend dead, just one more broken thing sprawled on a heap of broken things.

Taking a deep breath before she crossed through each doorway, Claire went from room to room, searching. Everything had been reduced to an oddly featureless mess. It was hard to remember what things had once been. In Charlie's bedroom, her pillows and duvet had been gutted, and goose feathers lay in drifts. The chair where she did her cross-stitch had been sliced to the heart, exposing its coiled springs. But no Charlie, not even when Claire risked peeking in the closet.

In the empty bathroom that lay between the two upstairs bedrooms, the intruder had efficiently destroyed two things at once by throwing Charlie's square bottle of Chanel No. 5 at the mirror, shattering both. The sweetish reek hung over Claire's bedroom, where every book had been thrown on the floor, every piece of clothing pulled from the dresser and closet. But still there was no sign of Charlie.

Back downstairs, Claire stepped gingerly through the dining room, where the sideboard lay overturned amid shards of china. In the kitchen, the flour and sugar canisters lay in shards on the floor, and the resulting mess had been walked through a dozen times. Two veal cutlets, now dry and curling at the edges, lay on the counter.

On legs that threatened to fail her, she came back to the living room, put the least damaged of the couch cushions back in place, and sat down. Something was bothering her. Although the house was like an echo of what had happened at her hotel room—had that only been this morning?—things seemed different. In New York, the damage had been, for want of a better word, functional. Things had been broken open or cut apart simply to verify that they did not hold the painting. But here, in her own house, things had been broken for the sake of breaking. Why else would someone pull the tulips from a hand-blown vase, lob the vase across the room so that it shattered against the wall, and then grind the flowers into the carpet until they bled crimson? Claire could almost feel the anger that had prompted such destruction.

The phone rang and Claire leapt to her feet, her heart jackhammering. She followed the sound of the phone until she found the handset wedged behind the refrigerator.

"Yes?" Her voice came out a cautious whisper, unready for another surprise.

"Claire? Is that you?"

"Dante?" At the sound of his voice, tears sprang to her eyes. Suddenly her suspicions of him seemed ridiculous. He was just a struggling painter, after all. There was no way he could be making bad things happen three thousand miles away.

"What's wrong?"

"I just walked in the door. Somebody broke in while I was gone. Everything's trashed. I think they were looking for the painting. But the worst thing is—I can't find any sign of my roommate." Claire gave words to her fear. "I'm afraid somebody kidnapped Charlie."

"Have you called the police?"

"I haven't even thought that far. It's all happening too fast."

"What about the painting?"

"I put it someplace safe. I was worried something like this might happen." Belatedly, Claire realized the mistake she had made. "Oh no."

"What? Are you okay?" His words were nearly on top of hers.

"I just realized that I called Charlie from the plane. Only now I don't remember what I said. Did I tell her I wasn't bringing it home?"

"Did you tell her where you were going to put it? Claire, where did you put the painting?"

Instead of answering, she began to wade through the debris in the living room, kicking it aside, seeking the black plastic base of the portable telephone. If they had listened to that!

It was half hidden by a gift-wrapped package, broken open to show a smashed pair of earrings, silver hoops reduced to broken curls of metal. Claire had forgotten that tomorrow was her birthday. Just surviving until the end of the day was beginning to seem problematic.

Dante's voice was insistent in her ear. "Claire, Claire, are you okay?"

"Yes." She answered absently, turning the phone's base over. The light on the built-in answering machine shone a steady green. Her call from six thousand feet had been listened to, then. But who had done the listening—Charlie, or the people who had destroyed the house? And where was Charlie now? What exactly *had* she said on her message? *Had* she said anything about the painting? Exhaustion fogged Claire's brain. She scrubbed her face with her free hand.

Dante's voice, insistent now, interrupted her thoughts. "Claire!

Claire! I think you should leave the house now and go to the police. And listen, I'm gonna come out there. I'll take the first flight I can get. I should be in Portland by early afternoon your time. Three at the latest. Tell me a good place to meet you."

"You shouldn't do that," she said, not knowing what she felt. Would she be crazy to trust him? She felt so alone, and trouble was multiplying all around her.

"Just tell me when and where."

Before she could decide on an answer, the doorbell chimed, startling her so that she nearly dropped the phone. Claire crunched her way to the front door and looked out through the tiny panes of beveled glass that marched in pairs across the top.

Only six inches away, a pair of eyes the color of washed silver met her own. Their owner stepped back a bit, revealing a good-looking man about her own age. She saw white teeth bracketed by narrow lips, the upturned collar of a beige trenchcoat, the lapels of a dark suit. He flipped a black wallet open to show a gold badge and pressed it against one of the panes. PORTLAND POLICE was stamped on the shield. Claire's knees loosened.

"Listen, Dante, I've got to go. The cops are here. It must be about Charlie."

"Wait—tell me where I can meet you!"

She picked the first public place she thought of. "Three o'clock at the Lloyd Center ice skating rink. Any cabdriver should be able to get you there." She could decide later if she was really going to show up.

"Okay, Lloyd Center ice rink, three o'clock, see you then. And Claire—be very careful. Somebody is serious about this."

"I will," she said, but the connection was already dead. There was no place to set the phone down, so she tossed it on the couch. Before she opened it, she put the chain on the door, thinking it was rather like locking the barn door after the horses had headed for the hills.

"Good evening, ma'am. Paul Roberts, detective with the Portland Police Department." He closed his wallet and slipped it inside the breast pocket of his jacket.

"Do you know where Charlie is?" Please, please, let her not be dead.

"Charlie? Who's Charlie?" the detective echoed. "I'm canvassing Sonia Wallin's neighbors. The woman who was killed Friday."

"So you don't know anything about my roommate?" Claire's anxiety started to return.

"No, I don't. But perhaps you can explain to me what you mean while I ask you about Ms. Wallin."

"Can't we do that here?"

"Through the door, you mean? Ma'am, I have a number of questions I must ask. I also have an Identikit that I'll need you to look at to help me identify any strangers you've seen in the neighborhood. I would really rather do this sitting down."

His weary, bureaucratic way of speaking decided her. Claire took the chain off the door and opened it.

She thought that when the detective saw the mess he would ask what in the hell had happened, but that apparently wasn't how he operated. Instead he pulled out a narrow tan notebook and began to ask her a few routine questions—her name, her date of birth, her phone number, her occupation. His slow, methodical plodding, his serenity in the face of disaster, were surreal yet oddly comforting.

The detective's first set of questions required no thought, so Claire was able to study him as he carefully noted her answers. He reminded her of someone, but she couldn't think of who it was. Then it came to her. Evan. Evan had that same careful, step-by-step approach to life. And if he was anything like Evan, there was no sense in hurrying him, even if part of her was screaming, *Charlie! But where's Charlie!*

Detective Roberts was about the same age as Evan, too, and his hair was also blond, but there the resemblance ended. Every inch of him was stylish in ways that Evan would be oblivious to—pressed where Evan would be rumpled, 100 percent merino wool where Evan would have settled for a blend. His voice was as measured and precise as his manner, every syllable equally weighted, which had the effect of making him sound like a very articulate foreigner or a computer-generated voice. But it was his eyes that were truly distinctive, a color so pale that they were neither blue nor gray. Whenever he looked up from his notebook to her face, his eyes flashed like mercury.

They sat in the ruins of the house while the detective carefully noted all the facts, numbers and dates that circumscribed Claire's life. Exhaustion weighted her eyelids, and after each blink she found it harder and harder to open them again. A surreptitious half-turn of her wrist allowed her to catch a glimpse of her watch. Nearly midnight. But if she were to go to bed right now, she knew her eyes would refuse to close, burning holes into the darkness.

Finally the detective said, "So, Ms. Montrose, please tell me what has happened here. And who this Charlie is, and why you think he is missing."

"I think maybe someone was looking for a painting and took Charlie instead." She watched his reaction carefully, but his face stayed expressionless as he wrote down the word *painting* and underlined it. His eyes remained guileless as he looked up, pen poised.

"A painting?"

"A little painting I recently inherited." She took a deep breath. "I think my finding the painting is related to everything that's happened."

"And may I see this painting, please?"

"Is that really necessary?" Uneasiness brushed her. Had it been a mistake to tell him about the painting? But she had to, didn't she, if she wanted Charlie found?

His voice was peevish. "I am attempting to obtain as complete and accurate an understanding of events as is possible. And to do that, I'll need to see the painting."

"I don't have it." Claire took a deep breath, exhausted by the thought of explaining how she had hidden it in her office, then having to take him there and introduce him to Bruce the security guard.

Before she could say anything else, his face began to change. Suddenly his long white teeth and pale eyes reminded her of a wolf. "What?" It was as if the functionary who existed only as a tool to take down her words had been put away, and something more feral—and more real—was taking its place. "Where is it, then?" He leaned forward and grabbed her wrist, enunciating each word through clenched teeth. "Where is the painting?"

Before Claire's mind could react, her body did. She watched her wrist move down and then back up, rotating toward his thumb, breaking his hold. Claire was on her feet and almost to the door before she felt his hand again close on her arm. Like a dancer executing a showy move, he brought her back to him with a snap.

A squarish silver shape loomed in the corner of her eye, and she reared her head back to see what it was. A gun had appeared in his right hand. At least she thought it was a gun. Although maybe if he wasn't a police detective—which was beginning to seem pretty likely—maybe this wasn't a real gun. Claire had never seen one up close. Maybe it was a lighter or a squirt gun, a novelty item purchased for $3.99. A play gun purchased at the same place he had bought the shiny gold badge that he'd probably paid an extra dollar to personalize.

Then he pressed its cold open mouth against her temple, and she knew it was real.

Everything was moving in slow motion. Claire had once gone scuba diving on a cheap package tour to Hawaii, and this was how it had felt. The claustrophobic sound of her own breathing, heavy and slow, filled her ears. It was the sound you heard in disaster movies when the shark was about to make an appearance. Only this shark was already preparing to take a bite.

Paul Roberts—if that was who he really was—hooked one foot behind her ankles, locking Claire in place, then moved his left hand from the small of her back and ran it roughly under her arms, between her legs, over her breasts. The world narrowed to his groping hand. This was it, then, he was going to rape her, probably right here on the floor amid the shattered remains of her life.

"What *is* this?" She realized he had been frisking her. His cool fingers fumbled under her chin, then with a jerk he unzipped her jacket, exposing her forgotten backpack. It now hung, slack and half-empty, over her black turtleneck.

"It's the painting," she said, striving to make her voice dejected. "See?" She didn't give him time to react, simply pulled the backpack's zipper open just far enough to allow her hand to wiggle in, past pens and PowerBars and a paperback mystery, until her fingers closed on a cylinder the size and shape of a cigarette lighter. It was Evan's gift from last Valentine's Day—a canister of pepper spray. With a jerk, she pulled it free, pointed it in his direction, and then closed her eyes and mouth and turned her head away as she depressed the trigger. Acrid droplets pricked her face, and her eyes and nose immediately burned and began to run.

"Shit!"

Claire felt more than saw him loosen his hold on her, and she was off. One foot landed on a magazine and sailed out from under her, but she somehow managed to break her fall and bounce back to her feet again in a single movement. *Weebles wobble but they don't fall down*, she thought. She waited for a bullet to drill into her flesh. There was a crash behind her as her assailant tried to navigate the same obstacle course more or less blind.

Outside, her slitted eyes revealed a world that was not nearly dark enough, lit by a three-quarter moon and the distant spangle of stars. The cold, fresh air relieved the stinging in her eyes and nose a bit. Claire ran past her Mazda, then a late-model white four-door parked behind it. Complete with a portable police light resting on the driver's side of the dash. Did that mean the man who was now chasing after her really *was* a cop?

Claire risked a glance behind her in time to see him stumble to the doorway. She turned back and ran harder than she ever had in her life. Across the empty street, between the neighbor's overgrown arborvitae, across their yard, over a low fence, through an apartment parking lot, past the neighborhood fire station. She could run in there for help, and for a moment she could picture it—brawny men leaping up to protect her—but Paul Roberts, whoever he was, was such a smooth talker that he could probably flash his badge and reclaim her over any protests she might make.

Lungs burning, she ran on, thankful that she had chosen to wear her Nikes to breakfast with Troy, nearly twenty-four hours ago. Past Mañana's Mexican restaurant, dark for the night, through the pumps of the closed Chevron station, and then right on to Barbur Boulevard.

She risked a glance over her shoulder, but the dip in the road hid her house. No white car, though, at least not yet. No cars at all, in fact, which posed another problem. Paul Roberts would probably be less likely to shoot her if there was a potential witness. But Barbur Boulevard at nearly one in the morning offered the exact opposite of what Claire needed. It was both too empty and too bright to offer her any protection, lit by neon signs advertising businesses that were shuttered for the night.

While her mind fretted over what to do, her feet made their own decisions, determined to put as much distance as possible between Claire and danger. She darted from shadow to shadow, behind the

Subway shop, past a sour-smelling Dumpster, through a motel parking lot, behind a darkened mini-mall offering a variety of useless services. Her left Achilles tendon knotted up. In her mouth was the faint coppery tang of blood. She imagined capillaries in her lungs popping under the pressure.

A tan car passed her, then a purple compact going the other way. There was a white blur of a face turning to watch a woman wearing street clothes running flat out in the middle of the night. But no one stopped or even slowed down. What to do, what to do? Should she turn off Barbur into one of the sleeping residential neighborhoods that bordered the street? It would be darker there, but even more deserted. Too easy to draw attention to herself. She imagined crouching behind someone's garage while their slavering rottweiler held her at bay, just waiting for the police—in the form of Detective Roberts—to arrive.

Claire kept running, running, still not knowing where she was going, risking an occasional glance behind her. With all the muscles that ran down her left leg constricted, it was now more of a lurching lope than a run. She wanted nothing more than to sink down on the sidewalk outside the shuttered Boston Market, draw her knees up to her chest, and curl into a ball.

Just then she saw her savior in the turnaround at the Barbur Boulevard transit mall. A maroon-striped Tri-Met bus, idling.

L8RG8R

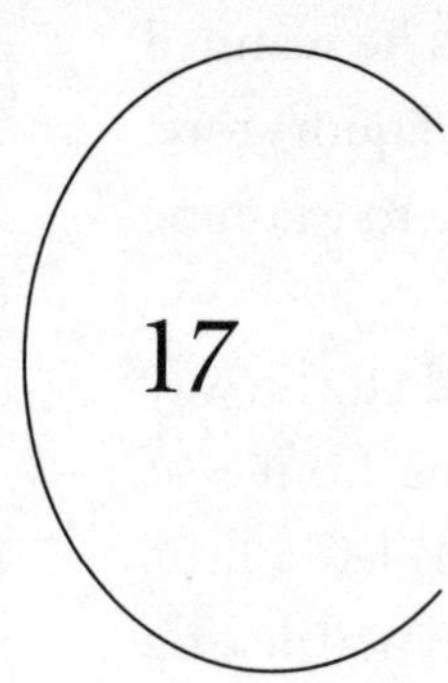

17

When Claire knocked on the bus's folding door, the driver started and dropped the paperback he was reading. She pressed herself flat against the side of the bus, her chest heaving as she sucked in great gulps of acrid exhaust. The driver looked at her curiously, then leaned forward and pulled a lever to crack open the door a half-inch.

"When are you leaving?" Claire managed to gasp out. That was a lot more important than where he was going. She risked a peek around the nose of the bus—was that a white car three blocks down the street?

"In twenty minutes I'm going to the downtown transit mall." The bus driver, a guy in his mid-fifties who looked like an Irish bartender—black hair, blue eyes, and a nose as big as a potato—leaned forward to pick up a tattered copy of *Pride and Prejudice* off the floor.

"Any chance I could talk you into going sooner?" It definitely *was* a white car, moving at a crawl, the driver's window rolled down.

The bus driver followed Claire's gaze. The white car was near enough now that she could make out the burnished glow of Paul

Roberts's hair and the rectangle of a black cellular phone pressed against his ear. His head was turned away from them as he scanned the parking lot shared by Barbur Boulevard Foods and a liquor store. In the next few seconds he would surely swivel his gaze to examine the other side of the street.

"Like that, is it?" the driver said, and the door sighed all the way open. Claire scrambled on board and crouched on the front seat behind the driver. "I guess it wouldn't matter if the bus left a little early. You're the first passenger I've had on this route in at least a month." The book thumped on the dash, and he shifted the bus into gear.

When they passed the white car, Claire raised her head far enough to watch Paul Roberts's eyes flick right past the bus as he drove farther down the street.

Thirty minutes later, Claire stood in front of the door to Evan's apartment, licking clean the plastic square that a few seconds earlier had been filled with neon orange processed cheese, part of a cheese and cracker "Snak-Pak" she had discovered in the bottom of her backpack. Snak-Pak. Good Lord. No wonder American kids couldn't spell. The cheese, like the crackers before it, tasted wonderful, salty and greasy and even a little bit sweet. She realized the last thing she'd eaten had been a Flybees turkey sandwich on unadorned white bread.

After three pushes on the bell, she finally heard Evan shuffling to the door. Claire hastily stuffed the empty cracker packet in her pocket, then took a half-step back so Evan would be able to see her clearly through the peephole. Locks clicked and chains rattled before the door finally opened to reveal Evan in his blue cotton-poly pajamas, eyes screwed half shut. The back of his hair stood up in a rooster tail. Claire had never been so glad to see him. She ran forward to give him a hug.

He gave her a half squeeze, then pulled back from her grasp.

Then he frowned at the black digital Timex that never left his wrist. "It's one-seventeen in the morning." Evan did not appreciate being woken in the middle of the night, as Claire had discovered on their first trip out of town when she had tried to awaken him after having had a sexy dream. "What's the matter?"

At his question, something clicked within her. She was finally safe, safe enough to contemplate the magnitude of what had happened. Tears began to stream down her face. "Oh, Evan, God, I'm in trouble. I came home and Charlie's missing and someone trashed our house and maybe killed our neighbor instead of me and now some guy with a gun is chasing me and I think he's a cop!"

"What?" He scrubbed his face with his hands. "What are you talking about? Slow down and start from the beginning."

Claire realized she didn't know where the beginning was. A half-century ago, when Göring had used his newly acquired power to assuage his lust for art? Or had the whole thing really been set in motion by her aunt's death two weeks ago? Or should she begin with Avery's and the appraisal of her painting as a fake? Or the moment she had first seen a painting so very much like hers—only hanging on the walls of the Metropolitan Museum of Art?

The last time Claire had talked to Evan had been when they argued about her going to New York. How was she supposed to explain everything that had happened in between?

Claire decided to tell the story more or less in chronological order, beginning with the appraisal at Avery's. She tried, but once Evan realized the painting might be real he kept stopping her to quiz her about how much it could be worth. When was the last time a Vermeer had come on the market? How much had it been sold for? Did she know how much that translated into in today's dollars?

On her walk from the bus stop, Claire had imagined Evan taking her in his arms while she sobbed out her story. Instead he got the calculator from his desk and began to tap in numbers, not even looking at her while she talked.

And there was no way to tell her story without mentioning Troy and Dante, much as she was reluctant to. Here in Evan's practical apartment, all hard-edged modern furniture that could be wiped clean with a sponge, the two men seemed like insubstantial ghosts. They both cared so deeply about art, while the only art Evan owned was a reproduction abstract—shades of gray and black with a single slash of red—that had been the same one used in the furniture store's display.

Even though he was now paying more attention to her words than to money, Evan didn't make telling this part of her story any easier. He quizzed her from a chrome-armed chair while Claire sat on the equally uncomfortable couch across from him, holding her head in her hands like a penitent. She was so exhausted that her cheekbones felt as if they had been replaced by balls of lead.

"Do you mean to tell me that you went out with *two* different men in the *five* days you were in New York?" Well, she hadn't meant to tell him that at all, but it had been impossible to avoid mentioning what she had learned over wine or espresso or bagels with lox. Evan continued to ask question after question, but about nothing that Claire considered important. What did this Dante do for a living, exactly? Why had she gone out to breakfast with this Troy instead of prudently arriving at the airport several hours early?

While Evan fixated on the wrong things, a part of Claire tried to make sense of the things that were really important, asking herself the questions Evan didn't know enough to. Were the break-in at her hotel and the destruction of her house related, or had two different people been behind them? And why would someone blow up her neighbor's car—especially if killing Claire would probably mean destroying the painting at the same time? And what about the man who had told her his name was Paul Roberts? Was that his real name? Was he a real cop? Did he know what had happened to Charlie?

The more questions Claire thought of, the more she realized she didn't have the answers. There was only one thing she was certain of. The painting must be real, or else why would it be causing her so much trouble?

A sound in the hall behind Evan made Claire straighten up, her mind blank with panic. Footsteps. Someone else was in this apartment, then. She had been foolish to think she had escaped. Paul Roberts must have broken in. She imagined silver eyes leveling on her again, remembered the way the gun had bit into her temple.

Moving faster than a thought, she ran for the door and began to fumble with the locks. Too slow. Too slow. Behind her, Evan was silent and she imagined his shock as he faced a gun—one of his feared statistics coming to life. She braced for a bullet that never came. Finally—although it was really only a matter of seconds—Claire turned to confront whoever had entered the room.

It took her a minute to recognize Marcia, Evan's receptionist from Kissling Insurance. For one thing, she lacked the strappy four-inch heels she habitually wore. But she was still dressed in a Marcia-ish way, in black satin tap pants and bustier, topped by a red satin robe that she made no attempt to close. Her legs were as impossibly long and slim as a Barbie doll's, and like Barbie, Claire saw that she was forced to walk on her toes, her Achilles tendon shortened by too many years of too-high heels.

Despite her outfit, or lack thereof, Marcia wasn't flustered at all. She sat on the arm of Evan's chair and regarded Claire coolly. Evan was the one who blushed, pulling at the collar of his pajama top as if he wanted to cover up the few blond hairs that sprouted there.

"What is *she* doing here?" It was Claire who should have said those words, but Marcia who spoke them, as calmly as if she were in her own apartment. Claire wondered how long she had been coming here. Since Claire had found the painting, she was seeing sides to people she would never have guessed existed.

"Nothing," Claire said. "I'm not doing anything at all." She sprung the last lock and stepped out into the hall. It was only as the door clicked closed behind her that she wondered where she would go.

IRITEI

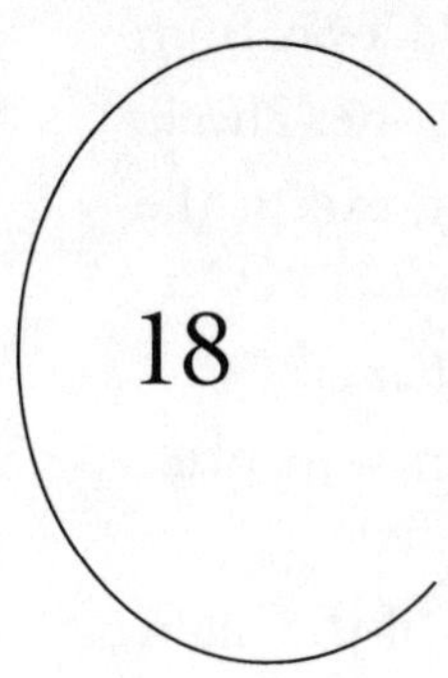

18

Trouble, Claire realized, would best be faced by someone who was familiar with it. Someone who knew what to do when the police might be out to get you and old friends couldn't be trusted. Someone who knew how to keep his mouth shut. And it didn't hurt if that someone was *family*—someone like J. B., Susie's live-in boyfriend.

Claire called him from a pay phone on the corner, facing out, reflexively checking the passing cars to make sure none of them was a white, late-model four-door. Less than fifteen minutes later, J. B. was pulling up in his beat-up red pickup. At the sight of J. B.'s untrimmed beard, face pitted with acne scars and tattered blue-and-gray Pendleton that predated Nirvana by at least two decades, Claire felt her tension begin to unravel. And unlike Evan, J. B. didn't seem driven by a need to know exactly what had happened to leave her stranded at two in the morning on a downtown street corner with no money, no car and no desire to go home.

"Mind if I smoke?" J. B. asked after they had ridden five minutes in silence.

"Would it be okay if you waited until we got to your place? I'm so hungry I feel nauseated." The last time she had used the word had been when she corrected Troy in Cri du Coeur, a world away from this battered pickup. The side window was cold against her cheek. She would have pulled her legs up on the bench seat, except the space was occupied by her nephew's dark blue car seat.

"So it sounds like the first thing you need is food. What else?"

"What?" Claire started, then realized she had been someplace between waking and sleeping.

"You called me. You're out all alone in the middle of the night and jumpy as a cat. I figure something is wrong. So what else do you need?"

Exhaustion engulfed her. "I need so much there's no point in starting to list it all."

J. B. shrugged, his skull-and-crossbones earring flickering in the passing streetlights. He and Susie lived on the southeast edge of town in an area where house fires were often fatal because people couldn't find the key in time to unlock their barred doors and windows. He pulled to a stop in front of the small turquoise-painted house he and Susie rented. The driveway was full of vehicles in various stages of decrepitude, with several more cars parked along the curb.

J. B. turned off the ignition, but made no move to get out. "Why don't you just tell me what you need."

"Okay." Claire took a deep breath and decided to take him at his word. "I need something to eat. And a car. And a little bit of money. Oh, and a place to sleep where no one will come looking for me. And . . ." Claire's voice wavered on the edge of hysterical laughter, but she brought it into line. "I need to look like a completely different person. Think you can manage all that?"

EZ4U2SA

൭൬

What she needed first, according to J. B., was an omelet. He paid no attention to her protests that she would be happy to eat something uncomplicated, like a bowl of cereal. Soon she was sitting at the Formica-topped table in their miniature dining room, marveling at the enticing smell of sizzling butter.

"Won't we wake up Susie and Eric?"

"Wouldn't kill either of them if we do. They both like to see you, and they neither one of them get the chance much."

That was true enough. Claire had only been to this house once before, when she helped them move in. And that had been before Eric was born. She watched as J. B. tilted the pan back and forth, then used a spatula to pick up the edge of the omelet and let uncooked egg run underneath. Giving the pan an occasional shake, he opened the refrigerator with his free hand and took out a Tupperware container. He shook something brown and glistening into the center of the omelet, folded it in half, and then let it brown on both sides before sliding it on a plate and placing it ceremoniously in front of Claire. Total elapsed time: five minutes.

With the first rich and woodsy forkful, her mouth filled with saliva.

"Mmm—what is this?"

"Chanterelles. We went out in the woods by Estacada to pick them today." He looked at the clock built into the oven. "I guess I mean yesterday. Then when we got home, I sautéed them with butter and a little sherry and diced Walla Walla sweet onions. We had omelets for dinner, so that's just leftovers."

If so, they were the most delicious leftovers Claire had ever tasted. "How'd you know what mushrooms were safe to pick?"

"Oh, chanterelles aren't tricky. Even if you don't know much about mushrooms, you can't go wrong with chanterelles. Or morels. There's nothing bad that looks like either of them. My dad taught me lots of stuff you can eat that grows wild in the woods."

"What happened to him?"

"He got killed in a logging accident when I was thirteen, and my mom moved us here. From my mom, I learned how to grow pretty much anything."

Including, Claire thought, but tactfully refrained from saying, the basement full of marijuana that had put him in jail for eight months nearly ten years before. That had happened right after he met Susie. Claire had thought Susie was a fool for sticking with this man with his long hair, tattoos and what struck her as an affinity for trouble. But now that J. B. knew Claire had her own problems, he was revealing a new side to himself.

Her plate was clean except for a gloss of butter when a soft touch on her shoulder made her whirl around.

"Claire? What are you doing here?" Susie stood behind her, hugging herself in her purple terrycloth bathrobe.

J. B. answered for her. "She needed someone to help her."

Susie raised her eyebrows. "And you called here?"

Claire was embarrassed at her inability to find an answer. For a moment they simply looked at each other, each gazing into a nearly identical pair of blue eyes. Then Susie's question about calling sparked a memory in Claire. In her mind's eye, she saw Paul Roberts's carefully manicured hand as he wrote down all the numbers that circumscribed her life. Including her mother's phone number and address.

"Can I borrow your phone?"

Claire's panic grew as she listened to ring after ring. But on the sixth ring, Jean finally picked up, her voice drugged with sleep. Claire warned her not to answer the door to any strange men, especially good-looking men with silver-blue eyes. With or without a policeman's badge. In monosyllables, Jean agreed that she wouldn't. She seemed too tired to be annoyed by having been woken up, too tired to ask why Claire, always cast in the role of the good daughter, now seemed to be on the lam.

When she put down the phone, J. B. said, "Hey, Suze, Claire needs some different clothes. And some different hair. Do you think you could help her out?"

"I've got some of my fat clothes from after I had Eric she could have." Claire wanted to protest that she wasn't fat, and that besides, anyone would look fat next to Susie, who was whittled down to nothing by cigarettes, but she held her tongue as Susie continued. "I don't know about the hair, though." She picked up one of Claire's apricot-colored ringlets. "This is the kind of hair people pay good money for and you got it for free." Claire could hear an ancient edge of jealousy in her sister's voice. "Why do you want to change it?"

"My hair's too easy to spot. Anybody could scan a crowd and pick me out in a second. That's not what I need right now. Do you still cut hair?"

"Now and again. I'm not licensed or anything, so I only do it under the table for some of the neighbor ladies. But I like it. I could give you a cut and color if you want. You're lucky, 'cause I've still got some dye I bought for someone up the street but didn't end up using. You feel like being a brunette?" When they were kids, Susie had spent hours with her Kut 'N' Kurl Barbie. She had a talent for anything practical with a clear and immediate application. Whereas Claire had been good at calculus and English and sociology, subjects that hadn't taught her to do much except long to go to college, which they couldn't afford. Once she got of school and into real life, Claire found out no one cared if you could do three-dimensional calculus or name the periodic table. And the only thing her big vocabulary had been good for was in helping her understand some of the more obscure license plate references.

Susie disappeared and came back with a worn sheet to pin around Claire's shoulders. "How come you don't do this for a living?" Claire asked.

Susie sighed. "Oh, I'd have to go to school and get licensed, which costs money. And then you have to buy a station at an established salon, and that costs more money."

The sensation of the comb traveling across her scalp was unspeakably soothing. Even Susie taking her to the sink and spraying her hair with the vegetable sprayer failed to jolt her back into alertness. Claire kept her eyes closed and surrendered herself to the snip of scissors, followed by more combing, more parting, more snipping. As her sister began to massage dye into the remains of her hair with plastic-gloved fingers, Claire nearly fell asleep. She kept her eyes closed as Susie led her for a second time to the sink, opening them just long enough to see water the color of ink running down the drain.

Then there was the whir of the blow dryer, as calming as a white noise machine, and the touch of Susie's fingers as she scrunched Claire's hair with one hand and wielded the dryer with the other. Finally, everything ceased. When Claire opened her eyes, Susie handed her the mirror with a shy, satisfied smile.

Claire's mouth fell open. Her now-black hair sprang up in a little cap of curls, providing a dramatic contrast to the pallor of her skin and her large blue eyes.

"You look a little like Winona Ryder," J. B. said. It was the first time he had opened his mouth in over an hour.

"Only older," Susie added.

Claire reflexively pressed her lips together. Then Susie caught her eye and she realized her sister was teasing. All three of them began to laugh, the kind of laughter fueled by exhaustion.

"Suze, this is really great." Claire tried and failed to remember the last time she had praised her sister.

"Thanks." Her sister met her eyes, then looked down at the floor.

"All I really need now is a shower. And maybe show me where you keep those extra clothes. I've been in these for the last twenty-four hours."

❧

J. B. made up a bed for her on the couch while Claire took a shower. She stayed under the spray for a long time, trying to wash her mind blank, but it was too crowded with questions. Who had turned her hotel room upside down and then her house? Who were the good guys and who were the bad guys? Had Troy been lying to her when he insisted the painting was a fake? Was Dante coming to Portland because he wanted to help her or because he wanted another chance to get the painting? Were either of them working with Paul Roberts? And if he wasn't a police detective, then who was he?

When Claire pulled back the shower curtain, there was a split second when the sight of a dark-haired stranger caused her throat to close in unthinking terror. She pulled on the nightgown Susie had left on the counter, reaching back reflexively to lift the weight of her hair from the collar. Her hands met only air.

When she opened the bathroom door, the rest of the house was dark except for a small table lamp beside the worn maroon couch, now made up with a pillow and blanket. Claire turned off the lamp, then tried to arrange herself comfortably. The couch was just short enough that when she lay on her back she could not stretch out full length unless she bent her knees and rested her feet on the armrest. In vain, Claire tried to relax. She breathed in through her nose and out through her mouth. Concentrated on moving her belly button with each breath. Tensed various parts of her body and then released the tension. Nothing worked. She was too conscious of her various organs working to keep her alive, her heart pushing blood back and forth, her lungs sucking in air whether she thought about them or not. She bunched the pillow in half and rolled from her back to her side, pulling up her legs to get them to fit. The pillow smelled like dust. Something poked her in the back and she reached behind the cushions and pulled out a Matchbox car that shone silver in the moonlight. With a sigh, she sat up, turned on the light, and rummaged around in her backpack until she found Aunt Cady's diary.

August 2, 1945

I went to the doctor today. A German doctor, since an Army doctor would give me an honorable discharge and no assistance, the opposite of what I need. It was a woman doctor, *eine Ärztin,* a word Al Patten taught me when he recommended her, and an even rarer sight here than at home. She practices in a semi-gutted room. The missing windowpanes have been replaced with X ray negatives of human chests. Lying on her chipped white-painted metal table, I focused on those cages of bones holding shadowed hearts and tried to think about anything else but what was happening.

I probably know less than two dozen words of German, but "baby" sounds much the same in both languages.

August 8, 1945

An hour ago, I told Rudy I couldn't see him anymore. His face went as still as a stone. I was sobbing, but he said nothing. Then I saw his face begin to crack a little bit, a muscle flickering in the outside corner of his left eye. At first I thought he might cry, but then I realized how angry he was.

Later—we heard about the bomb tonight. This might well mean the end of the war. Maybe that would be the best for me, to go home, to forget about things.

There were no more entries, only blank pages filigreed with mold. Claire had read at random through the diary, but now when she paged back she could find nothing that revealed how her great-aunt had come to have what might be a 350-year-old beauty in a suitcase. It wasn't hard to guess, though. Rudy must have given her to Cady as a little token of his affection, a painting so small it could be taken from the hoard he guarded with no one the wiser. He wasn't the kind of man to worry about who might have owned it before. He had cushioned it with whatever wastepaper came to hand—and in Germany after the war, what was less valuable than Nazi literature? And he could have thrown in a few things he thought might be valuable again one day. That would explain the death's-head ring.

Claire turned off the light again and closed her eyes. When she finally slept, her dreams made little sense, just fragments of memories playing in her head. She saw her dead neighbor, Sonia, raise her hand in greeting as they drove past each other in their matching cars. Charlie's face, drained of color, while she talked about what her family had owned "before." Green-eyed Troy, his voice an intimate whisper just inches from her ear, as Manhattan glided by the limousine's window like an underwater dream. She saw Dante turn his heavy white mug to rest the warmth against his cheek. The flat-faced man who had nearly knocked her down as he ran from her hotel. And finally Claire dreamed of Paul Roberts, with his eyes the color of washed quarters.

Again she felt the gun bite into her temple. In her dream, just as she had in real life, she closed her eyes, but when she opened them again, she saw that the woman in the painting had joined them, only grown to life-size. In her cornflower-colored dress and jacket of pale lemon, she stood in the corner of Claire's living room the same way she did in the painting, a piece of paper held tightly in her hands. The woman watched Claire and Paul with the same eternally enigmatic gaze, her full lips parted. And Claire realized that to the painted woman the onlookers who had gaped at her for three centuries were not even as real as dreams, that only the letter she held had meaning. That even if Paul Roberts were to kill Claire right now in front of her watching eyes, she would then turn back to those words on paper, because only *her* world was the real one.

And then in Claire's dream Aunt Cady appeared behind Paul Roberts, not as an old woman but instead the age she had been when she wrote the diary. A khaki cap rested on her French-braided hair, and her shoulders were square in her uniform. She reached out to take Paul Roberts's chin in her hand. Reluctantly, he turned, releasing Claire, and the two looked into each other's eyes for a long time without moving. In her dream, Claire turned to run out of the room, past the painted woman, who still stood watching. Paul Roberts turned back, his eyes now two round silver mirrors. Claire was just on the verge of understanding it all when she woke up.

The rest of the house was already awake. Claire looked at her watch. Six A.M., which meant she had had a little over two hours of sleep. She swung her feet to the floor. From the couch, she had a clear view of the dining room and kitchen. Eric sat in his high chair, eyes half closed, sucking dreamily on a bottle. J. B. looked up from the paper and nodded at Claire. Susie stood at the sink, running water into a teakettle. When she saw that Claire was awake, she set down the kettle and walked into the living room.

Eric's eyes went wide when he saw his mother walk past in her heavy purple terrycloth bathrobe. He pulled the bottle from his mouth and crowed, "Barney! Barney!"

Susie flushed and sat down on the arm of the couch. "J. B. started calling me that as a joke, but now I think Eric thinks I really *am* Barney. He just loves that stupid show. And since Mom has cable, he watches it three times a day. Have you seen it?"

Claire shook her head without speaking, still trying to adjust to the real world as opposed to the dream one.

"Barney's this big purple thing that's supposed to look like a dinosaur. But he's shaped more like a really fat woman with saddlebags. And the kids on the show are just like a McDonald's commercial—one black, one white, one Hispanic. Even one handicapped one, only of course he's just as cute as a little bug. It's all so sweet it's really sickening. The only good thing is that I hear by the time they turn three, kids *hate* Barney." Susie picked up Claire's blanket and began to fold it. "How does an Eggo waffle sound?"

As she ate, Claire's thoughts came back again and again to her dream. One face kept returning to her. Not Charlie's nor even the painted woman's, but the flat, acne-scarred face. The face, she realized now, of Troy's chauffeur. What had his name been? John? Had he been the man who had run from her hotel as she returned from breakfast? She remembered how he had kept his eyes averted from her even as she fell to one knee. John could have heard Troy mention fantastic sums of money when he talked about the painting. But did Troy know that his driver indulged in a little freelance breaking and entering on the side? Or maybe he did more for Troy than drive him places? Could that be the reason Troy had taken her out to breakfast—so that John would have a chance to steal the painting?

Still not knowing what to think, Claire said her goodbyes twenty minutes later. She hugged her sister for the first time since they were kids. Eric was next, and it felt like something in her chest was tearing when she felt his little arms slip around her neck. Then J. B. gave her a hug that lifted her feet from the floor.

Afterward, he pressed the keys to a twenty-year-old yellow Datsun B-210 into her hand.

OWTAHR

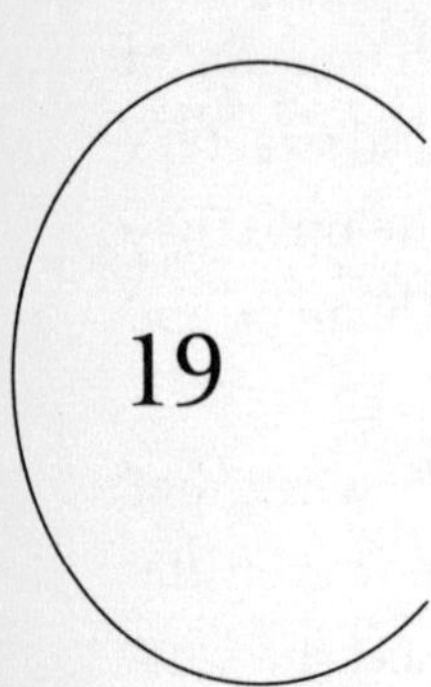

19

The thing about the B-210 was that in addition to the holes in the floorboard and the exposed springs in the upholstery, it had a stick shift. Claire had driven a stick only once before, a quick turn in a friend's car around a shopping center parking lot, and that had been on a day when she wasn't exhausted. Now she couldn't seem to get her left foot and right hand to do the correct thing at the same time. The car popped and jerked down the street. At least at 6:25 in the morning, the roads were mostly empty.

After a dozen blocks, she dared to use her shifting hand to turn on the radio. It seemed to capture only one station, KXL, and that faintly. KXL divided its offerings between easily digested snippets of "drive-time" news sandwiched between conservative talk shows. It was hard to imagine J. B. listening to Rush Limbaugh rant on about liberal wackos, but then again, Claire would never have guessed that he could cook an omelet or prove to be just what she needed.

As the car climbed the overpass that led to I-84, Claire felt a gust of wind slap the car. A minute later, KXL's traffic and weather report told her why.

"The time is six twenty-eight, twenty-eight past six. Traffic is still moving well on the inbound freeways. The weather might be another matter. We're expecting heavy winds today, peaking sometime in the next thirty-six hours. We're already hearing reports from the Aloha area of gusts up to forty miles an hour. Coming up next we have the national news, but immediately afterward we'll have more on the weather."

Claire snapped off the radio. Right now, it was hard to believe there were actually people who thought that the worst thing that could happen to them was bad weather.

ᘓ

It wasn't until she standing at the building's entrance that Claire realized she still didn't have her ID badge. And the same guard—she remembered his name was Bruce—still sat behind the security desk, just as he had the night before. Only now he had his head propped up on two fists and the vacant gaze of the half-asleep.

Claire took a deep breath and pushed open the door to the lobby.

"Morning, ma'am."

Bruce clearly didn't recognize her new look. Good. Maybe that meant she could fool the bad guys, too. "Bruce, can I ask you a big favor? I forgot my card again this morning. I need to get to thirteen. I came in early to catch up on some work."

"And you *are*?" His hair was cut so short she could see the pink shine of his scalp.

"Don't you remember me from last night? Claire Montrose? You let me up on thirteen?" Surprising them both, Claire let her sweater fall open to reveal Susie's old jeans (which were nearly too small for Claire despite Susie's comment that these were her "fat" clothes), and a T-shirt that depicted a leaping, spangled salmon under the legend THERE'S NO NOOKIE LIKE CHINOOKIE. The salmon was distorted from being stretched across Claire's larger breasts.

The security guard's eyes grew wide. "Damn. Sorry I didn't recognize you, but you don't look anything like you did last night. Did you have a makeover or something?"

"Or something," Claire agreed. "So—do you think you could let me up on thirteen again? I promise I'll bring my card tomorrow. It's just that I stayed, um, someplace unexpected last night." She dropped her chin and looked at him through her lashes. "Can you zap me up?"

Looking slightly dazed, Bruce agreed that would be no problem.

AXNU8D+

&

The elevator seemed to take forever to reach the thirteenth floor. Impatient, Claire willed it to move faster, anxious to have the painting back in her possession. What had seemed like such a good idea last night now seemed stupid. Who knew when the next workman would come along to fix the wiring, phone lines or air conditioning? Besides, whoever had torn apart first her hotel room and then her house could be counted on to make the next logical move and search her workplace. And if Claire could manage to outwit Bruce twice, then an experienced criminal wouldn't have any problem.

Her watch said 6:45. It should take about five minutes to climb on her desk, retrieve the painting, breeze past Bruce and get back in her car. Then she would weigh her options. Chance going to the police? Try to contact the FBI or the Justice Department? Lay low until Dante arrived, maybe hole up in one of the anonymous hotels on Sandy that rented rooms by the hour and try to catch a few hours sleep? Her thoughts chased themselves. Every time Claire thought of Charlie she felt frantic with worry, but she didn't know how to find her. J. B. had promised to put the word out among his biker friends. He seemed to still have some connections, a fact that up until today she would have said was a bad idea. She was still thinking when she rounded the last corner that lay between her and the Custom Plate Department.

Instead of empty shadowed cubicles, all the lights were on and the area was bustling with activity. A stocking-footed Lori stood on a chair, taping red and purple balloons to the edge of Claire's cube. Roland was trying to find the best place to display an outsize three-foot-tall vase of dark red roses with fat nodding heads. And Frank was already helping himself from a box of assorted Winchell's donuts.

Damn! Claire came to a stop. She had completely forgotten that today was her birthday. And about the tradition that the birthday boy or girl was supposed to arrive at work not one minute before their regular time, and then express amazement at the miraculous transformation of their cubicle.

Stepping lightly, she started to back up. Maybe she could escape without anyone noticing. She would regroup and come back again in the evening.

Just then Lori turned and saw her. She looked at her quizzically and then her eyes grew wide with recognition. "Claire, is that you? *Like* the hair!"

As fast as if something had crawled out of the cream filling, Frank snatched his hand back from the box of donuts and spun around. He let out a nervous bark of laughter. "Claire, is that really you?"

Roland's mouth had dropped open, but no sound came out. Instead, his gaze went from Claire's now-black curls to her Nike-clad feet, taking in everything in between. His thought processes were so transparent that she could tell that he both liked her outfit and thought it inappropriate. Knowing Roland, in a few minutes he would begin crafting a three-page memo on appropriate work attire, complete with minimum length requirements for skirts and a carefully worded stipulation requiring proper undergarments.

Lori jumped off the chair and slipped into her black pumps. "So what happened to you in New York? Send the girl off to the big city, and she comes back a new woman." She stepped forward to give Claire a hug. "Oh, and before I forget, happy birthday. At least your birthday gives us the chance to celebrate, since the state's too cheap to give us Columbus Day off."

Claire returned her squeeze, but her eyes were fastened on the square of ceiling tile that hid the painting. It was only ten feet away—but it might as well have been a mile. Just then a heavy hand fell on her shoulder.

"May I see your badge, miss?" The hand slid down to her upper arm and tightened.

Claire turned. The speaker was a security guard, a big man whose chest strained against his white polyester shirt.

"I don't have it with me today. But these are my co-workers"—she gestured at Lori, Frank and Roland, who all wore their ID badges on cords around their necks—"and they can verify that I work here."

"I'll vouch for her, Officer." Roland stepped forward. "This is Claire Montrose and she's one of *my* employees."

The guard shook his head. "I'm afraid we've had an alert in this area. And the rules clearly state that anyone lacking an ID badge must come down to the security office and fill out Form Number 115-96C."

Confronted with a greater force—required paperwork—Roland's half-hearted defense of Claire melted. "Maybe it would be best if you went with him, Claire. To minimize any delay of our little celebration."

"Oh, come on." Lori put one hand on her hip and appealed to the guard. "It's her *birthday.* Can't you just fill out Form Number Whatever by yourself and bring it back up here for her to sign? If you do that, I'll let you have your pick of donuts." She picked the box from Claire's desk. "Even a maple bar."

He was unmoved. "I'm afraid she's going to have to go with—"

Just then Claire came alive and tried to twist out of his grasp. "Let go of me!" Her co-workers stared, but Claire's brain had finally realized what her eyes had been trying to tell her. This man was no security guard.

What had given the game away were his shoes. They weren't the cheap all-black running shoes favored by the real security guards, but instead reddish-brown oxfords. Exposed by the cuffs of the man's too-short black polyester pants, they looked as big as boats. Suddenly, Claire had known where she had seen the shoes—and the man now wearing them—before. Only then he hadn't been a security guard in her office building. Instead, he had said his name was Karl Zehner. And the last time she had seen him, those shoes were planted on the floor of her great-aunt's trailer, while their owner asked if she had by any chance come across a painting among Cady's things.

Her eyes were level with his chest, and as she struggled in his grip, Claire saw that his name tag read BRUCE. Claire spared a brief thought for the real Bruce. This man might be wearing his uniform, but she hoped Bruce hadn't had to die to give it up.

Her struggles had had no effect. Still holding her arm, Karl started to march her down the hall that led to the elevator. "If you're not careful, miss, you're going to have to fill out another form for resisting lawful detainment."

"I know who you are! Let go of me!" Karl half dragged her to the elevator. She turned to appeal to her co-workers. "Help me! This guy's a fake! He's trying to steal something from me!"

Frank looked at Roland and Claire watched as he mouthed the word "Drugs!" Roland pursed his lips and nodded, as if he had been handed the key to both her new downmarket appearance and her recently altered behavior. Only Lori, standing with her hands balled at her sides, seemed at a loss for what to do.

"Lori! Please!" Claire called back over her shoulder. Karl had marched her to the elevator doors. For a moment she pretended to match him step for step, until he took one step forward and she deliberately took one step back, donkey-kicking her other foot behind her as hard as she could. It only reached his shin, and Karl didn't even grunt when her foot connected.

"Wait a minute!" Lori ran in front of them. "If Claire says you're not really a guard here, I believe her. Give me some proof, buddy."

Just then the elevator doors opened, revealing Ed, the nominal head of their license plate kingdom. He had a black briefcase in one hand and a copy of the *Oregonian* under his arm. He appraised Claire and her captor with narrowed, bloodshot eyes. "Is that you under that wig, Montrose? You can run, but you can't hide. Good work, Officer." He held the elevator open as Karl began to force Claire inside.

"What? What are you talking about?" Lori demanded. Frank and Roland hung back.

"This woman's a wanted fugitive. Here, see for yourself." Ed thrust the paper into Lori's hand. Frank and Roland crowded around. Claire managed to catch a glimpse of the headline before Karl pulled her into the elevator and hit the CLOSE DOOR button. WOMAN SOUGHT FOR QUESTIONING IN NEIGHBOR'S DEATH, ROOMMATE'S DISAPPEARANCE.

"I am warning you. If you do not keep quiet, I am going to hurt you." Karl jabbed the button marked *B* as soon as the elevator doors closed. He was using a voice Claire hadn't heard before, not the prissy inflection of Aunt Cady's supposed friend or the officious intonation of a security guard, but something rougher and angrier. Maybe she *had* hurt him when she kicked him. She certainly hoped so.

"Who are you working with?" Claire demanded. "Paul? Dante?

Troy?" Karl held her in front of him, so she couldn't see if his face changed, if any of the names resonated. "Do you know where Charlie is?" He kept silent.

In only a few seconds the doors would open and he would take her someplace where no one could hear her scream. Did Karl have any weapon beyond his brute strength? At least she knew that poor Bruce's uniform didn't also come with a gun.

"Okay," Karl said into her ear, "we are going to walk out of this building, and we are not going to make a fuss." He slid his hand down to her wrist and pulled it up behind her back until she grunted. "Try to get away and I will break your arm. Minimum."

The elevator doors opened to reveal a crowd of workers clutching nylon lunch sacks, athletic bags, briefcases and purses. Claire knew a few of them by sight, but none by name. And none of them seemed to recognize her, even though several held copies of the *Oregonian*.

Karl gave Claire a little push and she began to walk. He kept his body so close to her that they could be mistaken for boyfriend and girlfriend, wrapped in each other's arms. In twenty more steps she would be in the underground garage, and once Karl had her in his car, chances were good she would never be seen again. After he had forced her to tell him where the painting was, he would probably kill her. She imagined a new *Oregonian* headline: BODY FOUND IN SHALLOW MOUNTAIN GRAVE.

Her thoughts spun as they passed through the crowd and made their way down the low-ceilinged hallway that led to the parking garage. The door ahead of them opened to admit another state employee. He held a ubiquitous Starbucks coffee cup, wrapped in a napkin to shield him from the heat. Before she had even consciously decided what to do, Claire's free hand was reaching out. With a flick of her thumb, she popped off the white plastic lid, then threw the contents over her shoulder.

Karl bellowed in her ear and let go of her hand. Claire whirled and pushed her fists into the soft dough of his belly. Already off-balance, his red, scalded face dripping coffee, Karl went down on his butt. His head hit the wall with a *thunk.* Claire burst past the startled worker and caught the door just before it closed.

For the second time in less than twenty-four hours, Claire ran for her life. Her legs had not yet recovered from her run down Barbur Boulevard, and when she tried to kick them out it was like ordering a paralyzed man to walk. She half lurched, half ran through the garage, up the stained concrete stairs, and out onto the street, her left Achilles tendon grating at every step.

Claire ran to the B-210, jumped inside, and reached down to pull the key from her jeans pocket. Something was already clutched in her fingers, a souvenir of her struggle with Karl. It was a state-issued ID card, with the word SECURITY in bold black letters on one side. And a picture of Bruce—the real Bruce—on the other.

MSTBF8

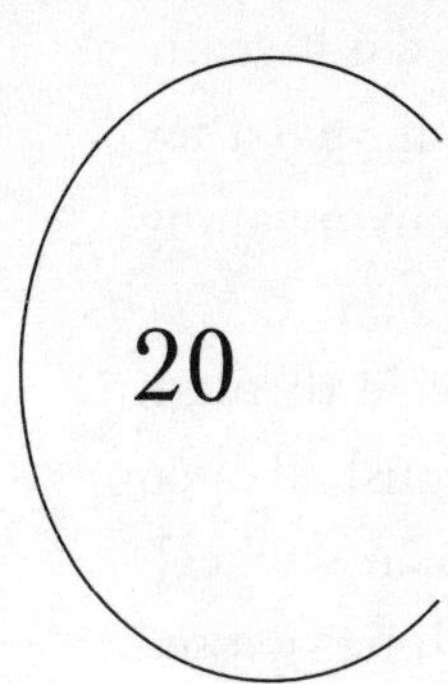

20

The Lord Is My Shepherd Assisted Living Facility said the flaking letters painted on the side of a concrete building that possessed all the charm of a warehouse. Since it was located in the industrial area of northwest Portland, it probably *had* been a warehouse.

Claire checked the printout again. After she had slipped the painting in its hiding place the night before, she had had just enough time to look up Al Patten—Aunt Cady's old hometown pal—on the state's computer. It had been a long shot, but it had paid off when the listing showed that he had still been around a few years before. "License revoked 5/19/93," it said. And after a c/o it gave the address she now stood in front of.

After she pushed the door open, she found herself in a small reception area bracketed by swinging doors. The sharp smell of disinfectant battled with the faint tang of urine. In front of her was a battered wooden desk, unoccupied, topped with an old typewriter. Mounted on the wall above it was a large white sign. "You are at The Lord Is My Shepherd Assisted Living Facility," it said at the top. The next line read, "The season is *fall*," with the word *fall* Velcroed into place. "The weather outside is *cool*. Today is *Saturday*." Since it was really Monday, Claire wondered how long it had been since anyone had paid attention to what the sign said. And did it really matter? If the people who lived here were so out of it that they didn't know what season it was, would reading it have any meaning for them?

"Hello?" There was no answer, and no one was visible through either of the swinging doors. Choosing at random, she pushed open the door on the left. An old woman sat slumped over in a wheelchair in the middle of the hallway, which was lined with half-closed doors. Each door was decorated with a large wooden cross, and on the cross a ceramic Jesus writhed in what seemed to Claire a little too clearly pictured agony. In the middle of the corridor lay a cart stacked with breakfast trays, and at the end of the hall was another sign: NO SINNER MUSIC MAY BE PLAYED ON PREMISES. Despite the wheelchair, the woman didn't seem to be paralyzed, since the footrest flaps were turned up and she was slowly shuffling forward.

"Excuse me, do you know where—" Claire began, but stopped when the old woman looked up. Caught in a net of wrinkles, her eyes were wide and wild. Claire looked away.

Wham! The old woman rolled her wheelchair over Claire's left foot and banged painfully into her shins.

"Hey! Be careful!" Claire said, taking a step back.

The old woman looked up at her, and something seemed to stir in her faded eyes. She took her hands from her lap, put them on the wheels and rolled over Claire's foot again.

"Stop that!" Claire took two quick steps around the woman's chair, so that she was now directly behind it.

"Sister Edna! Are you bothering people again?" A young woman came out of a room at the end of the hall. Her white long-sleeved uniform fell past her knees, and was buttoned up to the top of her neck. On top of her thick bun was pinned something that looked like a white doily. "Can I help you, sister?"

Claire crossed her arms over the saying on her T-shirt. "I'm looking for Al Patten. I think he's a resident here." She sidestepped as the wheelchair grazed the back of her knees.

"Sister Edna! Stop that! You need to get back in your room." The young woman stepped around Claire and grabbed the back of the old woman's wheel chair. "He's in Room 112 Are you a relative?"

Claire tried to think of the most plausibly distant relationship that might result in a visit. "A great-niece." After all, if this stranger could call her sister, it wasn't that much of a stretch to claim kinship with a man she had never seen.

The aide spun Edna's chair around and began to push her back the way Claire had come, accompanied by the old woman's frustrated whimpers. "His room's down this way. I didn't even know he had any relatives. I don't think he's had a visitor the whole time I've worked here."

Claire followed the aide or nurse or whatever she was back through the reception area—still empty—to the other side of the building, which was a mirror of the first. There was the same long corridor, the same deserted food cart, even the same hand-lettered sign warning about "Sinner Music." The aide nodded at a door halfway down the corridor. "Room 112 is right in the middle. Would you mind helping Brother Al with his breakfast? We're kind of short-staffed today."

"No trouble at all," Claire said, and picked up a tray. With her foot, Claire nudged open the door to 112. It held two hospital beds, each with its head to the barred window. On one an old man sat hunched over, dressed in threadbare pajamas. His eyes were closed, his face pinched, and he was rocking the upper half of his body back and forth, rocking, rocking. He reminded Claire of a TV show she had seen once about autistic children.

The other man was sitting in a chair beside his neatly made bed. He was dressed in a thirty-year-old suit, and his hair had been combed back with water, the white curls rippling like corrugated cardboard.

"Al Patten?" Claire asked him, fearing he wasn't. The rocking man didn't pause, but the dapper man leaned down and began to pull a suitcase from under the bed.

"Am I getting out today?" His muffled voice was unexpectedly low and melodious, like an old-time radio announcer.

Claire felt a stab of guilt. "No, Mr. Patten, sorry, not today. I've brought you some breakfast, though."

With a sigh, the old man pushed his suitcase back under the bed. He began to pat his jacket pockets, then reached for a wallet that wasn't there. "Would you mind spotting me, darling? I seem to have misplaced my wallet."

Claire realized he now thought she was some sort of waitress. "That's okay. I've got it covered." She sat the tray on the table between the bed and the chair, and then took a seat on the edge of the bed. Only then did the old man straighten up and look her full in the face. He sagged back in his chair with a little cry.

"Cady! What are you doing in this place?" With a palsied hand, he reached out to touch one of the wisps of dark hair that framed Claire's face. "Why have you changed your hair?"

Claire remembered standing in front of the bathroom mirror in her aunt's trailer, marking the similarities between her face and her aunt's fifty-year-old photo. What would he tell her if he thought she was Cady? "Do you like it this way?"

"Oh, sure, honey, sure. You can fix your hair any way you want, because you'll always look good to me." He looked at the table and gave a little grunt of surprise. "Oh, look, breakfast." He reached for a glass of what looked like Tang and took a sip. A dreamy smile crossed his face. "Where have you been keeping yourself? I haven't seen you for . . ." Al looked away and then back with a mixture of confusion and discomfort. It was clearly an effort for him to stay fixed in one time, not go slipping backward or forward. "For ages," he finished. "And when's Rudy gonna come by? You tell him I have a little deal I need to talk to him about."

A deal. That seemed to be in keeping with the Al Patten Aunt Cady had written about fifty years before. "Actually, that's why I came by to see you. I need to ask you something. Do you remember that little painting Rudy gave me—"

"That girl with a letter? She's got those big blue eyes like yours?" Al laughed. "Rudy said that would get you talking to him again."

So that was it. Rudy must have given the painting to Aunt Cady to persuade her to come back to him. A darker thought occurred to Claire. Or maybe Rudy had given Aunt Cady the painting as a bribe, to make it harder for her to turn him in for looting from the storeroom he was supposed to be guarding.

"So where did Rudy get it from? Did it come from—"

A plaintive wail from across the hall interrupted her. "My shoes! Where are my shoes! Bring me my shoes!"

Claire wondered if something should be done, but Al's roommate never stopped his rocking and Al himself was tucking a napkin under his collar without paying the least bit of attention.

She finished her sentence. "Did it come from the train that had all of Göring's stuff?"

He shook his head, looking confused and upset. Was it that he didn't know the answer or that he didn't want to talk? Then his face cleared. From under overgrown eyebrows he gave her a sly look. "Is there any way you can get me out of here, Cady? I'll make it worth your while."

"Where are we?"

For an answer, he rolled his eyes and blew air through pursed lips. "The lockup, of course. I don't remember exactly what I did, though. Was it a 'drunk and disorderly' again?"

Claire hesitated and then offered him a half-smile, unwilling to give him either a lie or the truth. "I want to ask you again about that painting. Where did it come from?"

"All I know is that it was in the warehouse." Al was now more interested in his oatmeal than stolen masterpieces. "Things are always going in and"—he lowered his voice to a stage whisper—"coming out. Every Nazi has a thing or two that he took from the Jews and now he's either turning it in or hiding it in his cellar. They got it from someone else, and now we take it from them. What's that old Latin saying?"

"'*Veni, vidi, vici*'?" Claire asked, resigned to the fact that she might never know what happened. "'I came, I saw, I conquered'?"

"You were always better in school than me, but that isn't it. All I remember is the English. 'To the victor goes the spoils.'"

∾

Claire found the I-Spy Shoppe in a Barbur Boulevard strip mall, sandwiched between a Thai restaurant and a tanning salon. J. B. has said he could get her a gun if she wanted, but she had declined the offer. But now she was feeling the need for some kind of protection. As she got out of the car and slipped on her backpack, she could still feel Al Patten's soft goodbye kiss on her cheek. She had promised to tell Rudy to come by. For the first time, she wondered what had happened to Aunt Cady's former lover. Was he dead now? In a nursing home like his old Army buddy? Living in a trailer in a remote area, just him and his pit bulls and his Nazi memorabilia?

A bell tinkled above her head when she pushed open the door to I-Spy. From behind the cash register, a brush-cut clerk glanced up at her and then went back to reading his magazine. The one-roomed store, with its blank cream-colored walls and industrial gray carpeting, had an air of impermanence about it, as if the next day it might become a quick copy shop or an Iranian deli. The only fixtures, in addition to the cash register, were a half-dozen glass display cases scattered around the room.

The store was like an old-fashioned magic shop that had been infected with a 1990s brand of technology-flavored paranoia. At first Claire's hopes slid as she examined the case nearest the door, which held a variety of items designed to conceal valuables. A fake rock. A false-bottomed planter. A completely unconvincing cement-colored dog turd that looked more like a gag gift. There were safes made from hollowed-out books, car batteries and a giant can of Fritos. Everything was slightly off and thus unconvincing. Like how often did you see a *can* of Fritos? The stuff seemed designed more to appeal to a nine-year-old boy than to deter thieves.

She spun the revolving display filled with books on lock-picking, disguises and secret codes, all with forty-year-old clip art on the covers. Next to the books was a pyramid display for the Bionic Ear, "the sound collector with a thousand uses." The package showed an Aryan-looking young man, clad in camouflage, his brow furrowed in exaggerated concentration as he listened to a pair of earmuff-like receivers.

Some of I-Spy's wares seemed to have been transported directly from the back of an old comic book. There were invisible inks and a two-headed nickel with the legend WIN EVERY TOSS!

Claire slipped on a pair of rearview sunglasses. The black plastic frames stuck out three inches on either side of her head, and were about as unobtrusive as a pair of 3-D glasses. The insides of the lenses were coated, offering a faint, oily reflection of the store behind her. She put them back on the display.

At she moved to the back of the store, the contents of the cases became sleeker and more expensive, designed to appeal to men with James Bond fantasies. At least Claire hoped they were fantasies. There were car bomb detectors, night-vision goggles, vehicle trackers, and a briefcase that promised to greet any unauthorized user with 10,000 volts. Telephone recording devices were displayed side by side with scramblers that disrupted telephone recording devices.

Claire ended her circuit of the room back at the register. "Excuse me. I have a problem and was wondering if you could give me some advice."

The clerk looked up from a magazine ad touting the benefits of bulletproofing your car. "Lady, maybe you should be telling your problems to a lawyer instead of to me." His affectation of world-weariness was at odds with his inability to grow a convincing goatee.

Claire wasn't sure where to begin. "This isn't exactly a lawyer-type problem."

He nodded knowingly. "I hear that all the time." He had a narrow, rabbity face. She had the feeling he didn't have many opportunities to talk to women.

"I'm being followed, and I need some kind of, I guess you'd call it a personal protection device."

"Have you thought about going to the police?"

"Well," Claire began. "There may be a problem with that."

He surprised her by slapping the magazine down on the counter. "Of course there's a problem with that! A piece of toilet paper will do you more good than one of those worthless restraining orders. I should know. I get the guys they are taken out against all the time in here, looking for stuff to get back at their ex-wives. The only one you can rely on is yourself. You have to be ready to use anything in your environment."

The clerk crouched in a way that was presumably supposed to represent catlike readiness, but the position only emphasized his incipient potbelly. "If you think you're being followed, the first step is to try to keep cars, trees, any kind of a barrier between you. Don't be afraid to make a scene. Set off an emergency alarm, honk a car horn, even throw a rock through a window. Do what you have to do to attract attention. Your trained assassin doesn't want witnesses."

He seemed to have forgotten that she was presumably the victim of a jealous ex-husband. "I would highly recommend the rearview sunglasses. I saw you considering them. At a minimum, learn to use the reflective surfaces around you to see what's behind you. Look in car and shop windows when you're walking. Check the plastic strip at ATM machines."

He straightened up, accompanied by an audible pop from his knees. "And remember that in a pinch, anything can be a weapon. A handful of dirt. A roll of quarters held in your fist." He made a "pow!" sound as he threw a shadow punch, then fished the keys from his pocket. "Slip your keys between your fingers, and use them to rake your assailant's eyes." He clawed the air and Claire took a step back. Then the salesman's instinct returned. "Or if you'd like to try our weighted gloves, you'll find they're very reasonably priced. And there's something else I'd like to show you."

He used one of his keys to open a case, then pulled something from it with a flourish, as if performing a magic trick. It looked like a cross between a beeper and an electric razor—small, black, curved to fit the hand. "How about a stun gun?" he asked as he pressed a button. Electricity arced between two wires, crackling and sparking.

N4CR

From behind the brushy green curtain of her neighbor's overgrown arborvitae, Claire had spent the last ten minutes casing her own house. Yellow crime scene tape was crisscrossed across the door, and her Mazda still sat in the driveway. At this time of day, the neighborhood was deserted, people swallowed up by the new American reality that demanded every able-bodied adult hold down a full-time job in order to sustain a reasonable standard of living. Mothers worked, teenagers worked, and even the elderly stood behind McDonald's counters in their orthopedic shoes.

One quick burst across the street, down the driveway and through the gated fence, and then Claire was in the shelter of the backyard, sucking lungfuls of air. The last time she had run for pleasure had been her final morning in New York, just a little more than a day ago, although it seemed more like a decade. She ran her fingers under the edge of the deck until she found the nail that held the key to the back door. Even with her belief in the power of an imaginary dog to guard her house, Charlie would have laughed at the idea of using a fake turd to hide her key.

The reality of what had been done to the house, of the violation of her sanctuary, engulfed Claire when she opened the door. Everything was in the same sorry mess it had been when she ran from it. Had that only been last night? Her fingers itched to make just one thing right, to get out a broom or set a chair back in place. Instead she made her way to the kitchen with its floor covered in spilled flour.

She knelt down and tried to read the scuff marks. She thought of ancient hunters in primeval forests who could read the story told by every bent twig. It wasn't as easy for her, especially since a half-dozen people must have walked through this space since she had been here last. But finally, Claire found what she had half remembered from the night before. Next to the refrigerator was a huge footprint, half again as big as any of the other tracks.

And Claire could only think of one man mixed up in this affair who had such huge feet. Karl Zehner. So Karl had been here then, here before Claire came back from New York. He had to have something to do with Charlie's disappearance. Had he stashed her someplace as a bargaining chip? Had he killed her when he realized she didn't know where the painting was? Claire thought about Charlie, tried to imagine her life snuffed out, and failed. Wouldn't she know if this woman who had been like a second mother to her was dead?

Before deciding it was safe to leave, Claire spent a long time peering out each window. No cars came down the street and the neighbors' houses were still and presumably empty. Still, she couldn't shake the idea that someone was observing her. She looked at her watch. In another ninety minutes, she was scheduled to meet Dante. She wanted to arrive at their meeting place ahead of time. She would watch, wait and make sure he was alone and she wasn't followed. And she would decide whether she should try to trust him. After a deep breath, she slipped out the side door.

A white van squealed into the driveway. Doors were flung open and a man and woman leaped out and began to run toward her. Claire had never seen either one of them before. No matter. She knew what they were after. Acquiring what might be a twenty-million-dollar painting was a sure way to make a lot of people decide they needed to separate you from it.

Something squarish, black and mechanical was balanced on the man's shoulder. *My God!* Claire thought wildly. *A rocket launcher?* The woman clutched a black wand, and now she pointed it directly at Claire.

Claire grabbed the stunner from her jacket pocket. The clerk's instructions from an hour before flashed through her brain.

"Roll tape, Brad!" barked the woman. Even without heels she would have been taller than Claire, but in her cream-colored pumps and matching suit she was terrifying and beautiful, an Amazon warrior queen. Claire didn't wait to figure out what she meant, just ran forward to meet her. Remembering the I-Spy clerk's instructions, she aimed for a spot just above the tan and freckled cleavage.

It was as if the woman had run full-tilt into an invisible wall. She fell backward so hard that gravel sprayed from the impact. One of her shoes flew past Claire. The woman's hands rose to clutch her chest, tears washing across her face. Her glossy lips opened and closed, emitting no sound.

Remembering her other would-be assailant, Claire went into a crouch and pivoted to wave the stun gun menacingly at Brad. But he had eyes only for the stunned woman lying on the ground. She had progressed to making a faint mewling sound. He threw his giant weapon down on the driveway, then knelt next to his fallen comrade, pressing his fingers to the tops of her heaving breasts as he searched for the wound.

"What did you do to her? What did you do?" He leaned forward, shouting. "Liz, can you hear me? Liz? We're going to get you to a doctor right away."

Liz's lips moved, and they both leaned forward to hear. Although the salesman at I-Spy had assured her that the stun gun would leave no lasting damage, Claire was beginning to worry.

The woman struggled to form the words. "Get the shot."

The shot? Claire grabbed Brad's weapon before he could. As her fingers fastened on the handle, she finally recognized it for what it was. Not some strange futuristic weapon, but a videocam.

Understanding opened in her like a ragged seam. Liz must have thrust a microphone toward her, not a weapon. Which meant that these two were—"You're TV reporters?"

XQQSME

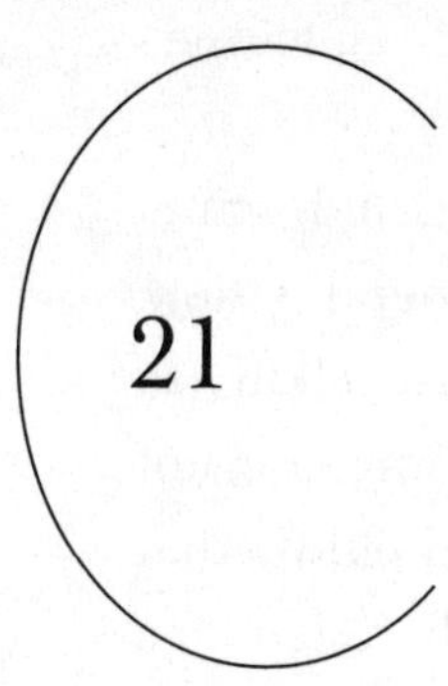

21

"Just let me get a peek at the little one." The old woman tried again to elbow her aside, but Claire clutched the handle of the baby stroller even tighter. Under the shelter of a multicolored canopy, the blanket-wrapped bundle didn't stir. Which wasn't surprising. The whole setup—stroller, blanket, and Baby Newborn—had been purchased twenty minutes before at Toys "Я" Us.

Claire tried to mimic the no-nonsense tones of an experienced mother. "I'm sorry, but if Jessica wakes up, I won't be able to get her back down again."

"And when are you due to give her a brother or sister, dear?"

Too late, Claire tried to step back, but the liver-spotted hand landed on the high arc of her belly.

The old woman, who had already confided in Claire that she had had "seven of my own," clearly knew that something was amiss. Under the lip of her clear plastic rain bonnet (which was tied firmly over a wig in a particularly unconvincing shade of tan), her eyes widened. Her mouth opened and then closed again. Finally, she turned on her heel and walked away, muttering and shaking her head.

With a sigh, Claire sat down on the bench outside Meier & Frank.

It offered a clear view of the Lloyd Center Mall skating rink, one floor below. In the basket of the stroller lay her backpack and Susie's old clothes.

Her new belly, encased in a virginal-looking pink-and-white-flowered maternity top, protruded into her peripheral vision, startling Claire for a moment. It had taken a bit of fast talking to persuade the clerk at Motherhood to allow her to purchase not only a maternity outfit but also the pregnancy-shaped pillow that hung from a hook in the dressing room. It had probably rested on a hundred tummies before Claire's, while newly pregnant women imagined how they would look with a cute little strap-on belly—forgetting to factor in the swollen feet, varicose veins and stretch marks. Claire had told the spiky-haired clerk that she wanted to scare an old boyfriend, and the girl had allowed herself a small smile before agreeing.

BBNBRD

∾

Her new disguise had been prompted by the fact that too many people knew what she looked like now, with dark hair and Susie's clothes. Her co-workers, Karl, KMDR-TV's Liz and Brad—and potentially all of Portland, if Liz and Brad broke their promise and aired Claire's reluctant interview tonight instead of three days from now.

First they had tried to lure her by promising to tell her side of the story. When that didn't work, they had threatened to broadcast footage of her lunging at Liz with the stun gun. For emphasis, Liz had rubbed at the faint red mark on her chest, plaintively asking Brad if it would show on camera. At Claire's insistence the negotiations had taken place inside the van, which Brad had driven several miles from Claire's house.

They had finally made a pact: KMDR would hold off for at least three days before airing any footage of her. In return, Claire would agree not to talk to any other reporters—and to allow them to film the painting a new anonymity might allow her to retrieve. Liz's azure eyes—a little too riveting to be real—had gotten even wider as she contemplated the idea that this "exclusive" might catapult her into a larger media market. Their two-person "news crew" broadcast local news twice a day on a station that devoted the rest of its airtime to the Home Shopping Network. She was meant for better things than KMDR, Liz had confided to Claire, while Brad watched her with what seemed to be lust-tinged amusement. Things like her own talk show or anchoring a program like *Hard Copy* or *Inside Edition.*

Despite their promise, Claire thought the chances were about fifty-fifty that Liz would give in to temptation and decide that half a scoop was bigger than none. But even if she didn't show up on KMDR's newscast tonight, Claire's new look was already overexposed.

Then she had remembered Lori's complaints five years before, when she had given birth to her son Max. "It defies the laws of physics," Lori had said. "I can push the stroller right through a crowd—and no one looks at me. It's as if I've become invisible. Guys in suits, teenagers, working women—it's like I don't exist for them at all." The funny thing was, now that Claire had a stroller—adding an additional pregnancy had been her own inspiration—she noticed how many women like her crowded the mall. There were dozens of other women piloting their own strollers, often with an extra kid reluctantly being pulled along by the hand. She had never taken notice of all these mommies before, but they must have surely been here.

For the fourth time, Claire ran her eyes over the people who encircled the ice skating rink. There! Was that Dante's dark head?

Something loosened inside her as she realized it *was* him. Among predominantly milk-pale Portlanders, Dante's olive skin and long dark curls looked even more exotic than they had in New York. As she watched, he craned his neck to scan the faces of the people sitting on the benches on the upper level. Without pausing, his gaze swept past her face.

Claire gripped the handle of the stroller harder. She had to decide now—did she trust him or not? Had he been the one who had followed her through the museum and then broken into her hotel room in New York? Could he somehow be involved in the terrible things that had happened here? Had he really come to Portland to help her? Or was he just looking for another chance to get his hands on a priceless and beautiful object?

Without making a conscious decision, Claire found herself on her feet. Before she could even raise her hand, Dante swiveled his head to look at her. His face suddenly creased into a smile. He gave her a little nod before taking the escalator stairs two at time.

"And how's the little mother?" he asked, bending down to kiss her cheek. His cool lips left behind a humming patch of skin.

"It's a long story." She suddenly realized how hungry she was. Her last full meal had been J. B.'s omelet, some twelve hours before. "Can I tell it to you over a plate of pasta?"

"Certainly. Will there be two or three of us at dinner?"

It took Claire a second before she realized he was referring to the stroller's occupant. "Baby Newborn doesn't really require food. But I know a neighborhood place where they'll let us park the stroller next to the table."

"I kind of like you as a brunette," Dante said as they left the shopping center. He had taken over pushing the stroller and his black satchel was now stashed in the stroller basket on top of Claire's things. "And I think the pregnancy gives you a certain glow." His smile, made raffish by his gold earring and mended tooth, was replaced with a swift, serious sideways glance. "But can I ask about the painting? Is it safe? Do you have it with you?" He cast a glance at the jumble of packages that filled the stroller's basket.

"It's not here. And I think it's safe. At least for now." She felt a prick of doubt. She wished Dante had asked about how she was doing—although it was clear that she was okay—or at least about Charlie.

At 4:00 P.M. on a Monday afternoon, the sponge-painted ocher walls of Raphael's held only empty tables, two waiters and a busboy. While they perused the menus, their waiter brought a bowl of olive oil and a hand-formed loaf of bread. Dante watched with an amused smile as Claire dipped slice after slice in the fragrant oil, alternating bites with bits of her story.

When their food came—Claire had ordered smoked salmon chowder and Dante pasta with sausage and red peppers—she eyed his plate hungrily before picking up her soup spoon. As soon as she lifted it to her mouth, she realized she had made an inspired choice. Each mouthful offered a new flavor: smoky caramelized onions, feathers of fresh dill, tiny new red potatoes, smoky slices of salmon, kernels of fresh sweet corn that popped between her teeth. When Claire finished, it was hard not to pick up the bowl to drink the last drops. Using the last piece of bread, she compromised by wiping the bowl clean.

Dante pushed the remains of his pasta toward her. "Still hungry?"

"Well, if you don't mind . . ." Claire realized she had been making little sounds of delight when she ate. She flushed as she remembered Troy's insinuation that a woman's reaction to food foretold what she would be like in bed.

Luckily, Dante couldn't read her thoughts. "So you think this Avery guy's chauffeur broke into your hotel?"

"I'm not absolutely sure, but yes, I think so. What I don't know is whether Troy knew. And if so, did he put the guy up to it? I mean, why would he want to steal it if he thought it was a fake?"

"Two possibilities. One is that he told you it was a fake so he could buy it from you cheap and then auction it off as his own fantastic find. The other is that it really is a fake, but that he was hoping to pawn it off on someone gullible he knew from Avery's. There's a lot of people who would be willing to pay a fortune to own a secret Vermeer, even if they could never show it to another soul."

"You're forgetting a third possibility. What if the chauffeur got the idea himself? After all, he heard us talking about the painting and he knew exactly where I was staying."

"But where does this Karl guy come into the whole thing? Do you think he kidnapped Charlie?"

"I know he was in our house. No one else has feet that big." Their waiter was busy telling a joke to the busboy, so she risked taking a sip of wine from Dante's glass. She wasn't up to listening to any lectures about endangering the health of her imaginary unborn baby.

"Which probably makes him the one who searched your house."

"But what about Charlie?" Claire pressed her fingertips against her closed eyes. "She's seventy-eight years old! She only weighs about ninety pounds. I don't even hug her hard. This guy's so much bigger—he could hurt her without even meaning to." Her fingers pressed harder. Bursts of red and orange light exploded behind her eyelids. She dropped her hands to the table, and Dante reached out and covered one briefly with his own.

"But you didn't see any sign that she'd been hurt, did you? Maybe she's hiding just like you are. She came home, saw what had happened and took off. With her history she probably doesn't trust police too much. And even if this guy Karl *did* kidnap her, I think he'd keep her safe. He knows she's the one sure way to get to you."

Claire felt a little better. "I'm just afraid he killed her. I couldn't stand it if she were dead."

"I don't mean to be blunt, but if she were dead, wouldn't he have left her body there? After all, he didn't mind attracting a lot of attention when he killed your neighbor."

"So you think Karl's the one who did that?"

"He seems a pretty likely suspect. Or maybe that guy Paul who told you he was a cop." Dante had asked if they should call in the local police, but Claire was too frightened, and he didn't push it. She remembered Paul Roberts's engraved badge and the police light on the dash of his car. What if he really were a cop, bought off by someone who knew about the painting? Claire took a deep breath and explained where she had hidden the painting. Dante's next suggestion was that they retrieve the painting and fly back to New York, where there were international art experts as well as a police force more experienced in dealing with art crimes.

"There's one thing I don't understand about what happened to my neighbor," Claire said. "To Sonia. If they thought she was me, why weren't they worried about blowing up the painting, too?"

"I'll have to admit I don't understand that either." Dante tilted his head back to drain the last of the wine. His white shirt was open at the neck, and Claire watched the muscles move in the column of his throat. A tuft of wiry hair was just visible at the base. She tried to ignore the wave of heat that ran from her breasts to her belly.

"What do you think we should do next?

Claire liked the way he said "we." It made her feel less alone. "I wish I knew if the painting were real or not. If it were a fake, I might just be tempted to burn it."

Dante set his glass down hard. "Burn it! Why?"

In quick succession, Claire saw Charlie's face, the hotel maid's frightened eyes, Sonia's hand raised in greeting. "So much evil is being done to try to get it."

"But if it is real, you can't destroy it. And I think it is very real. Remember those photos I took? I've carried them with me ever since." He reached for his satchel and took out a manila envelope.

Inside were the color photographs he had shown her earlier. He ran the tip of his index finger over the curve of the woman's cheek. "There were dozens of Dutch genre painters, but a woman in a Vermeer painting is something extraordinary. Cool, remote and absolutely beautiful."

"Like a still life. That's what you said when we first met."

"You remember that?" He gave her a surprised look that lengthened into a smile. "And it's more than just a feeling. I told you that a Vermeer matching this description was sold at the famous Dissius auction three hundred years ago. There are stories that it turned up later with a French king's mistress, that a Hapsburg duke lost it at a gaming table. But there's a few more things I'd like to check on." His next question surprised her. "Does your office building have any other tenants besides the state of Oregon?"

"The state doesn't own it. We just rent space there."

"What do the other tenants do?"

"There's a law firm and a temp agency and a building contractor—"

Dante interrupted her list. "Any kind of doctor?"

"There's a clinic on sixteen. They have about five or six doctors, but I'm not sure what they specialize in. I was only up there once when I closed my finger in a filing cabinet and I thought it might be broken. They X-rayed it and said—"

He interrupted her again. "Would that magic card of yours get us in there?"

"The one that really belongs to the security guard? I don't know. It might. Why?"

"I've been thinking about another way we could tell if what you have is a Vermeer. But to do it, I need an X-ray machine."

KPASAMD

൭൭

For dessert, the waiter brought her a slice of chocolate–peanut butter pie with a single candle flickering in it. She realized she had told Dante it was her birthday when she talked about what had happened that morning. His dark eyes reflecting the flame of the candle, Dante told her to make a wish. There were so many things to wish for. Claire tried to cover all the bases by closing her eyes and wishing simply that everything would turn out all right.

They dawdled over dessert and then several cups of coffee until the waiter simply left them alone, having given up all hope of turning their table. While Dante paid the bill, Claire called her mom from the pay phone to let her know that she was all right. Jean reported that she had hung up on an *Oregonian* reporter and turned another away at the door. When Jean began to worry about whether Claire would be safe, she finally reassured her that she was going to her own building, which Jean knew was accessible only by card key.

Claire and Dante got to the building's parking lot at 7:30 P.M., just as the last car was leaving, and walked down the parking garage stairs to the basement entrance. After hours, the basement door opened only to card key holders, so it was a good way to test—without witnesses—whether the twice-stolen card still worked. It did. They took the elevator straight from the basement to the thirteenth floor, bypassing the front desk entirely. The pillow was still strapped across Claire's belly and Dante pushed the stroller. She figured that if they were challenged, the props might provide a precious moment or two of confusion.

Their luck held on Claire's floor. Her cubicle was still half-decorated for the birthday party that had never happened. A single jelly-filled donut had even survived Frank's assault on the Winchells box, and Claire ate it while Dante retrieved the painting.

When he climbed down to stand beside her, the bubble-wrapped painting in his hands, she noticed how his breathing had quickened more than could be expected from a climb on and off a desktop.

Dante's fingers hovered over the tape. "Mind if I take another look?" he asked. Claire nodded. Standing so close, she noticed he smelled like cinnamon. He slid the painting out. For a long moment, they both stared at the woman, caught in a moment in time, with her wide eyes and slightly parted lips. In turn, she regarded them without surprise.

"Whoever painted this knew the secret of light, didn't he?" said Dante, breaking the silence. "Look at how the light flows into this room and creates a dozen different shades of every color it touches. Even the shadows are rich with colors."

"Did you notice she doesn't have a shadow? Charlie pointed that out to me."

"She's got a good eye. The best painters make you think you're looking at reality by showing you something completely different."

"Are you one of the best painters? Someday I'd like to see your work."

An expression she couldn't translate crossed Dante's face. "I'm afraid you'd probably be disappointed." He turned away from her and delicately slid the painting back into the bubble wrap.

Claire's stolen key card again worked its magic on the clinic's door. They took a quick walk around the office, which was laid out for maximum efficiency. A central nursing station was surrounded by four exam rooms, each barely big enough for an examining table, a stool, and a countertop with sink. Behind the receptionist's desk were a couple of physician's offices, each with two desks. A third room held the X-ray machine, which was mounted on a movable arm attached to the ceiling. Dante raised and lowered it, a thoughtful expression on his face. Then he went back into the reception area and retrieved his satchel from underneath the stroller.

He began to lay out a series of tools in a neat row on the receptionist's desk. There was a black headpiece with magnifying lenses, a roll of white cotton wrapped in paper, some orange sticks, a sheaf of white heavy paper, a stoppered bottle of red-tinged fluid, and what Claire guessed was a scalpel. "I brought some things with me that might help me figure out what we're looking at."

"You mean whether it's real or not?"

"It may not be that simple. In real life, there are a lot more shades of gray than there are blacks and whites. Say this really is a Vermeer, or at least it began life that way. Any three-hundred-and-fifty-year-old painting will have changed since it left the artist's easel. The question is—how much repainting has to take place before it is no longer a Vermeer?" From the satchel, he took a black case not much bigger than his palm. "So this could be a Vermeer. Or it could be a Vermeer that has been so heavily repainted that it really isn't much of a Vermeer at all anymore. Or it could be a painting by someone else who was painting at the same time as Vermeer. Or it could be an out-and-out forgery painted last week."

Dante opened the carrying case, revealing a small portable light. "In some ways, we have it easy. If this were a possible Rembrandt, it would be even more complicated. Rembrandt ran a painting school, and as part of their training, his students used to copy his paintings, or paint their own works in his style. That means there are literally hundreds of paintings floating around that are the right age, done on the right kind of canvas with the right paints in the right style. They're just not Rembrandts. And to make it even more complicated, Rembrandt used to make corrections directly on his students' work, showing them how he would do it. So some paintings might be ninety percent student and ten percent Rembrandt. And if a student's painting was really good, Rembrandt might just sign it himself."

"So how can anyone even tell if a painting is a Rembrandt or not?"

"Sometimes even the experts don't know. Still, everyone agrees there are hundreds of real Rembrandts. But there are only thirty-two undisputed Vermeers, with maybe another dozen arguables. Some of those may have something in common with Rembrandt's work. After he died, people forged his signature on paintings that weren't his but might have been. Not only is it a lot easier to fake a signature than a whole painting, it's also a hell of a lot harder to detect."

Claire remembered how closely both Troy and Dante had examined the painting. "But there isn't a signature."

"That's one thing that makes me think this may really be a Vermeer. If you had created a forged Vermeer, you'd want the whole world to realize it."

Dante plugged in his portable lamp and turned off the overhead light. They were left with a single narrow focused beam of light. He propped the painting on a thick copy of *Physicians' Desk Reference*, and then dropped to his knees and began to inspect it from below, holding the light nearly parallel to the surface.

"What is that?" Claire knew there was no need to whisper, but it seemed natural in the darkness.

"It's called a raking light."

Some parts of the painting stood out in high relief, while others fell in dark shadows. The fine cracks that glazed the painting now appeared as deep canyons. It reminded Claire of photographs of the moon, with their revelations of mountains, ridges and craters. "What are you looking for?"

"With a raking light, you see not only the damage, but you can also spot any overpainting."

"You mean things the artist changed?"

"Sometimes. Or a new owner might decide to change something to suit him. Three hundred years ago a painting was just part of the household furnishings. They weren't treated as valuable museum pieces. People might cut one up to fit a new frame or have someone repaint a face to match their daughter's. The raking light helps you see stuff the original painter didn't do. And that guy from Avery's was right, the upper right-hand corner has been repainted. I also see some other raised areas. Not too many, though. Probably just touchups where there was a little rubbing over the years. And I think some of the highlights have been redone. But on the whole the paint layer is in very good condition."

"But there are so many cracks," Claire protested. "Are there supposed to be that many?"

"If you were three hundred and fifty years old, you'd have a lot of cracks, too. And luckily the suitcase under your great-aunt's bed must not have been near a heating vent. Fifty years in a more or less climate-controlled environment. It's the pattern of the cracks that I'm interested in."

"The pattern?" Claire echoed.

"I did some research into your Troy's theory that this is a fake by Van Meegeren."

Claire wanted to protest that he wasn't "her" Troy, but she let Dante continue.

"He faked his cracks by baking his paintings in a two-hundred-degree oven. Then to crack them even more, he wrapped them around a cylinder and pressed on them with his thumb. The only problem is that this resulted in very regular cracks, more like a grid."

Claire took a closer look, not at the cracks themselves, but at the pattern they made. If anything, they were like spiderwebs. "So this isn't one of Van Meegeren's forgeries, then?"

"I can't say for certain. He got better at removing the paint but leaving on the old ground. Then he'd coax the old cracks to come up through the new paint." Dante turned his face to her, the light hollowing out his cheekbones and eye sockets. "Despite what that guy from Avery's says, I still don't think this painting is a forgery. But even though it seems real, it still might be a fake."

"Aren't they the same?"

"A forgery is something done on purpose—for example, if your friend is right and this was painted to look like a Vermeer, doctored to make it look old, and then palmed off as the real thing. A fake, on the other hand, is something that didn't begin life as an imitation Vermeer, but somehow became that.

"Every couple of years, an 'unknown masterpiece' pops up on the art markets. It's either snatched up by some eager collector, or an art expert like that guy at Avery's denounces it. The auction house withdraws it and makes a lot of noise about how sorry it is. Then a year or two later, the same painting resurfaces, usually in another part of the United States, sometimes in another country altogether."

"Isn't that illegal? Selling something that has already been proven false?"

Dante shook his head. "Fakes and even forgeries, in and of themselves, aren't illegal. You can copy all the old masterpieces you want, age them artificially so they look old, even sign a famous painter's name to them. You can even tell your friends that they are the real thing. All that *is* legal. The only thing that isn't is to sell them as the real thing. So prudent forgers or people who own forgeries don't sell them on the open market. There are enough rich and gullible collectors who are willing to buy gray-market art, especially if they think they're getting a bargain."

He pulled on a pair of white cotton gloves. "I'm going to remove some of the surface dirt and then clean up her jacket. It will give us an idea of the color in the light areas and the gorgeous depth of the blacks." He picked up the stoppered glass bottle filled with red-tinged fluid.

"What's that?"

"It's a very diluted synthetic solvent mixed with a little turpentine. It will take off the dirt and any old retouches, and then get us down to the varnish."

By rolling a piece of cotton onto an orange stick, Dante created what looked like an outsize Q-Tip. He dipped it into the solvent, then tapped off the excess. With the utmost delicacy, he used his thumb and forefinger to roll the swab gently over the spotted fur that trimmed the woman's jacket. He worked for about ten minutes, changing swabs twice, before breaking the silence.

"What if I'm wrong and that Avery's guy is right? If this painting turned out to be a forgery, how would you feel? Would you like it less?"

"The first thing I thought when I found it was how beautiful it was."

"And would that beauty be gone if you found out that someone painted it fifty years ago instead of three hundred and fifty? It would still be the same painting."

"But somehow it wouldn't be same," Claire answered slowly. "It wouldn't be a painting Vermeer had created of someone he loved. It would be completely different, a deception by someone who only wanted to make money."

"Vermeer probably painted to make a living, too, even if he wasn't successful. And if the painting itself hasn't changed, isn't it still beautiful? Even if it's not a Vermeer?"

It was hard for Claire to explain what she felt. "In the past week I've learned a lot about Vermeer—mostly thanks to you—and that has made this even more beautiful than when I first saw it. When I hold it in my hands, I think, three hundred and fifty years ago Vermeer was doing the very same thing. But if it's not a Vermeer, then there's no link to his past."

Claire had been watching Dante's rapt face and not what he was doing. When she dropped her gaze to his work, she saw that the dozens of utterly delicate passes were beginning to have an effect. The rich colors and cut of the woman's costume were emerging. Claire could almost feel the plush black-spotted white fur between her fingers.

He created another swab and began to roll it delicately over the woman's face. Her skin grew milkier, her large eyes a brighter blue.

"Take a look at her mouth." Dante handed her the headpiece and she slipped it on. "What do you see on either side?"

Without magnification, the mind's eye filled in what was missing or worn, saw the loveliness of the young woman's expression without noting the tiny patch of missing paint on her cheek. Magnified, the painting was an altogether different creature, and far more fragile. At first all Claire saw was rivulets of cracks running through tiny lozenges of paint. Then she began to see the image again. "They look like . . . little dots of pink paint."

"Don't they make her mouth look juicy? Whoever painted this certainly knew what he was doing." Dante put his homemade Q-Tip down and picked up the painting. "Maybe I'm just biased, but it seems like something Vermeer would do. He was obsessed with light, and that includes his approach to painting highlights."

"Circles of confusion," Claire said.

"That's right." He smiled at her, clearly pleased that she had again remembered something he had said. "Now there's one more test we can do to see if this might be a Vermeer." He picked up the painting and carried it back to the room that held the X-ray machine, with Claire following.

"See if you can find where they keep the X-ray film." She finally located it in a flat storage case behind the shield that would protect the X-ray tech. "Now put it down on the exam table." Dante turned the painting upside down and carefully lowered it into place until it lay directly on the film. He positioned the X-ray machine a few inches above the painting, then took Claire's elbow and pulled her behind the shield. When he pressed the button, the warning buzzer made Claire jump, and he slid his hand up and down her arm reassuringly.

"How did you know what to do?" Claire asked.

"Graduate students specialize in learning things that will never be useful in real life. I actually learned how to X-ray paintings at school."

It took only a minute for Dante to run the film through the automatic developer. The X-ray image looked familiar and strange at the same time, the same painting rendered with a new palette that reflected thickness rather than color. Dante showed her how the film registered varying shades of gray as the paint decreased in thickness and tapered off into shadows. Claire's eyes began to pick out the differences between what she could see on the surface of the painting and the different truth the X ray revealed.

"There are some paint losses here," Dante said, pointing at a dark shadow revealed just beneath the woman's hands. "And these light gray spots in the highlights of her hair and on the brass bowl show where he laid the paint down thick." He pointed at the wall behind the woman's shoulders, the wall that had previously been bare. "What do you see there?"

"It looks like the corner of a painting. A painting within a painting." Claire brought her face closer to the X ray. If she squinted, she could just make out the outlines of a plump leg and a fallen arrow. "But I'm not sure what it is. Maybe a fat little leg and an arrow?"

She started when Dante let out a jubilant shout. "I know what it is. That's got to be Cupid! This really could be a Vermeer! He always made changes to the underlayers, and it would be just like him to paint out something he thought was too obvious."

"Like Cupid?" Claire asked.

"Like Cupid. It would spell out that the woman was in love, that she was holding a letter from her lover, and probably Vermeer decided he didn't want his audience to know even that much." Dante turned his attention to the bottom edge of the X ray, which was almost translucent. "You know what the other thing I notice is? This looks like a double thickness of canvas here. I think part of this painting has been folded up."

He had already picked up the painting again, and now he ran his thumb over the frame. "After looking at that X ray, I'm guessing this frame is old, but probably not original." He turned it over. Affixed to the covered back of the painting was a single rusted ring, about an inch wide. The back itself was pale gray, worn rough in places, smooth in others, the edges dark and grimy from years of being handled. He took the painting back to the tools lined up on the receptionist's desk, picked up a penknife, and set to work. Finally, with a little *pop,* the bottom edge of the frame came loose, accompanied by a puff of dust.

A piece of paper fluttered to the ground from inside the frame, and Claire bent over to pick it up. It was about two inches tall and three inches long, as soft as cotton, imprinted with the face of a stern-looking man with a long nose and a hat in a style no one had worn for centuries. Her heart began to race.

"Look, Dante. I think this is money. Old money."

Dante answered absently as he took the painting from its frame and laid it on one of the sheets of white paper. "People used to use the space between the stretcher and the canvas to hide things. Love letters, keys, rings. And money." His white-gloved fingers gently exposed the bottom edge of the painting, which, Claire saw, had indeed been doubled back. The newly revealed piece didn't show anything exciting, though. It was simply the bottom edge of the carpet-covered table.

"Someone must have decided to use this frame, but the painting didn't quite fit. I'm not going to unfold this all the way. If I do it will crack like crazy. I just want to look at it for a second." He slipped on the magnifying headpiece.

"What are you looking for?"

"A signature. Not that Vermeer always signed a work. There are a few pieces we are nearly a hundred percent certain are his, yet they're not signed."

"But if—" Claire started to say, but Dante held up his hand.

He was silent for a long time, then he slipped off the headpiece and handed it to Claire, his fingers trembling as they brushed against her hand.

"What do you see there? Just at the edge of the table."

And then Claire saw what had caused Dante's fingers to tremble. A monogram, elaborate curlicues that formed two letters nearly lost in the painted shadows.

"It looks like an N and an M. What would that mean?"

There was a pause before he answered her. "Nicolaes Maes."

All the breath left Claire's body. "So it's not a Vermeer, then?"

Dante didn't answer, just took the magnifier back from her and slipped it on.

"Who's Nicolaes Maes?"

"He painted at the same time as Vermeer. And they both did a lot of genre painting. And for a long time, his paintings were very popular. Two hundred years ago, a Maes was far more valuable than Vermeer. Same with Terborch or Metsu. But tastes change. Now people think only of Vermeer, and Maes is forgotten."

He dipped the Q-Tip in the cleaning solution again, only this time he ran it gently over the painted flowers made of tufts of carpet. Right over the spot where Nicolaes Maes's monogram had been painted. Claire could pick it out now without the magnifier. But the N was already dissolving. And while the M held fast, above it appeared a single straight line ending just above the downward V of the M.

"What does that mean?"

"He rarely signed his paintings the same way twice. I've seen this in another of his paintings, a signature where he played with the shapes of the letters. The Meer with a vertical line above the V of the M, suggesting both the V and the J."

"Then Nicolaes Maes didn't paint this?" Claire was too stunned by the events of the last few moments to know what to think.

"Vermeer used to be the name you replaced if you wanted to get a good price. Of course, if whoever did this was alive today, he'd be too busy painting IV Meer on every halfway decent mid-seventeenth-century Dutch genre painting he could find."

"So," Claire said, taking a deep breath and finding there wasn't enough air in the room, "this really is a Vermeer. A lost Vermeer."

Instead of answering her, Dante put down his swab, slipped off his magnifier and put his hand behind her head. He brought his lips to her mouth, sealing up all the questions that had crowded into her mind.

FX108

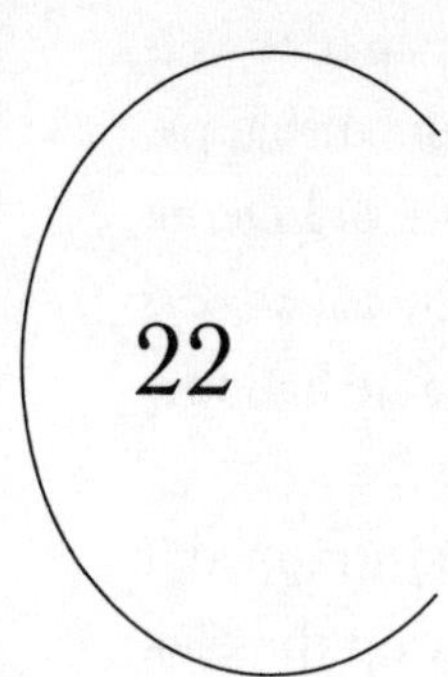

22

With her fingers, Claire combed her hair into place, thinking that short hair did have its advantages. In the mirror just above the metal shelf for urine specimens, her own reflection gazed back at her, eyes wide, lips swollen from kissing. She pushed one last curl into place, then opened the door to the bathroom. Trying to hold her stomach in without being obvious, she walked back into the reception area wearing only a smile. Dante greeted her with a kiss on the tip of the nose.

"Hi."

"Hi."

She felt shy, conscious of their naked bodies, her pale, nearly translucent skin a contrast to his swarthiness. Dante had already put his tools back in his satchel, and now she watched as he slid the bubble-wrapped painting in after them. He gave her another kiss before he, too, went into the bathroom.

Claire went into the exam room where their clothes littered the floor and sat down on the edge of the brown vinyl exam table. In a theoretical way, she knew she must be tired, but instead she felt relaxed, with a subterranean hum of energy.

She could hear him splashing in the tiny bathroom as he tried to replicate the effects of a shower with only a fistful of paper towels and a bottle of hand soap at his disposal. He didn't seem unhappy, though. He was half-singing, half-humming "Layla," the old Derek and the Dominoes song. *"What'll you do when you get lonely, and nobody's waiting by your side? . . ."* His clear baritone trailed off where he had forgotten a word or two.

Claire slid to the floor, cast around for her watch and strapped it on her wrist. She pressed the button on the side to light up the dial. Two in the morning. They would clean up here and then head straight to the airport to take the first available flight to New York. Should she wear her pregnant clothes or the outfit Susie had loaned her? While neither choice was appealing, the maternity smock had the advantage of serving, if necessary, as a semi-disguise while they left the building. She resolved to buy new clothes in the airport, even if she ended up in New York wearing a MY GRANDPA WENT TO PORTLAND, OREGON, AND ALL HE GOT ME WAS THIS LOUSY T-SHIRT T-shirt.

Her clothes lay mingled with Dante's, and the sight of their pantlegs intertwined made Claire smile. While she was pulling her own pants free, Dante's wallet fell out of the back pocket of his Levi's. She paused for a second, listening. The water was still running and Dante was still singing. *"Darling, won't you ease my worried mind . . ."* One little peek wouldn't hurt. Did he have a library card? An old girlfriend's phone number? She walked to the light of the doorway and flipped it open.

Her heart made a terrible twist in her chest. In the very first vinyl window was a photo of Dante and another woman. If that was all it had been, Claire could have accepted it. After all, he had had a life before her, just as she had. But this photo showed a Dante she had never seen, his hair combed back into a ponytail, formally dressed in a black tuxedo, the dazzling white of his shirt punctuated by black studs. His head was turned slightly as he looked at something off-camera, and his arms lay loose around a woman's waist, her hands clasped in his. Her wide-spaced blue eyes looked directly at the viewer. In any other circumstances, Claire would have liked the woman's confident grin, but not now, not when its blond-haired owner's face was framed by a wedding veil.

All the blood rushed to Claire's own face. She had been so stupid! If people had been willing to kill her to get their hands on a twenty-million-dollar painting, would it be so hard to sleep with her? Dante had gotten her right where he wanted her, had even managed to assure himself of the painting's value. And now the painting rested in his satchel. She wondered where he planned on leaving her. Outside the building? In the airport?

Only a few seconds had passed, but everything had changed. Claire quickly shuffled through the rest of the contents of his wallet, trying to figure out what other lies he had told her. Her fingers found his driver's license. Dante Bonner was really his name, he was the age he had told her, his hair and eye color weren't the result of dyes or tinted lenses. He had two Visa cards, a Chevron gas card, an AT&T calling card, a three-quarters-filled card that would eventually entitle him to a free book at a bookstore in Greenwich Village. And he had money—two $1 bills, one $5, nine $20s, three $50s and a $100.

He also had a scrap of paper pushed to the very bottom of the bill compartment. All doubts that she might have been jumping to conclusions vanished. It seemed to be notes from a telephone conversation, block printing on a torn piece of yellow lined paper. Reading it, Claire felt a snake uncoil in her belly. *"IFAR has no records, thus prob. of living claimant slim. . . . highly collectible, highly portable . . . easily worth $25 mil +. . . . buy w/no provenance & no proof of ownership?"*

Claire returned Dante's wallet to his pants, but kept the piece of paper. By the time he knew it was missing she intended to be long gone. Moving quickly, she went into the next room and transferred the painting from his satchel to her backpack. Then she went back into the X-ray room and pulled on her pants, slipped on her shoes. Since her maternity outfit lacked anything as practical as a pocket, after she got dressed she tucked the note in her bra. Over the drone of the wind outside, she became aware of the sound of her own breathing, shallow and fast, with a little moan at the end of every exhalation.

The water was no longer running in the bathroom. *"Like a fool, still in love with you. You've got my whole world upside down."* Dante was moving around, wiping away the traces of his having been there. He probably wished he could do the same thing with her, make it be so that she would forget all about his existence. No wonder he had so easily speculated about Troy's intentions—he had already thought it all through himself. Was he planning on flying to Europe, where he could sell the painting clandestinely through a disreputable dealer in a former Communist country? Or did he already have a buyer lined up in the United States, a collector with lots of money made in the stock market or software, who wouldn't question too closely where such a beauty had come from?

Claire walked over to the window, ready, when the bathroom door opened, to pretend she was admiring the lights of the city. A good poker face had never been one of her strengths.

Outside, the streetlights revealed a world in motion. The awnings of the conference center across the street flapped in the wind. The black branches of the trees that bordered the parking lot lashed the pavement like whips. The window itself hummed with the wind, which was like the roar of a vacuum cleaner that occasionally sputtered and then surged to life again.

Although it was the middle of the night, the streets weren't deserted. There were a few cars driving down Martin Luther King Jr. Boulevard, and even a man standing under a streetlight in front of the shuttered Burgerville across the street. A man holding binoculars to his face as he scanned both entrances to the building.

When he took the binoculars away from his eyes, even from sixteen stories up and half a block away, Claire recognized him immediately.

Troy.

Troy Nowell. Well. The man who had told her her painting was worth nothing must have changed his mind in a big way, enough to make him eager to track her down. The wind couldn't ruffle Troy's close-cropped hair, but it had turned his buttoned-up trenchcoat into a sail.

The door to the bathroom opened, and Dante came out, wearing only a pair of black briefs. The dark hair on his chest was in the rough shape of a butterfly. *"Layla, you got me on my knees, Layla, I'm begging darling, please . . ."* He stopped singing when he saw Claire's face. "What's the matter?"

At least now Claire had an answer for him. She pointed out the window.

It was, Dante argued, unsafe to leave the building while Troy was watching. They would wait until morning, then mingle with the office workers and slip away. Claire privately decided that might be a good time to lose Dante, too, in a place where she knew every street and alley. While he sketched out his plan, Dante's hands kept touching Claire, stroking her shoulder, patting her knee, combing an errant curl out of her eyes. At one point he even leaned over to kiss her cheek, and Claire couldn't help but think of Judas. How could Dante betray her with such ease?

"You're being awfully quiet."

Claire offered him the smallest possible smile, then walked into the reception area. Without warning, it felt as if the world was falling away from under her feet. Her stomach lurched, and she reached out to grab the edge of the receptionist's desk. "Do you feel that?"

"What?"

"The building. It's moving. I can feel it swaying under my feet."

Dante nodded, seemingly unfazed. "Tall buildings are designed to do that. I read someplace that the average skyscraper can move eight feet in any direction."

Claire felt sick. Now that she knew the building really *was* moving, the swaying seemed more pronounced. She wanted to be back on solid ground. To avoid making conversation with Dante, she snapped on the radio that sat on the receptionist's desk, twisting the dial until she picked up KXL.

After a few minutes of sports talk, the weather report came on.

"The time is two twenty-eight, twenty-eight past two. Repeating our top local story: the National Weather Service has issued a high wind warning for the Willamette Valley. The storm is scheduled to set down here sometime in the next two hours. It has already hit Newport, and our reporter, Bob LeBart, is on the line. Bob, what can you tell us?"

"Well, Diane, it's a pretty amazing sight. I went outside a few minutes ago and could barely stay on my feet. We can all be very thankful that this storm has hit in the middle of the night, when most people are at home asleep. Otherwise it might be far more serious. We've just had a report that a metal roof was lifted right off a Shari's restaurant, but we don't know if anyone was hurt. So many telephone lines are down that it may take some time before we really know the extent of any damages. One thing is sure, though—there will be plenty of property damage. And as soon as more information is available, we'll bring you an update. This is Bob LeBart in Newport, Oregon."

"And this is Diane Harburg in the KXL studio. In Portland, forecasters are telling us they can't exactly predict whether the storm will pack the same punch as it has in Newport. If it does, we may be looking at something the size of the famous Columbus Day storm—" Claire snapped off the radio. She didn't want to be reminded of the day she was born. Here she was, thirty-five years old, and she still couldn't judge men.

Dante patted the exam room table. "Why don't you come over here for a second."

"I don't know about you, but I need to sleep." Her words were curter than she had intended. Did her voice betray her new knowledge?

"Then I'll make us up a little bed." He rummaged in the cupboard and came up with a couple of modesty drapes, which were like undersized sheets. "And I'll behave like a perfect gentleman. I'd love to watch you sleeping."

It was Dante who slept, however, and Claire who watched. They slept in the X-ray room, which offered the widest exam table, but it was still so narrow that they were forced to nest together like two commas. Claire tried to will herself to relax so that Dante wouldn't feel her tension. Against the cage of her ribs, she felt the slow beat of his traitor's heart. After she heard Dante's breathing slow and deepen, Claire raised herself up on one elbow and looked at him for a long moment. His generous mouth was slack and vulnerable, the bridge of his nose more prominent with his dark eyes shuttered. Even from a few inches away, Claire found herself observing Dante as if from a great distance. He was still a beautiful man, but she told herself that his beauty no longer had the power to reach her.

What plans did Dante have for her? Wouldn't it be a lot simpler to have her out of the picture altogether, no inconvenient woman coming forward with tales of how a painting should really be hers, some blabbermouth who might make even a secretive collector reconsider? Could he be thinking of silencing her forever? And what part had he played in the death, destruction and disappearances that had haunted her since she opened that suitcase? As she watched

Dante's seemingly open face, the building groaned and swayed under them like an old ship on rough seas.

∾

"Claire!"

The sound broke through the skin of Claire's restless sleep.

"Clai—!" The voice was abruptly muffled, but Claire had heard enough to know whose it was. Charlie, with her characteristic rolled *r* that turned her name from something plain into something exotic.

Dante laid a cautioning hand on her arm as she started to get up. "Wait!" he hissed in her ear. "It might be a—"

Claire shook his hand free and got to her feet. "Charlie!" She ran into the next room, not thinking, only knowing that her darkest fears were evaporating as quickly as her fragmented dreams. Charlie was alive!

She stopped short. There was Charlie, but Paul Roberts's hand muffled her mouth. When he saw Claire, he looped his arm around Charlie's neck in a parody of friendliness, grinning humorlessly. On Charlie's other side stood Karl Zehner, his gun drawn.

"Claire, don't come out." Charlie finished her sentence almost under her breath. She wore what appeared to be a large man's white T-shirt that billowed around her knees. On her feet were her trademark pink tennis shoes, now smudged and dirty.

Paul's eyes took in the stroller and Claire's maternity top, slack without her strap-on belly. He waved his finger in mock admonishment. "One baby and another on the way—haven't you heard about overpopulation?" The smile fell from his face. He turned to Karl and held out his hand for the gun. "Tie them up." Where was Dante, Claire wondered. And then hoped that he had sense enough to stay put in the unlit X-ray room. He might have been planning to steal the painting from her, but at least he had never pointed a gun in her direction.

Karl pushed Claire into a faded orange waiting room chair. While he used the flat cord from one of the telephones to tie her hands behind her back, Claire kept her eyes on Charlie. "Are you okay?" Her friend's face was pale and pleated with tiredness, but Claire couldn't see any bruises or other marks on her body.

"I'm surviving." There was the ghost of a smile on Charlie's lips. It disappeared when Karl jerked her hands behind her and began to lash them together.

Claire's eyes swung between the two men. "So you two work together?"

Paul answered for them both. "He works for me."

Karl made one last knot, then stood up and took the gun back from Paul. He gestured in Claire's direction. "We will ask the questions. Where is the painting?"

"In a locker at the airport." Claire tried to sound as if she meant it.

"No, it isn't. You were watched there. And we have searched your house—twice. So tell me where the painting is, unless you would like to see your friend die now."

He pressed the gun against Charlie's temple, hard enough that Claire saw the skin dimple. Her friend's faded blue eyes regarded her calmly. Outside the flags cracked in the wind.

Claire's decision had been made for her the moment she saw Charlie was still alive. "You don't have to make threats." With her chin, she motioned at the stroller behind the two men. "It's in that bag."

Smiling a cat's feral grin, Paul delicately slid out the painting and weighed it on his fingertips. "Twenty million dollars, and it doesn't weigh over three pounds." Overhead, the lights flickered and dimmed. Looking down, he addressed himself to the painted woman, still cushioned by her protective wrapper. "You're just as beautiful as I thought you would be." His eyes didn't move, but his next words were for Claire. "Bubble wrap. I'll have to remember that the next time I transport a painting."

"The next time you transport a painting?" Claire echoed. "Then I take it you're not a cop."

"No." He looked up and then smiled, dangerously playful. "And my name isn't Paul Roberts. My real name is Rudy Miller."

"You—you're alive!" The room reeled. She remembered the man whose photos had decorated her aunt's mirror. That was where she had seen those quicksilver eyes before. In fifty years, Rudy Miller hadn't changed.

All playfulness vanished. He took a half-step toward Claire. "You know who I am?"

"Cady wrote about you. In her diary."

"That woman kept a diary!" His mouth tightened. "Grandpa should never have taken up with that stupid bitch."

"Grandpa." Claire blinked. "Then you're—"

"Rudy Miller." He lifted his chin, making the resemblance even more pronounced. "The Third."

"Is your grandfather still alive?" She tried to imagine what the man before her might look like in half a century.

Rudy shook his head. "Dead for six years. He was a smart man, my grandfather." His voice warmed into boastfulness. "No education, but he knew something beautiful when he saw it. He liberated a king's ransom and sent it home wrapped in plain brown paper, courtesy of the U.S. Army Post. But after the war ended he saw which way the wind was blowing. The Germans were becoming friends with the Americans again. Jews were in power all through this country. People began to ask what had happened to certain collections that had gone missing during the war."

Understanding broke. "That's why my neighbor was killed. You didn't care if you blew up the painting, too. It was more important to you that no one question its source."

To her surprise, Rudy shook his head. "Don't lay that at my feet. It's been years since anyone really cared. That was all *his* doing." He gestured with his chin at Karl, whose face reddened. "And he was acting without orders. He was supposed to get the painting back, not destroy it."

The big man protested, "You said you didn't want anyone to know! You didn't want anyone to start asking questions!"

"Only because I wanted a chance to get the painting back before anyone knew what it was. You were supposed to get it from the old lady's trailer, but you screwed up and got there too late. I never told you to blow up a twenty-million-dollar painting. You thought up that clever twist all on your own."

Claire interrupted their bickering. "But won't a potential buyer care if the painting was stolen by the Nazis?" Then Charlie bandaged Claire's chafed wrists.

"My grandfather said that the more time passed, the less people asked about where things had come from. If he'd waited a few more years, he probably could have stayed right in the U.S., instead of moving to Argentina."

Now Claire understood Rudy's precise, colorless speech. The perfect uninflected command of English that only a non-native speaker possessed. "And everything originally came out of that warehouse he was supposed to be guarding?"

"Who did all that belong to? No one. At least not any longer. The only reason the United States had it was because they had won. Do you think they took everything from that warehouse and gave it back to its original owners?" He snorted in derision. "Go look in any museum and ask yourself where the paintings on its walls came from. The Louvre has dozens of paintings acquired courtesy of the Nazis, and they are not working too hard to find out who used to own them. The greatest galleries and auction houses in the world sell art taken during the war. Some even note it on the provenance. After all, what does it matter who owned something two generations ago? What is it they say here? Possession is nine-tenths of the law?"

"So if you don't care if people know your grandfather stole a bunch of paintings from the Nazis, why are you so eager to get this one back?"

Rudy's laugh sent a chill sliding down Claire's spine. "Still determined to play the innocent, are you? My grandfather was not an educated man, but he liked beautiful things. In Germany, he bought 'degenerate' modern paintings the Nazis despised for a few marks. Twenty years later he sold them for millions. In the eighties, he sold Impressionists to the Japanese before the market bottomed out. And as he learned more about paintings, he realized what he had lost." He turned the painting to face them, resting the top edge against his chest. Claire stared at the woman's image through the bubble wrap and wondered if this was the strangest scene she had witnessed in the last three hundred and fifty years. "He had *given* your aunt a *Vermeer*, when there are only thirty-two others in the whole world. He even wrote to her, offered to buy the painting back—and he was the one who had given it to her in the first place. She refused. But even though he knew how much it was worth, he was a fool. He refused to take it from her, made me swear that I wouldn't either." A bemused expression crossed Rudy's face, and Claire realized that he had actually loved his grandfather. "But I never promised that things wouldn't change once she was dead. I sent Karl to retrieve it, but he botched it. And by the time I came up here, you were gone. I figured we could trade your roommate for the painting."

"But how did you figure out where I"—Claire almost slipped and said *we*—"was tonight?"

"You probably thought you were so smart—taking the same ID

card from Karl that he had taken from the guard. Instead it just led me straight to you. When I flashed my policeman's badge at the security guy out front and told him I was investigating this morning's incident, he was more than willing to let me look at his computer. And that led me straight to you."

"So now what happens?" Claire asked.

Karl answered, "We kill you, of course."

Rudy shook his head and laughed. "Of course we do not kill them, Karl." He set the painting down on the desk. "We leave them tied up here. By the time someone comes into this office, we will be out of the country. We got what we wanted—and we do not need any more trouble. Two more deaths will just make the police more eager to find us."

Karl's face reddened again. "But they will talk. And that talk will spoil any sale."

"Oh, it will, will it?" Rudy made a disparaging *puh* sound. "If anyone pays attention to what these two nobodies have to say, it will just drive up the price. Use your head for once. The people I sell to already know they have to keep our little deals a secret. Any publicity will simply give the painting more cachet. Everyone wants to own something famous."

"Don't laugh at me." Bright spots of color appeared on Karl's cheeks. He took a step back and gestured with his gun in Claire's direction. "Just because they are women and this one is pretty, you just do not want to do what is necessary." He hesitated, then with a slow deliberateness he aimed the gun at Claire. Time seemed to stop.

Crash! In the corridor behind Karl's and Rudy's backs, Claire saw a stool fly out of the X-ray room and land in the exam room across the hall. Their argument forgotten, Rudy and Karl ran to investigate. Not to the X-ray room, but to the room where the stool had landed. As soon as they began to crowd into the narrow door,

Dante—still clad only in his briefs—charged up behind them with a yell. He jammed a wastebasket on Karl's head, and then swung a heavy lead apron as hard as he could at Rudy's face. The weighted apron wrapped itself around Rudy's head and shoulders, and he fell to the floor like a stone.

Forgetting that she was tied to her chair, Claire tried to get to her feet to help. The telephone cord bit into her wrists and the chair's weight dragged her back down. Karl was bellowing with rage, the sound echoing, hollow and metallic, as he scrabbled at the edges of the wastebasket. The gun fell from his hand, hit the wall and spun away on the floor.

"Dante, get the gun!" Claire shouted. "Get it!"

But it was Rudy who made the next move, suddenly coming alive. Still lying prone, he swept his arm out in a blind arc until his hand connected with Dante's ankle. He yanked. Dante's head hit the doorjamb with a horrible hollow *thunk,* and he went down in a slack tangle. Rudy pulled the apron from his face and got to his feet, his fingertips gingerly exploring his already swelling face.

A second later, Karl succeeded in pulling the wastebasket from his head and flung it in the corner. Angry at finding his enemy already vanquished, he lifted one of his huge heavy shoes and kicked Dante in the ribs. Then again. Claire could hear bones cracking, but Dante didn't stir.

Dear God, was he dead? All the anger she had felt earlier drained from her, leaving only a terrible sense of loss.

"Did I not warn you?" Karl said to Rudy, somewhat irrationally. "Did I not tell you that you had to take care of things before they got out of hand?"

"The women did not do anything," Rudy said wearily. "It was this guy." He lifted his foot and pulled it back as if he, too, were going to kick Dante, but then dropped it to the floor again. He looked over at Claire. "Who is he, anyway?"

She decided to keep her answer simple. "My boyfriend." Charlie looked at her and raised one eyebrow, but kept silent.

"Well, he is not doing you much good now, is he?" Karl said. Claire froze as he reached down to pick up the gun and then aimed it—almost casually—at Dante's sprawled form.

"You are not in the secret police anymore, Karl." Rudy held out his hand, palm up. His voice was steady. "I do not want to leave a trail of dead bodies behind me."

Instead of handing over the gun, Karl raised it and took a step backward into the reception area. "Do not do this, Karl. Do not do that," he mimicked in a singsong voice. "I am tired of you telling me what to do." His huge hand hovered over the receptionist's desk. Then in one quick move he picked up the painting and tucked it under his arm.

"What are you doing?" A note of panic had crept into Rudy's voice. Claire thought of the sorcerer's apprentice, setting into motion what he ultimately couldn't control. "You give that—"

As he was speaking, the lights went out.

For a long moment, everything was silent except for the keening of the wind. It was completely dark—no light in the room, no windows glowing in the buildings around them, no spangle of lights on the hills that lay to the west. The moon was far away, a white thumbprint against the inky sky.

There was the sound of a body running into something—Claire thought it was the receptionist's desk—followed by a grunt of pain or surprise. Rudy, Claire guessed, trying to grab the painting from Karl.

"Give it to me, Karl. You would have no idea what to do with it."

Karl's voice sounded stronger, more certain, as if he were gaining courage from his own rebellion. "After five years, I know your buyers as well as you do. And one thing I have learned is that they are not choosy. They will buy from whoever has the goods. Which in this case would be me."

As Claire's eyes began to adjust to the light provided by the distant moon, she strained to see what was happening. Next to the window a dark smudge moved against the night sky. Karl, she guessed, not talking now, simply concentrating on circumventing Rudy as he made for the door.

Rudy must have caught sight of him, too, for suddenly there was the rush of feet running, and the sounds of a struggle. "Give it to me, give it to me!" Rudy cried, but Claire didn't know whether he now meant the painting—or the gun.

When the gun went off, the sound was even louder than the roar of the wind outside. The first shot shattered one of the floor-to-ceiling windows, letting the outside in. The wind was so fierce it was hard to gulp a breath. Glass stalactites glinted in the moonlight. Eyes watering from the wind, Claire watched the two figures reel back and forth amid a swirl of loose papers that had risen up from the receptionist's desk and now whipped through the room. The sound of the wind was nearly deafening, but still, the second shot was even louder.

The bigger figure—now Claire could just make out Karl's pale face—staggered backward, off-balance, one arm flailing, the other still clutching the dark shape of the painting against his chest. Just below it, a black stain was spreading across his once white shirt. One huge foot stepped back into space. Karl seemed to hover for a moment, his free arm reaching blindly and finding only air. Then he was simply gone.

Claire tried to scream, but the wind tore the breath from her mouth.

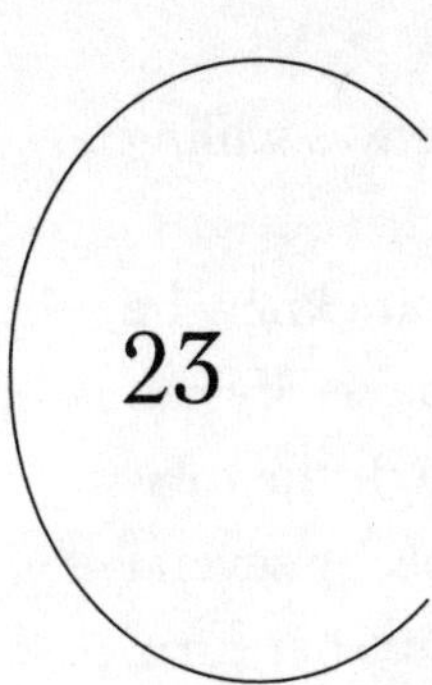

23

When Rudy walked slowly from the shattered window to stand in front of them, Claire was sure it was the end. Dawn was just beginning to wash the sky. She could see the silver glint of the gun, now held loosely by his side, but because Rudy had his back to the window, his face was in the shadows. She was never to know what he was thinking at that minute. Was he reluctant to add more dead bodies to his troubles, even though they had just witnessed him commit a murder? Did he think of whatever had existed between his grandfather and Claire's great-aunt? He only stood looking down at her for a long minute. Then he turned on his heel and left.

Claire looked over at Charlie. She had expected to find her slumped against her bonds in exhaustion or residual terror, but instead Charlie's face was intent as her shoulders twisted back and forth. "Try and get behind me. If you can put your foot on this one part of the rope, I think I can get loose."

In a painful progress of tiny hops and drags that left her fingers numb, Claire was halfway to Charlie when a hand fell on her shoulder. She cried out.

But it wasn't Rudy having second thoughts. Instead, Dante stood swaying beside her. He looked terrible. One side of his head was matted with blood, and his left hand cradled his ribs.

"How are you?" Claire asked. For that moment, she was willing to forgive him anything, because he was alive.

"I'm surviving." He gave them both a smile, and Claire knew he was consciously echoing Charlie's earlier words. "Let me see if I can find something to get you loose." He rummaged through the cabinets and reappeared with a scalpel. Although he had to stop several times to rest, Dante finally sawed Charlie free. When it was her turn, Claire was alarmed to hear his ragged breathing, louder than the dying wind. He finished cutting her loose about the same time that Charlie came back from her own raid on the doctors' supplies, her arms full of bandages and tape. She had him sit down in the chair Claire had just vacated, and then ran her fingers lightly over first his ribs and then his head.

"Three or four cracked ribs and a good-sized cut on your head. But it's not fractured. You must have a very thick skull."

"Ask Claire about that." Dante sucked in his breath as Claire put a generous dab of antibiotic cream on his cut.

They gathered up their things and then descended the darkened stairwell, guided by the flashlight Claire had retrieved from her backpack. When they reached the shelter of the building's entrance, they found Troy, looking out at Karl's body. Now covered by a sheet, it lay in the middle of Broadway Boulevard, bracketed on one side by an ambulance and on the other by a police car. The sirens were silent and both drivers were behind the wheel talking into handheld radios. Otherwise, the street was deserted. Through the litter of thousands of leaves and small branches, the wind—now a brisk breeze—scudded an occasional orange traffic cone or empty box.

Troy barely glanced at them. "Hello, Claire." His eyes were pulled back to the sheet-covered body. The fact that she had acquired two well-worn companions and bandages around her wrists seemed not to impact him at all.

"Troy." It took her a minute to remember what he was guilty of. When compared to Rudy and Karl, not very much. Just trying to steal the painting from her in New York.

"The painting's destroyed, you know. I went out to try to help this guy and here he is, holding your painting. Most of the middle is just . . . gone."

"What were you planning on doing with the Vermeer?"

He spoke absently, still mesmerized by destruction. "It wasn't a Vermeer, of course. But the beautiful thing about it was that it so easily could have been. All it needed was a signature. And that little detail could have been remedied. Ten minutes' work from John and I could have sold it for three million easy."

"John? Your chauffeur?"

An expression that under other circumstances might have been a smile crossed Troy's face. "John works for me, yes. Usually, he just adds or subtracts."

"What do you mean?"

"People bring paintings to Avery's that have been in the family for generations, but they still are completely undistinguished. A few years ago, I realized how little it would take to make them salable. It was easy enough to find an artist willing to finally make some money. You see, with just a bit of paint, old women can become young girls, unknown sitters famous generals, landscapes acquire a dog or a horse in the foreground—just the kind of revisions that make a painting worth several thousand instead of several hundred."

"You'd risk your entire career for a few thousand dollars?"

"Oh, but if you make three or four thousand every week, yes. Avery's isn't a place for poor people. Their pay scale is predicated on the idea that you're already living off Daddy's trust fund. Every day I see what money can buy. Do you know how hard that is when you don't have any yourself? And then you came in with that clever little pastiche. All it needed was a signature, which would be no trouble for John. There are a lot of gullible collectors out there who would be willing to spend three million or so for a painting by the great Dutch master Vermeer."

Dante spoke up. "I'll have to remember that next time we have dealings with Avery's."

Troy tore his gaze from the sheet that covered the remains of the painting. He looked at Dante, who had a bandage looped around his head. "I know you, don't I?"

Claire wasn't surprised by this. After all, thieves probably ran in the same circles.

"Dante Bonner."

"That's right, from the Met. Don't worry, I only work my magic for my private sales. Well-heeled Upper West Side matrons. The Fifis, if you know what I mean."

Now it was Claire's turn to stare, first at Dante, then at Troy. "He doesn't work at the Met. He's a painter. Only he had the same plan as you did—to steal the painting."

Dante pushed the hair out of his eyes and gave her his full attention. "What are you talking about?"

"I saw the photo of you and your wife!" Claire felt Charlie's arm slip around her waist. "And I found this." Claire reached into the neckline of her maternity top and pulled out the note. "You were making notes on who you could get to buy it."

"I was making notes on whether the Met would buy it, given its lack of provenance." Dante's dark eyes shot sparks. "And more important, if you're talking about the photo—which you must have found snooping through my wallet—that was from my sister's wedding! Did you really think I would make love to you under such false pretenses?"

"Don't give me that. Don't tell me that some blue-eyed blond is your sister!"

They had finally caught Troy's attention. He was swiveling his head back and forth as if he were at a tennis match, and Claire found herself wishing he would just go away.

"Remember—my last name is Bonner. My sister is a throwback to the German part of our family. And the only reason she's blond is that her hair has a little help." Dante shook his head, his jaw set with anger. "I can't believe how little you trusted me. And how stupid you thought I was. Did you really think I wouldn't notice something was wrong last night?"

A renewed flame of anger blazed up in Claire. "You're the one who lied to me! You said you were a painter."

"You asked me if I was and I told you the truth. It's just not how I make my living. I didn't want to tell you where I really worked because I didn't want to scare you off. When you first showed me the painting, I thought you were like that guy from Kansas whose family had a whole trove of stolen art. It might have disappeared again if I scared you off. But after I figured out the truth, I couldn't think of a way to tell you who I was without making you mad." He turned around and started to walk away, then stopped for a second. "Did you really think the only thing that attracted me to you was that damn painting?"

24

For the sixth time, Jean Montrose leaned forward to squint at her new VCR, making sure it was set to RECORD. It was. And after the tap-dancing bottle of toilet cleanser disappeared, there she was, Elizabeth—or Liz, as she had graciously told Jean to call her—with her riveting turquoise eyes. She sat behind a Lucite desk that revealed a pair of slim, tanned thighs draped in the tiniest of skirts. Jean had already pasted the article from this week's *TV Guide* in her scrapbook, the one that compared *Stop the Presses* to *America's Most Wanted.* Like *AMW*, it mixed interviews with re-creations—only with a focus on starlets, sex scandals and high society, with only the occasional murder thrown in for spice.

Liz straightened her shoulders and launched into the top story. "Good evening and welcome to the premiere of *Stop the Presses.* Tonight we bring you the story of a brave young appraiser at Avery's, the world-famous auction house." A photo of Troy Nowell appeared over her left shoulder, looking solemn, jaw set. "When a young woman came to him with an unlikely tale about where she had gotten a beautiful painting, he felt compelled to investigate. And what he found will surprise you. It's a story that's still being unraveled—a story of Nazi loot, secret deals for stolen art, and murder."

Jean leaned forward, enthralled. She had liked Troy from the moment she had first seen him through her chain lock, on the night of the big windstorm. At first he'd been all mixed up, thinking Jean was Claire's sister. "You're not her mother, surely?" he'd asked in that rich way he had of speaking. Then he explained about how he had met Claire in New York City and fallen head over heels in love. Intent on protecting her from some complicated-sounding but clearly urgent danger, he had followed her back to Oregon. It wasn't long before Jean had taken the chain off the door and invited Troy inside for a cup of coffee. And over a second cup, accompanied by some Ho-Hos she just happened to have, Jean had let slip where Troy might find Claire. She hadn't realized she was sending him in harm's way, but luckily everything had turned out all right.

She still didn't understand how Claire could have let Troy get away—although once he was interviewed by Liz any battle she might have fought was lost. Their whirlwind engagement was written up in *People*. Even Claire said Troy and Liz were meant to be together, although she muttered it in a way that made Jean wonder if her daughter really *had* had a crush on him. At the same time, Liz was shopping the story and her "exclusive access and footage" around to every TV magazine from *American Journal* to *Hard Copy*, looking for whoever would give her the best deal. The others had offered her cash, but it was *Stop the Presses* that had given her what she really wanted—an offer to be one of their on-air hosts.

Even with the worldwide publicity (LONG-LOST VERMEER FOUND!), there was still no clue to who had owned the painting before it found its way to the Army collecting depot. For a while a great-grand niece of Göring's had made noises that the painting should be hers by inheritance, but when no one listened to her, she had faded away. Jean watched as an actress portraying Claire—*her daughter!*—

appeared on the screen, kneeling by a narrow bed as she reached underneath to pull out a dust-covered suitcase. Her wig wasn't quite right—it was too red and too curly—but still, Jean was thrilled. While what followed wasn't exactly the story Claire had told her, it was much more exciting.

Jean munched her way through a bag of reduced-fat Doritos as the story unfolded, complete with black-and-white footage of windows being shattered on *Kristallnacht*, sad-eyed Jews being herded onto a train, and a torchlit Hitler speaking to a crowd of thousands. There was color video of Karl's body covered with a sheet, the camera panning up to show the shattered sixteenth-floor window. And, of course, film of Troy—the real Troy this time, no actor—bringing down the gavel as he made auction history by selling the long-lost Vermeer for a record $27 million.

Claire had told Jean one tidbit that was glossed over in the TV version—how when she was in the doctor's bathroom, she had replaced the painting with one of the full-size photos Dante had taken. The original—carefully laid between two sheets of acid-free paper—had gone into Claire's backpack, cushioned by an empty binder she had found on a shelf behind the receptionist's desk. Claire had thought her switch might buy her some time when she tried to slip away from Dante, but instead it had worked to fool Rudy. Viewed through the bubble wrap, the photo had looked like the real thing.

In a bit of poetic license, *Stop the Presses* had Troy rescuing a tied-up Claire and Dante (Charlie didn't even exist in this version of the story) while simultaneously fighting off Rudy and Karl.

Jean shed a few tears when the segment ended with shots of Liz and Troy's wedding, a celebrity-studded ceremony that had taken place just a few weeks before. Claire scoffed that the whole thing must be a publicity stunt worked up by their respective agents, but Jean told her that she might think about taking a page from their book.

Her daughter and Dante Bonner weren't even engaged, although Jean dropped enough hints. Some of the money from the painting could have gone to a truly beautiful wedding, but instead Claire had given most of it to the World Jewish Restitution Organization. Even though she was disappointed that Claire hadn't kept much of the money from the painting, Jean had to admit her daughter hadn't forgotten her family. Susie now had herself a station at Curl Up and Dye, and there was college money set aside for Eric when the time came. And of course there was the very home theater system that Jean was now watching the last few commercials on—a forty-eight-inch Goldstar with separate speakers.

Claire herself hadn't wanted anything for herself, and it was only at Charlie's insistence that she had set aside a little. It had been enough, however, to free her forever from the Custom Plate Division.

Finally, the credits began to roll. Jean saw what she had been waiting for all evening, the words that in the weeks and months to come would cause her to hit the pause button on her VCR dozens of times, just so that she could flush again with pleasure. "Special thanks to . . ." and there was her own name, Jean Montrose, right in the middle of the list.

∾

Claire reached for the remote and clicked off the TV.

"I think I like the real you better." Dante rolled over on his side to face Claire. He dropped a kiss on her right shoulder.

"You should be glad you like me better," she said, "since I heard that the actress who played me has just finished her third marriage and her fourth admission to the Betty Ford Clinic." She turned her face toward him for another kiss.

Outside the windows of Dante's Fourth Avenue condo, horns,

sirens and car alarms punctuated the ceaseless murmur of New York City. After a half-dozen trips here, Claire had gotten to the point where she almost didn't hear it anymore. Dante, on the other hand, still had difficulty sleeping whenever he visited Portland, finding the silence oppressive. They had talked about one or the other of them moving, but Charlie pulled Claire one way and Dante's job at the Met pulled him the other, so for now they made do with frequent visits. Claire snapped off the light and moved into Dante's arms. She didn't know where things would end up, but she was enjoying the trip.

NJYNLF

Key to License Plate Terms

1DRKNYT = One Dark Night
2RU LUV = True Love
6ULDV8 = Sexual Deviate
AMYSTREE = A Mystery
ANGLBB = Angel Baby
AXNU8D+ = Accentuate the Positive
BBNBRD = Baby on Board
BG BKS = Big Bucks
CC DDAY = Seize the Day
COWPOO = Manure
CUNQRT = See You in Court
DEVORSD = Divorced
EZ4U2SA = Easy for You to Say
FX108 = Affectionate
GETNAKD = Get Naked
H2OUUP2 = What Are (water) You Up To?
IMHERE = I'm Here
IRITEI = Right Between the Eyes
KPASAMD = What's Up (qué pasa), Doc?

L8RG8R = Later Gator
MSTBF8 = Must Be Fate
MYTB$$ = Might Be Money
NJYNLF = Enjoying Life
N4CR = Enforcer
OL4LUV = All for Love
OWTAHR = Outta Here
PP DR = Urologist
QS10ALL = Question All
RESQ ME = Rescue Me
RUD14ME = Are You the One for Me?
STAY2ND = Stay Tuned
SWMR = Swimmer
TI—3VOM = Move It (as seen from a rearview mirror)
TVZTRU = TV Is True
ULIV 1S = You Live Once
XQQSME = Excuse Me
YRUFAT = Why Are You Fat?
ZTHSIT? = Is This It?